THE GREAT DETECTIVE AT THE AT THE CRUCIBLE OF LIFE;

Or, The Adventure of the Rose of Fire

THE GREAT DETECTIVE AT THE CRUCIBLE OF LIFE;

Or, The Adventure of the Rose of Fire

From a Memoir As Told By

Allan Quatermain

Author of "King Solomon's Mines," "She and Allan," "Marie," ETC.

1881 Manuscript Recorded, Edited, and Supplemented by

John H. Watson, M.D.

Author of "A Study in Scarlet," "The Hound of the Baskervilles," ETC.

Edited, Supplemented, and Annotated by

Thos. Kent Miller

Editor of "The Great Detective on the Roof of the World" ETC.

WILDSIDE PRESS

THE GREAT DETECTIVE AT THE CRUCIBLE OF LIFE

Also, for Jayne and Douglas, this new service, this new hymn.

Wildside Press
www.wildsidepress.com

First Wildside Press edition: 2005

FIRST EDITION

In this great crucible of life we call the world—in the vaster one we call the universe—the mysteries lie close packed, uncountable as grains of sand on the oceans' shores.

—A. Merritt

A red light, a burning spark seen far away in the darkness, taken at the first moment of seeing for a signal . . . and then, as if in an incredible point of time, it swelled into a vast rose of fire that filled all the sea and all the sky and possessed the land.

—Arthur Machen in "The Great Return"

Remember, most loving and compassionate virgin Mary, it has never been said or heard that anyone who turned to you for help was left unaided. Inspired with this conviction, I run to your protection and stand before you penitent of my wrong doings, for you are my mother and the mother of all. O Mother of the Word of God, neglect not my prayers, despise not my words of pleading, but in your mercy, please hear and answer me. Amen.

—The Memorare: A Prayer to Mary

Travelers afoot in hot deserts should set their course toward shade!

—Junior Woodchucks' Guidebook

Dedication

To Sir Henry Rider Haggard (1856-1925)

My Dear Sir:

As you so often with sincerity dedicated your books to those you admired, I would like to offer this volume to you, though, as I place these words down for the record, you have been gone from us for more than three-quarters of a century.

Let me accomplish this by meandering a bit. During the early 1950s when I was a child, my father and older brother read Uncle Scrooge *comic books (published for ten cents at the time by Dell Publishing Co., Inc.). I received them as hand-me-downs and was enchanted and enthralled by the adventures of Uncle Scrooge McDuck and his nephews, Donald Duck and Huey, Dewey, and Louie. Though it was obvious that my father and brother enjoyed these stories, at some point I realized that somehow these illustrated tales of lost cities and civilizations touched a special chord in me that transcended mere enjoyment. I knew this because my reaction to them was fundamentally different; my father and brother forgot about them and lost track of them, whereas I treasured every panel, turned the pages reverently as I read and reread the stories, and considered them my most precious possessions.*

On the cover, prominently displayed above the title was the name of Walt Disney. What I did not know as a child was that during that era of comic book history the actual writers and artists who created the comic stories were anonymous. As an adult, I learned that Mr. Disney had little or nothing to do with Uncle Scrooge. Scrooge was the creation of a man named Carl Barks and the best Scrooge stories—the ones that haunted me, such as the Ducks's stumbling upon the Seven Cities of Cibola, the lost continent of Atlantis, and Tralla La—were written and drawn by Barks.

Furthermore, I didn't know—and didn't learn until still more time had passed—that it was you, Sir Henry, who was the man behind Barks.

He drew from you as surely as desert nomads draw from an oasis well. The magic he touched me with—as glorious as it was—was, in a way, recycled magic. You invented the magic—the subgenre of fantasy that has come to be known as the "lost race adventure."

Let me quote from the consummate historian and editor of fantasy literature, the late Lin Carter. In the introduction to a reprint of one of your novels, he wrote that you were the right man with the right idea in the right place at the right time, that time being the end of the nineteenth century at the height of a succession of momentous historical and archaeological discoveries.

"For even more exciting," Carter said, "than the discovery of lost cities of the past, dead and buried and forgotten for thousands of years, is the discovery of an ancient city tucked away in some far corner of the world—still inhabited!"

I cannot say why this subgenre you invented affects me so, but I suspect that somehow these matters are prearranged by a power far greater than ours, as perhaps you would agree. Be that as it may, because of the great joy I have experienced both from you directly in the form of your many "lost race" novels and indirectly through Mr. Barks (and not only Mr. Barks because it turns out that there are a multitude of others you have touched, among them writers named Edgar Rice Burroughs, A. Merritt, Talbot Mundy, James Hilton, and, more recently, of course, Michael Crichton)[1], I ask you to allow me to set your name upon this page and subscribe myself,

Gratefully and ever sincerely yours,

Thos. Kent Miller
Redwood City, California
December 1, 1988

Contents

Editor's Note to the Third Edition

The publication of this third edition of *The Great Detective at the Crucible of Life* coincides with the official joint announcement by the African states of Eritrea, Ethiopia, Djibouti, Somalia, Kenya, Uganda, Rwanda, The Democratic Republic of Congo, Burundi, Tanzania, Malawi, Mozambique, Zambia, Zimbabwe, and South Africa that great swatches of their countries are being set aside for the establishment of a vast African continental preserve—The Great Rift Valley Paleoanthropologic Preserve. The preserve, in principle, follows the East African Rift System that cuts north and south through most of these countries. The park extends a bit further beyond the southernmost aspect of the rift valley into South Africa and is roughly 3,500 miles long, averaging about 75 miles wide, for a total of about 265,000 square miles.

Given that much of this area has been in extreme political turmoil for years, and that death, civil war, and even genocide have been the windows by which the world has assessed much of the area, this unprecedented alignment seems little less than a miracle. This near-impossible task was, in fact, accomplished through the supreme efforts of the Wildlife Conservation Society, the board of directors of the Peace Parks Foundation, and United Nations Secretary-General Nicholi Lorenzo and a significant percentage of the staffs of the U.N. Environment Programme, the Institute of Human Origins, the National Science Foundation, the National Geographic Society, and the thousands of dedicated volunteers who believed in the unique value of this preserve.

The motivating principle behind the creation of the park is to preserve that unique spot on this planet where the human species arose. It has been shown over and again through a succession of historic paleoarchaeological finds (beginning in South Africa with

Raymond Dart and Robert Broom early in the twentieth century through the redoubtable Leaky family in Tanzania and Kenya; Donald Johanson, Tim White, and Yohannes Haile-Selassie mainly in Ethiopia; and numerous other investigators) that beyond a reasonable doubt, primates stood tall on their legs and walked fully erect all over this area beginning between six and three million years ago. Despite the fact that researchers are constantly quibbling about the details, timeline, and branches of our family tree, there is complete consensus that these first walking primates came into existence in East Africa. Then, through the ages, they lived their lives, slowly changing in response to changes in their environment. The general outline of this evolution is *Ardipithecus* to *Australopithecus* to *Homo hablis* to *Homo erectus/ergaster* to *Homo sapien*, the latter two being those who left Africa to spread across Asia, then Europe, and finally the Americas to populate the world.

In a sense, we are all Africans, and now this fact has finally been acknowledged by the modern countries that include and surround the rift system.

But, of course, it is far beyond the realm of possibility or even of the wildest dreams to expect such a preserve to have a literal, physical fence around it with admission gates, souvenir shops, and the like. Something so vast as this preserve, which crosses so many political boundaries, even to the extent of absorbing entire countries—Rwanda, Burundi, and Malawi to be specific—must be something altogether different than what we are used to thinking of as a preserve.

There is no doubt that The Great Rift Valley Paleoanthropologic Preserve exists. But if there are no fences marking its outermost boundaries, what is the nature of its existence? This preserve exists in the following manners:

- In the minds of the leaders and politicians of the fifteen governments who set it up at the urging of the agencies already mentioned, it exists as an entity within certain geographical points of longitude and latitude as measured by the Global Positioning System (GPS).

- In the eyes of the United Nations, it exists.
- In the minds of the people of the world, it exists.
- As a designated area on all new maps of Africa and of the world, it exists.

And to underscore its existence, each of the Preserve nations is even now setting up preserve offices staffed with scientists of all sorts, preservationists, administrators, and an "army," as it were, of preserve rangers, who, like similar personnel the world over, will educate and entertain visitors while also protecting their charge.

*   *   *

By now, I'm sure, some of the new readers of this book are wondering what this astonishing accomplishment has to do with *The Great Detective at the Crucible of Life.*

I'll satisfy that curiosity by briefly discussing the evolution, as it were, of this book and show how it has changed over its three editions.

In the beginning, by a circuitous route, the manuscript came into my possession *(see my original preface beginning on page 23).* Given the state of publishing these days, it was in itself a miracle that I was able to get first my agent, Gail Morgan Hickman, and then a publisher to even look at the book. Even so, once the publisher was persuaded to print Quatermain's story, for purely commercial reasons she balked at printing the rather extensive front matter and ancillary material, much of which was my contribution. Thus, the book was released as a paperback original with a print run of 10,000, and all concerned assumed that it would sell enough copies to make a modest profit or break even and then fade from memory, the unsold copies of course being stripped and recycled. But by one of those flukes that can never be predicted, nationally syndicated radio talk show host ("shock jock") Randy King by chance read the book and mentioned on his program that he had enjoyed it and found it thought-provoking. The net result was that the paperback publisher went back to press seventeen more times over the next two years.

The inevitable movie was released, of course . . . and then tanked. The film version (*The Rose of Fire*, starring Michael Caine, Gene Hackman, Sigourney Weaver, and introducing young Nigel Knox as "Will Scott," and costing in the neighborhood of $75 million) had a disastrous opening weekend, acid reviews, and then quickly disappeared. It came and went so fast that most people weren't even aware of its existence. Indeed, as of this writing, it still has not appeared on video or DVD.

But, naturally, the eventual fortunes of the film were not known while its advertising and promotion campaigns were being prepared. As the movie-tie-in edition of the book was being planned, I used my then not-so-insubstantial clout to suggest very strongly that the book be published as I had originally planned. As the publisher was quite distressed about this, I quietly reminded her of a particular clause in my contract, whereupon she sighed ever so deeply and made no further protest.

And then, in another twist of fate, the movie tie-in version of the book took on a life of its own.

Whereas the original paperback was accepted and thought of as a rather light true-life adventure story, the second edition (at first only a paperback, then reprinted in hardcover but with no further changes, as I had nothing more to add at the time) became a magnet for study. It seems the notion of a continental park was not new, that the groundwork had been prepared by many of those visionaries mentioned above, among others, and all that was wanting was a straw to cave in the camel's back, so to speak . . . and this little memoir of Quatermain's adventure proved to be just that. Educators, scholars, politicians, and heads of state, many of whom were affiliated with conservation groups around the world, found that Quatermain's record of the events in 1872 included an aspect that underscored the reasoning and the arguments that they themselves had pursued to no avail for years. Slowly, others of influence gravitated to the book, discussed its implications, and eventually more and more world leaders were persuaded that certain points brought up in the book warranted serious study.

In time, the East African Coalition came into being and the world community was able to provide certain inducements and guarantees to the fifteen preserve nations. The joint announcement is the unprecedented result of all that focused interest.

This third edition is, therefore, intended for those readers who are coming to the book for the first time. *The Great Detective at the Crucible of Life; Or, The Adventure of the Rose of Fire* has taken on a life of its own, to be sure, but I hope that it never be forgotten that it began as a true story of "rip-roaring adventure" shared among cultured friends before a crackling fire in upstate New York.

T.K.M.

Editor's Note to the Movie Tie-In (Second) Edition

Now that Allan Quatermain's history of his adventure with Sherlock Holmes will soon arrive to silver screens and multiplexes worldwide—but in drastically altered form, as is frequently the case when books are translated into film—I feel obliged to take advantage of this movie tie-in reprint edition to prepare the definitive collector's edition that I originally planned and include the original introductory material, which explains how the manuscript came into being and just how it came into my hands.

Many readers may remember that the book was originally published as a true-life adventure memoir beginning with what is Chapter One in this book. This seems natural enough, but unbeknownst to those readers, that edition omitted Quatermain's introduction, Watson's foreword, and this editor's preface, as well as much other ancillary material, the publishing wisdom of the time (and still is for that matter) assuming modern readers wanted only to jump into the narrative—front matter be damned!

I am grateful to my publisher for this new edition, allowing me to rectify that disservice to the shades of the principal parties.

What follows, therefore, is the complete manuscript that I had the good fortune to receive. As editor, I have made certain cosmetic changes according to practical and commercial decisions, such as incorporating a title with a more Sherlockian cast and eschewing the original:

Record of A.Q.'s narration concerning certain adventures that unfolded in east Africa during the early part 1872
As set down by John H. Watson, M.D.

In addition, for the sake of the modern reader, I felt obliged to add a few applicable epigraphs; to correct or update spelling (e.g., "Ethiope" to "Ethiopia" and "Chaka" to "Shaka"); to add clear editorial attribution to the many internal notes made by the three contributors; and to add appropriate chapter titles, footnotes, endnotes and other corroborative supplementary material.

In this vein, I am particularly grateful that this edition of the book will carry the title I originally gave it rather than the abortive, abbreviated version that both the original edition and the movie carry. Let's face it, *The Rose of Fire* makes it sound like yet another sequel to *Romancing the Stone* such as that silly confection *Jewel of the Nile*.

Let us embark, then, on a miraculous journey and enter the minds of some of the nineteenth century's most exciting individuals—but in a manner that I hope is more in alignment with their expectations of how their adventures should be presented to a discerning readership, and also in a manner that does no disservice to this editor's far-from-slight investigatory efforts aimed at putting the whole affair into the historical perspective that seemed wanting and which begged to be resolved.

T.K.M.

Preface

The Prodigious Phone Call

By Thos. Kent Miller, Editor

There is no doubt in my mind that there is a force in this world that some call "serendipity" and others "synchronicity."

It was my birthday, a Tuesday in October 1994. I was sitting at my desk rereading for the hundredth time a yellowing correspondence from the late Judy-Lynn Del Rey, who was up until her death in 1986—and still is, to be sure—considered one of science fiction's most admired and important editors. It so happened that this missive—which, in point of fact, was a rejection letter—was one of my prized possessions. It reads thus:

Del Rey Books
An Imprint of Ballantine Books

September 18, 1985
Dear Mr. Miller:

> Your idea of writing a double biography that blends the lives of Allan Quatermain and his literary representative H. Rider Haggard is indeed interesting. Unfortunately Lester's and my attempt to resurrect Haggard recently was an unmitigated disaster. Therefore, I must say that taking on your project would be economically unwise for us at this time. I sincerely hope your project finds a home elsewhere.
>
> Best to you,
> Judy-Lynn Del Rey[2]

I prized this letter for many reasons, but the most important was because Judy-Lynn had clearly *reluctantly* rejected my idea. It was gratifying that a person of her stature saw the merit in my idea.

For those of you who might not know, Allan Quatermain was the prototype "great white hunter," who in the mid-1880s wrote the enduring memoir *King Solomon's Mines*. It is his self-portrayal in that classic that propagated the likes of Jungle Jim, Congo Bill, and all those rifle-toting, safari-leading heroes such as Clark Gable in *Mogambo*, Gregory Peck in *The Macomber Affair*, John Wayne in *Hatari*, and even Pete Postlethwaite in *The Lost World: Jurassic Park* and Ernie Hudson in *Congo*.

My idea was to take the nineteen published histories that Allan Quatermain wrote (or inspired) mostly during his three-year hiatus at his estate, the Grange, in Yorkshire, England, and subsequently left behind (all except the last), and condense them into a formal biography. Listed in internal chronological order, these works are *Allan's Wife*, *Marie*, *Child of Storm*, "Zikali the Wizard," "A Tale of Three Lions," *Maiwa's Revenge*, "Hunter Quatermain's Story," "Long Odds," *The Holy Flower*, *Heu-Heu or the Monster*, *She and Allan*, *The Treasure of the Lake*, *The Ivory Child*, *Finished*, "Megepa the Buck," *King Solomon's Mines*, *The Ancient Allan*, *Allan and the Ice Gods*, and *Allan Quatermain*.

Yet, the story of Quatermain must always be intertwined with that of his friend, Henry Rider Haggard, through whose tenacity and great strength of personality Quatermain's histories saw the light of day. I think it can be said without fear of argument that Quatermain and Haggard were in many ways doppelgangers of one another, mirroring as they did each other's life so neatly — thus, my vision of blending the lives of the great adventurer and his literary executor into a single volume.[3]

So there I was, rereading Mrs. Del Rey's note, mourning the project that never happened, when the phone rang. That call was the first domino in a series of events that changed the direction of my life.

I had taken the day off from my job as the editor of a respected trade publication. It was ten in the morning, and the call proceeded in the following manner.

"Hello, are you Thomas Miller, the editor of *The Great Detective on the Roof of the World*?"

"Yes, I am," I said, delighted, for heaven knows I receive little enough feedback on that particular labor of love.

"Well then, I'm Jim Turner . . . . "

Excitement welled up within me and before he could finish his thought, I blurted out, "The publisher of Arkham House!"[4]

"Why yes. I'm flattered that you know me."

"Mr. Turner, I've been a fan of Arkham House for most of my life. Of course I know your name. What can I do for you?"

"Please call me Jim. May I call you Tom?"

"Of course."

"Tom, I'm not sure if this will interest you, but it turns out that a box of H.P. Lovecraft material was misplaced and went unnoticed for seventy some years after his death and has turned up in the Brown University archives—in the John Hay Library to be exact. Naturally, I was among the first to be notified.

"Among its contents was a book-length manuscript that Lovecraft had apparently received as a commission to revise or 'fix up' as he used to call it. It appears the manuscript was originally set down in script in 1881 and was received by Lovecraft in 1925. Lovecraft's revisions, such as they are, are rather sparse and unenthusiastic with the exception of a section dealing with meteorites. They are in his handwriting, so we know he started the job. We have no idea why it apparently was never completed."

"You are most definitely sparking my interest, Jim."

"It seems that in 1925, Lovecraft, with his wife Sonia, had traveled up to the Hudson River Valley area of New York state and had visited an unusual and rather lavish house called Olana—"

"I'm sorry to interrupt again, Jim, but are you speaking of the home of Frederick Church?"[5]

"Yes. I'm gratified you know that as well. You seem to be knowledgeable in a number of fields."

Ignoring the compliment, I hurried on to say, "This is marvelous! Before you go any further, I must tell you that my wife Jayne, our son Douglas, and I made what I call 'a pilgrimage' to the National Gallery in 1990 to the Church exhibit."

There was a long silence at the other end of the line.

"Jim?"

"This is fortuitous indeed."

"Please go on."

"Yes. While at Olana, Lovecraft and Sonia met with Sally Good, Frederick Church's daughter-in-law, who with her husband inherited the home at the time of Church's death in 1900. During the visit, when Sally learned of Lovecraft's vocation as a revisionist, she asked if he would be interested in undertaking a commission—namely to revise for publication a peculiar manuscript that she and her husband possessed, that they had inherited along with the house. Apparently Sally, though by no means feeling it was an urgent matter, nonetheless sensed that the manuscript had some historical or literary value and chose this opportunity to act on that intuition.

"Lovecraft seized the opportunity and took the manuscript home—and then it disappeared for more than seventy years until the archivists at Brown unearthed it last month."

"This is truly wonderful, but I don't understand what all this has to do with me."

"Yes, I suppose I ought to get to the point. The manuscript in question purports to detail an expedition to Ethiopia a century and a quarter ago. Indeed, the names of Allan Quatermain and Dr. John Watson are prominent. Naturally, as a publisher, I was overjoyed.

You can imagine all the permutations of publishing possibilities that flashed in my mind."

"Allan Quatermain! Dr. Watson!"

"Despite my excitement, I must be realistic. In a short time I will be leaving Arkham House to start my own publishing company. Arkham's plate is currently full, and my new company has more than enough to do at the moment. And this volume, as undeniably exciting as it is, and though it certainly has merit, is nonetheless a bit of an odd duck, and, as such, must wait in queue for some time, perhaps years, before we could get to it.

"When I began to think of who else might shepherd this volume into publication, I began to list editors with backgrounds in the subject. The list was very short. Then I remembered Leo Vincey's journal [*The Great Detective on the Roof of the World*] and also recalled that Vincey's literary executor was H. Rider Haggard, as was Quatermain's. And, insofar as fate had once arranged that you take up Haggard's baton, I realized that you of all people would be the most perfectly equipped to properly prepare this remarkable story to share with the world. May I send a copy to you?"

Somehow, through my breathless excitement, I was able to assure Mr. Turner that I would be delighted to receive the manuscript and take on the project.

In due course, a photocopy arrived at my door via UPS. On opening the box, the first thing I found was a sheet of Arkham House stationery with a cordial note from Mr. Turner more or less repeating what he had told me over the phone.

Below that . . . .

*   *   *

How can I express the pristine joy that filled me at what I saw next.

There, below Mr. Turner's note was a photocopy of an original typescript of an actual letter written by H.P. Lovecraft and addressed to "My dear Smith:—" who could only be Clark Ashton Smith, the northern California painter, sculptor, poet, translator, and author of whom Lovecraft once wrote, "In sheer daemonic strangeness and fertility of conception, Clark Ashton Smith is perhaps unexcelled by any other writer dead or living." As the letter I was looking at was dated June 1925, Lovecraft and Smith by then had been regular correspondents for slightly over three years.

Turner had scrawled at the top of the photocopy, "Derleth and Wandrei left this note out of the *Selected Letters*. I assume that was because the manuscript referred to could never be located and the letter would have meant nothing out of context. Of course, the original letter (which is lost) would have been in Lovecraft's dense, spidery script. This is a copy of the typescript they had prepared, as they did for all of HPL's correspondence that they were able to locate. If it had been printed, it would have started on page 19 of volume II where letter #188 to Frank Belknap Long currently is."

Let us, dear reader, simply be glad that the typescript remained in the publisher's files. The letter reads thus:

169 Clinton Street
Brooklyn, N.Y.

June 21, 1925
My dear Smith:—

On this cosmic & splendid Solstice Day, I bid you greetings. I bear news of the grandest sort! By way of preface, I will begin at the beginning & come to the delicious details in due course.

. . . . [6] Upon my wife's return from Saratoga Springs[7], we chose to celebrate in a most uncharacteristic manner. (But I mustn't prevaricate. The following voyage extraordinaire was also initiated, in part, with the transparent and terribly self-conscious goal of heading off my funk—or that part of it that remained following the burglary of my clothes.) Ol' S.H.G. & I were able to prevail upon the good nature of one Mrs. Renshaw, a client up from Washington, who seemed more than happy to act on behalf of this Lady & Gentleman in the role of chauffeur.

You may recall that last year I mentioned to you something to the effect of my having a real affection for scenes—landscape & architecture—as opposed to the company of transitory mankind. In point of fact, recently the craft & home of Frederick E. Church has come to my attention. You may recall that he was quite the rage three-quarters of a century ago, a veritable pinnacle of the Hudson River Valley School of landscape art. He built his retirement home not too terribly distant from here.

Thus, it turns out that our destination this very day—O! prodigious day!—was the Church home, which is built on a hilltop overlooking the Hudson River. Furthermore, "Olana," as the place is named, is one of the few places on earth where the separate disciplines of landscape & architecture cross with a vengeance.

The purpose of our visit was part satisfaction of architectural curiosity, part holiday, part celebration at S.H.G.'s return to health & home. Our host & hostess were expecting us, once again due to the good graces of the ever resourceful Mrs. Renshaw.

Even before we viewed the house, as we drove up the circuitous drive, at every bend we encountered the most fabulous scenes of the Hudson River or the Catskill Mountains. The man had actually planted thousands of trees in such a manner as to purposefully frame choice vistas just as though they were landscape paintings. Quite ingenious! Thus, you can imagine that when we made that last bend, the house itself was like a veritable jewel in the crown. Trust me when I say that when the house ("mansion" perhaps is too large a term) first came into view, I caught my breath at the audacity of it.

Though the underlying purpose of Olana was that of a sanctuary for his family, Church designed the house himself fueled by inspiration derived from travels to Persia & other exotic

Middle Eastern states. The name Olana I was told by Church's daughter-in-law, is a variation on "Olane," which she said was a fortress/treasure house in ancient Persia. The Oriental windows, the graceful pink & blue tile work, the bell tower & embellished doorways . . . . Believe me when I say I felt transported into the likes of F. Marion Crawford's "Khaled," or William Beckford's "Vathek," or George Meredith's "The Shaving of Shagpat." One would not do badly by quoting from "Vathek" in attempting to give the flavor of the place:

> "The palace named 'The Delight of the Eyes, or the Support of Memory,' was one entire enchantment. Rarities collected from every corner of the earth were there in such profusion as to dazzle and confound, but for the order in which they were arranged . . . . Here a well-managed perspective attracted the sight, there the magic of optics agreeably deceived it; whilst the naturalist on his part exhibited, in their several classes, the various gifts that Heaven had bestowed on our globe."

We were treated lavishly to be sure, fêting us not in the parlor but in the family's own sitting room. Though this lovely room had many features of significant note, the eye was perpetually drawn to, & eventually anchored by, a lavish, tallish painting above the marble fireplace of Petra's El Khasne, whose astonishingly detailed façade was carved, as you know, from a rose-colored sandstone cliff, & which in the painting, only a glimpse can be seen beyond the converging walls of a mountain cleft.

In due course, though, there came a time when the ever-merciless spectre of vile "business" appeared like a fungus & would not be shaken off—to blazes with mixing metaphors! Once our hostess learned that I made my livelihood primarily by revising the prose & poetry of others, she verily leaped at the chance to offer me a commission, that of, as she said, "turning an old manuscript into something worthy of publication."

I demurred, of course, but she was insistent. Between that

& the equally insistent prodding of S.H.G's elbow into my side, the end was that I agreed to see the MS. She was gone from the room for quite a while. When she returned, she had with her a rather dusty & discolored leather portfolio that had the appearance of being hurriedly wiped & which *still had the silken strands of spider webs clinging to its accordion folds!*

I took the portfolio, set it on my knees, & extracted a disorganized stack of heavy foolscap. Believe me I had no idea what to expect. I spent a moment straightening the sheets. They were written upon in ink in an inconsistent script—sometimes large & round, sometimes small & squeezed. It was difficult to determine if they were the same hand. As hackneyed as it sounds, it actually did take a few moments for me to realize what I held on my lap. That title page, which merely bore the fact that it was a "Record of A.Q.'s narration concerning certain adventures that unfolded in east Africa during the early part 1872" actually had the shattering audacity to additionally state "As set down by John H. Watson, M.D." Talk about an unexpected state of affairs. These poor people, for all their acumen within their particular social strata & business interests, really did not seem to appreciate—nay! simply had no idea—what they had, & which, I soon learned, had been occupying a convenient cubby in their wine cellar for a quarter of a century!

As you know, I am immune to so-called matters of providence, yet I swear a tingle possessed my spine for those few moments when all this first made itself manifest. Providence or not, coincidence or not, the fates of the whole known Universe or not, I—me!—myself!—happened to be the right person at the right time in the right place when this particular MS. changed hands!

I took the commission, of course, & I have to tell you I was in quite a state, an uncharacteristic one, I assure you—S.H.G. tells me I even flirted with rudeness—until I could focus on the thing.

But to conclude Olana . . . . Our hosts toured us around their home, or at least the downstairs—the upstairs being strictly personal—& we left after dark.

O! most dire of circumstances! Understand that Renshaw, gracious lady that she is, has installed within her automobile a splendid lamp to satisfy the nocturnal reading requirements of her sundry passengers during longish rides. Yet the lamp this night was not functioning! I had no choice but to wait before I could peruse the document further. In due course, over the lonely roads, I found myself mentally framing this missive to you &, having come home only minutes ago, have set it down forthwith, knowing that first to last you'd appreciate the magnitude of this . . . this . . . *discovery!* Having said that, I will now get back to the MS.

I can hardly contain myself. Wait a bit. . . .

* * *

I calmed myself down enough to look over the MS. & I have now had an opportunity to study the document well enough to give you the broad outlines. As I said, it is authored by Watson (or claims to be). But, as I scan through the first half, I must admit to being puzzled. Throughout, as you would expect, there are references to "Holmes," but as far as I can tell, they don't refer to the *correct* Holmes, but another one entirely. Indeed, the person of Sherlock seems altogether absent. . . . Furthermore, the document is primarily a memoir of Allan Quatermain. (You remember him, of course—he penned 'King Solomon's Mines' back in the '80s. Several of his memoirs were brought to print by Rider Haggard in those days.) It seems Watson's role in this particular instance was that of transcriber.

O! This will be fun! A new Quatermain adventure in Africa. I was promised a fair wage for my dabbling; but I feel almost as though I'm stealing from Church's relations. I do see, however, much need for my poor workmanlike efforts. Watson was always a bit quick, don't you think? I often thought he would have benefited from a good polish.

I am posting this immediately & will offer the sequel (when there is one) "in the fullness of time."

Yr most oblig'd & obt. Servt.

H P L

My eyes reached the end of this epistle and lingered on HPL's abbreviated closing. I must say that I was deeply affected by being so privileged to have access to this otherwise unknown letter. Silently I thanked Jim Turner to the skies—and then found I didn't want to turn the page.

I was gripped by the plethora of the emotions one feels when delving into the unknown—fear, joy, dread, excitement—but the predominant terror, if you will, was that of dread that what I would find next would be anticlimactic and not meet my heightened expectations.

Eventually I mastered myself and did in fact turn the page, finding another sheet of stationery on which Turner had scrawled the following:

Sad to say that no "sequel" to this letter has yet turned up, and it is unknown why HPL apparently made no further mention of this commission again in other correspondence. Neither is it clear why he didn't pursue, let alone complete, the project. You'll note that his crabbed scribbles—not even finished edits—are most evident on the pages dealing with meteorites and astronomy.[8] Perhaps it is no coincidence that his accepting this commission predates the writing of "The Colour Out of Space"[9] by almost exactly two years. It is certain, however, that his initial enthusiasm must have waned rapidly, otherwise his revision would have been far more extensive. The more interested he was in a project, as you know, the more likely he would have undertaken nothing less than a complete rewrite. Perhaps he was intimidated by the notion of rewriting a proven master, or, perhaps, just the opposite, he felt himself above dabbling with the work of a senile hack who couldn't even keep his dates, wounds, and wives straight[10] and who frequently diminished himself to the level of a mere romance writer.[11] Doubtless we will never know. Thanks for your interest and your agreement to help.

Agreement to help! I would have paid handsomely for this opportunity!

I flipped the page and came to another sheet of paper—yet another one that affected me profoundly. There lay before me this note:

Dear Mr. Church,

The account given by Mr. Quatermain in your sitting room seemed to impress and affect us both to such a degree that I took the opportunity presented by our long sea voyage back to England to set it down on paper. This effort was made all the easier due to the presence of Mr. Quatermain himself who indulged me by responding to my every question.

In memory of your delightful hospitality and your boundless enthusiasm for Mr. Quatermain's tale, I have arranged that a copy of the ms. be made and be sent to you forthwith for your pleasure and also as a memento of that fine evening.

I have notified Mr. Quatermain of my intent and he sends his regards.

Yours ever faithfully,
John H. Watson
February 4, 1881

Whereupon, I settled in to read the manuscript from beginning to end, and soon realized the ultimate irony of ultimate ironies. What neither Lovecraft nor Turner had mentioned—and therefore probably didn't realize—was that Watson had indeed recorded a real Sherlock Holmes adventure—*a full month before he had even met Holmes!* Their famous encounter at St. Bartholomew's Hospital on March 4, 1881, had not yet happened! Yet this was undeniably a full-length account of a teenage Sherlock Holmes traversing the hellish deserts of Ethiopia.

Can you imagine my state? I was holding a document that was, without doubt, both a new Allan Quatermain memoir and a new Sherlock Holmes tale. Furthermore, it was a story of the most prodigious journey the mind of man could fathom—dwarfing in its way even Magellan's circumnavigation of the earth and Apollo 11's journey to the moon—for the adventure described was nothing less than a journey to the City of God!

T.K.M

Foreword

By John H. Watson, M.D

February 1881

My dear Church,

As I prepared a copy of the following ms. for your special enjoyment, it occurred to me that it would be advantageous for you to understand exactly in some detail how it was Quatermain and I happened to appear on your doorstep last month, and then I will summarize for posterity (or perhaps for no more than merely our own faulty memories) the gist of that evening.

It was with great delight that I heard my new friend, Mr. Allan Quatermain—only shortly after he had settled into the Grange, his new home in Yorkshire—invite me to join him on a transatlantic voyage to America. We had been introduced only a few weeks earlier by his son, Harry, a medical student at St. Bartholomew's Hospital, and we had found that we had much in common.

"John," he began, "I have business to transact in Boston and New York City, and I fear that such a trip alone to lands unknown I would find daunting and I would be honored if you could contrive a way to join me."

I found amusing the thought that this man who had trekked over all of the wilds of Africa—to and from since he was but a mere lad—would find anything at all daunting. Nevertheless, I myself had only just returned from war duties in Afghanistan and found London sufficiently stultifying that this proposed adventure to the New World had much appeal. Unfortunately, such meager finances that were my wound pension allotment at the time, and my sole income, prevented my accepting Quatermain's invitation.[12] I muttered something banal in an attempt to obfuscate my way out of this embarrassing situation that my friend had inadvertently placed me in. But before I had completed the lie, Quatermain said, "Of course, I understand the financial imposition such a trip would entail, and Heaven knows that it was only a short time ago that I lived so close to the land that supper enough to fill my stomach only became a reality if an antelope happened to wander by or if I could strike up a trade with whichever Kaffirs happened to be in my neighborhood. But I've made my pile now, and I can afford to be generous. Consider my invitation to be on me, and, pray, please accept this without a second thought and don't let it be a matter of discussion. Any further discussion on the subject I will take as a personal affront."

Well, when faced with this decree, I can honestly say that I threw polite humility to the wind and without further hesitation I agreed to put my affairs, such as they were, in order so that I could indeed join Quatermain for the requisite amount of time, which would be about four or five weeks. I did insist, though, that once my practice was established and running smoothly I would repay his generosity.

Before a month was out, and after an uneventful ocean voyage of ten days, we found ourselves disembarking the steamship *Virginian* in Boston Harbor. Quatermain's business, having to do with investments involving the diamonds he brought back from the mines of King Solomon, took us to New York as well, and it was concluded within a few days. Eventually we found ourselves with time on our hands. It was a Friday night, then, when we were strolling down a lane quite bursting with a variety of entertainment choices when we came upon an art gallery. We entered and walked slowly through, gazing upon paintings by Monet and Renoir and Cézanne and the like. Though he was silent, I could tell that Quatermain was disgruntled.

"Allan," I ventured, "you're restless."

"John, what am I to make of these pictures? What are these blurs and blobs? What has happened to art? Isn't the point of a picture to represent *something*—some reality?" He fell silent and I could see the muscles below his left eye twitch slightly as he mused. "I remember there was an exhibition when I was last in London about ten or eleven years ago. *[Editor's note: This would have been before Quatermain's retirement to England, of course.]* Now that was art! Straightforward, clear, no doubt what you were looking at. I forget his name . . . it was a Mexican scene, I think, of a raging volcano with a jungle and a waterfall in the foreground. Blast, I wish I could remember the artist's name. It was one of those names that is also a word, something like Temple or Hall."

The proprietor of the gallery happened to hear Quatermain's remarks and said, "You must be referring to Church, Frederick Church. He did a number of Mexican and South American scenes, some of which toured Europe. He lives just upstate, you know, in the Hudson River area."[13]

"He does? Now there's a man whose hand I would like to shake. In fact, his pictures would fit well within the Grange. Now there's an idea! Where, sir, could I purchase one or two?"

The proprietor's face shifted from a smile to a frown. "Well, now, his work has been out of favor for some years now. Also, it isn't so easy to find one available these days."

"Well, then," I offered, "Perhaps we can trek 'upstate' and see if we can get one from the source, and then you could indeed shake the man's hand!"

Of such small resolutions, big things happen and, within four days, after making inquiries, we found ourselves approaching Olana, which we first perceived as an exotic palace set on a snowy hilltop surrounded by trees.[14]

Let me set the stage once again, the better to savor memories of that most pleasant evening. You had been alerted by wire of our visit and awaited us in the foyer of your home. In short order we met your wife and four children, ate a sumptuous supper and retired to your perfectly appointed sitting room.

As we entered this room, and Quatermain's and my gaze took in our new surroundings, something peculiar happened. It was a small thing, and I doubt anyone else would have noticed. I did because I was already medically attuned to my friend's smallest behaviors. His gaze stopped abruptly at the painting above the hearth, and I saw him start. He quickly regained control and we continued in. I quickly forgot it, and remember it now only because, in retrospect, its significance is clear.

As the evening progressed, the fire bloomed, warming your guests as did the delightful spirits clinging to the sides of the crystal goblets in our hands.

"I dare say, Mr. Church," Quatermain said, "that your hospitality and fellowship have made our journey to America more than worth it."

"That is very kind of you to say, Mr. Quatermain," you replied. "Likewise, the company of one as worldly as yourself gives me inestimable pleasure."[15]

As I relaxed, I couldn't help but notice that the entire decor of the sitting room was clearly chosen to complement the painting that was over the mantle and that had riveted Quatermain's attention. Judging from the extreme care of rendering of minute detail, this work, I determined, must be one of your own.

I said as much and inquired as to the subject.

"Ah," you said, "this is the ancient treasury house—carved in red sandstone—of El Khasne in Petra. Some call it 'the rose red city half as old as time.' It is quite the amazing place, located as it is amongst some cragged mountains in the middle of a desert wilderness south of the Dead Sea. We traveled there thirteen years ago. The place has special meaning for me, but I suppose that's obvious."[16]

I noted aloud that the rendering of the painting seemed somehow unusual, showing as it does a mere fragment of the glowing treasury house on the far side of what looked to be a great crack in a cliff face, the rock sides of the crack dominating two-thirds of the painting and rendered in a dark, opaque, almost oppressive fashion.

"But, you see," you said, "that is just the way it is. The gateway to Petra is a crack in the mountain wall. The crack leads into a narrow canyon a thousand feet deep where the sun seldom shines, and the canyon leads into the city. That is part of the wonder of it. An entire fabulous city hidden from view, protected from enemies. Besides which, it is also the very spirit of civilization, or, at least, so it seems to me, which is why it is so central to this room. From the point of view of the artist, the dark cliff walls force your eye to the sunlit façade beyond, which was my intent."

For a few moments, we were all lost in our thoughts. Then Quatermain broke the silence, venturing, "Though hardly a connoisseur of art, Mr. Church, I have nonetheless formed a distant and great admiration for your paintings. I am a straightforward man, and take my enjoyment in a straightforward manner. This new impressionism is simply a confusion, if you ask me. But, sir, when you paint a leaf, a leaf it is and nothing more. When you draw a mountain or valley, there is no doubt of what you have represented. By chance do you have a work in progress you would care to share or, perhaps, even one that I may purchase for my own home?" Then he added almost shyly, "I'm in the position now of being able to afford the finer things in life."

You smiled wistfully. "Perhaps I should have mentioned it at the outset, but I have retired from the business of landscape painting, as my arthritis makes it increasingly difficult to ply my craft. For well over a decade it's been now. Which is not to say that I have stopped painting altogether. In fact, in the corner behind you, Quatermain, propped on an easel by the window is a new one. It is, I'm sorry to say for your sake, spoken for already."

You rose, crossed the room, and removed the covering from the painting. My first impression was that its oils still looked wet in the firelight. The image portrayed a fairy city, noble and pristine in the brilliant distance, while in the deep shadows of the foreground a man stood at a curious fountain.

You were saying that your plans for Olana would eventually include a formal art studio with proper lighting. In the meantime, you still dabbled, as it were, in your Manhattan studio, and that you had brought this nearly completed landscape to Olana to view it in the light of the country, since you never considered a painting complete until you had viewed it in the light of both city and country.

As for the subject matter, you said it presented an idealized view of Constantinople with a fountain called El Ayn. It was realized from sketches and notes you had placed in your sketchbook some thirty years earlier during your journey to that part of the Old World. "I call this one *The Fountain*," you said.[17]

I recall that Quatermain studied the picture at length and finally sat back down with his brandy. The three of us were quiet for a time. For my part I was content in the company of these world-class men. I noticed that Quatermain's eyes returned over and again to *The Fountain* and also to Petra's ancient treasury house over the fireplace.

"I must admit," he finally said, "that these particular works of yours, Mr. Church, call to mind an interesting interlude in my life, wherein I was required to traverse through a mountain cleft much as you've rendered there . . . only to encounter a most fabulous city and a fountain as well—but one of a very different character, I dare say." Then he shook his head as though shaking off the memories that had intruded themselves into his mind.

"But that has nothing to do with anything," he said with finality. He abruptly stood, saying, "Mr. Church, I fear we have overstayed our welcome. I merely wished to make acquaintance of a man whose artistic technique so closely parallels my own concept of an organized universe. That and to perhaps purchase a painting, but I can see that that is easier said than done."

Somewhat taken aback by the abruptness of Quatermain's leave-taking, I was about to rise, but you would have none of it. "*Mister* Quatermain, please sit back down. Humor me, please. Your comment interested me. I am flattered that my work would evoke memories in one—that is to say an adventurer—such as yourself. I hesitate to be so bold, but may I inquire about this 'interlude' you mention?"

To this Quatermain at first demurred, but our insistence prevailed and thus it happened that we sat before that wonderful fire, partaking of your delicious spirits long into the night. Quatermain turned back the hands of time while you and I sat enthralled, experiencing vicariously so many entirely new sights, sounds, and feelings.

Thus, because his experiences seem to me worthy of permanent record, I have set them down—and I only hope my attempt will be deemed acceptable in your eyes and in those who may chance to follow in time to come.

—J.H.W.

THE GREAT DETECTIVE AT THE CRUCIBLE OF LIFE;

Or, The Adventure of the Rose of Fire

Ethiopia shall soon stretch out her hands unto God.
—Psalm 68:31

In some older strata, do the fossilized bones of an ape more anthropoid (manlike) or a man more pithecoid (apelike) than any yet known await the researches of some unborn paleontologist?
—T.H. Huxley

A new animal was abroad on the planet, spreading slowly out from the African heartland.
—A.C. Clarke

Introduction

As Told By Allan Quatermain

It was Christmas morning 1871 [Quatermain began] as I was preparing to leave the Black Kloof, the dreadful, dark and haunted gorge that was the home of Zikali, "The Opener of Roads," the formidable and clever black dwarf who was the wizard Zulu kings most held in awe, where he'd had me stay for several days and nights telling him every last detail of my recent adventures to Heu-Heu land—where he had sent me to procure a certain medicine for him. As I say, I was preparing the oxen and wagon to leave the area when two of his immense guards came to me and explained very politely in their Zulu language that Zikali wished to see me one additional time before we rode off.

Now, when Hans, my faithful Hottentot[18] servant, heard this, he clamped his hands to his head and moaned, "Baas! Oh Baas, leave now while we have the chance. No Baas! The Opener of Roads must have another grocery errand for you down another long road and I am sick to death of his errands."

Hans was a little Hottentot fellow who had been my companion through most of my adventures, even when I was a lad. Indeed, my very first memories include him, as he was aide-de-camp for my father. Hans was strong, quick, and agile, also clever—extremely so—and quite astute when the need called for it. Otherwise, he remained quite content to drink when he could, and when he couldn't, he tended to get himself into mischief in the most ingenious ways. In any case, his eyes were always bloodshot from the drink, which was, if he had any choice in the matter, gin, which he called "square-face" after the shape of the bottle it came in. Nevertheless, he was devoted to me, as he was to my father before me. Sad to say, he is gone from this world now and I miss him, but that is another story, and neither here nor there, and has no pertinence to my tale.[19]

So it was that I looked at the two enormous men who stood waiting patiently and said to Hans, "If you think either or both of these fellows will take 'no' for an answer, then you may be my guest in the execution of your plan."

"No, Bass, for I think now that you have a point and because I think 'execution' is just the right word to describe our poor futures if we deny these huge fellows."

The end of it was that I was soon once again seated before the shriveled old dwarf, who said, "Macumazahn"—which means "Watcher by Night" and is what the natives call me—"thank you for returning to speak to this Old Cheat, as I know you call me at every opportunity. There is another matter of which I wish to speak.

"The reason I called you back is this: Last night as I slept, my spirit flew much farther than it does most times—halfway to the stars it seemed—and when I looked down upon the face of the world, I saw not the world of forests and mountains and deserts that are the coin of the world, but instead a giant bowl, its edges aflame. Then fiery stones fell from the sky with horrible roaring sounds and poisonous smoke and crashed into the bowl."

I sat listening to this nonsense, wanting only to be on my way, for the truth is I become impatient with Zikali and his ilk very quickly. "So what does this have to do with me?" I asked. "Do you have another errand for me?"

"Why, Macumazahn, I am talking about how your life, as pale and feeble as it is, as humble as it is, will soon have an encounter with the gods, or rather, a god. That much I know from the dream. But let's look further into the matter."

Here he grabbed some ashes from the circle of dying embers that surrounded the small fire that burned forever it seemed before his crouching figure, poured them on the dirt floor and patted them flat. I should say here that my acquaintance with Zikali began when I was quite young, hardly a boy, but even then he looked much the same as he did during this encounter, a shriveled dwarf with eyes of fire and an enormous head from which granite white hair fell in lavish braids. I have often thought that this particular posture of his, which I dare say is the only one that I can recall seeing, made him look much like an evil, aberrant toad.

He clapped his hands, and a servant appeared, one of those who had requested our return, with Zikali's catskin medicine bag and handed it to the wizard, who rummaged inside and pulled out his yellowed knuckle bones, those that he kept near him at all times and used for divining, or at least supposedly so, for I don't take much stock in such tricks that are the stock in trade of Africa's wizards. Then he shook the bones in his cupped hands for a bit and threw them down into the ashes.

Here he did something that I certainly didn't expect, and can say in truth I never witnessed before or since. He actually flinched as though startled. This was especially unusual because Zikali's whole existence was one of control. In many ways, he was like the puppeteer who controlled the marionette strings of his minions over all Zululand and beyond. I pretended I hadn't noticed and he continued to peer at the bones in the ashes.

"Ah!" he said, "more than a mere encounter. Much more. You will become an honored familiar to a great goddess. No, not a great goddess. *The* great goddess," he said, cocking his head and glancing at the bones from a somewhat different angle. Here he began to chant under his breath in a hypnotic wavering drone and rocked back and forth on his haunches. I sat impatiently for several minutes waiting for him to say what he had to say. I must have dozed, for the next thing I remember is seeing that he had a figurine cupped in his hands. The figurine, only about three inches in height, was one of those fertility goddesses that one sees so often these days in drawings of artifacts that have been dug up from archaeological sites all over the world. This, as those, possessed heavy drooping breasts, wide hips and a pregnant, prominent belly. Zikali dug a small indentation in the ashes and there placed the figure carefully before him. He then waved his hands in wide large movements, fanning the fire and bringing some of the smoke up from the fire to himself where it circled his head then drifted down to the figurine and began to encircle it, a horizontal ring of smoke that formed a kind of halo above that bit of carved black stone. All this while he had been chanting, and after some time, it was almost as though he had gone to sleep himself, with only the occasional audible mutter communicating that he may be alert still.

His murmuring eventually stopped, and he stirred himself and coughed. Then he reached into his medicine bag again and withdrew a handful of roots that he began to deliberately place into the fire, one by one, and each flared with a different colored flame and smoke. In a few moments, a rainbow of flames emanated from the little fire and the small hut was thick with the complicated, changing patterns created by the intermingling columns of many-hued smoke.

Before long I thought I was seeing an image in the congealing smoke. It was really quite a complicated illusion, and I must admit that for a short time I almost believed the image was real. What I thought I was seeing was this: I was standing alone on an enormous plain, when suddenly a burning stone fell from the sky with a shriek, hitting the ground and setting fire to a nearby thorn bush. Then, lightning flared all around the flickering flames of the bush and a voice like thunder spoke my name, "Allan, O Allan!"

And I responded in my dream with, "My Lord, why have you brought me hither?" At this, I began untying my boots and awkwardly slipping them off my feet, for it seemed the right thing to do, though I felt rather foolish.

"O Allan, she who is mother to all, she who is mother to all the world needs your aid. Go to her and I charge you with her care while you are with her. I also task you with discharging the great responsibility that she will require of you."

"What responsibility, Lord?"

And the response was an enigmatic one. The voice from the fiery bush said, "You are but a cog in the wheel of life and in the fullness of time you will exercise my will, though mayhap you will not know it."

At which point the fiery bush began to smoke terribly, and then the smoke was the smoke in the hut. It was choking me and I had no choice but to jump up and run out into the air.

When I returned some minutes later feeling somewhat better but still confused and shaken, the smoke had cleared, by what manner it was done so fast I don't know. I returned to my sitting position in the dirt before Zikali. I noticed that though the fire still flickered, for it never went out entirely, it was now mostly glowing embers, and the bones and small idol and medicine bag had been cleared away. Zikali himself was motionless but making a peculiar sound. In time I decided he was laughing, "Ho, ho, ho, ho!" When he quieted down, he said, "O, White Man, who is so brave as is his whole race, I can see into your mind. You are saying, 'He is nothing but an old repulsive Kaffir cheat and magician. I saw nothing of consequence except that which was suggested to me while I was somehow drugged and made to dream.' But you are also wondering now how can "the thing that should never have been born" know of such things?*

"Verily, Macumazahn, I had little to do with any of this. I have heard that your people have something called a magic lantern that projects pretty pictures that you all gather round and make surprised sounds at. Consider then that I have only been a magic

---

* Editor's note: 'The thing that should never have been born' was a title mockingly given to the wizard some fifty years before by the great Zulu emperor, Shaka, as there was "bad blood" between the two.—T.K.M.

lantern through which one greater than I caused you to see that which you were intended to see."

By then, I was vastly confused and said as much. But it really came down to one simple question: "Zikali, why did you want to see me and ask your messengers to bring me back here before you? Always you want me to help you for some selfish end. What do you want of me?"

The old wizard finally stopped laughing and peered at me with his infinitely black eyes. "O, Macumazahn," he began, "you always think so poorly of me! I have nothing to gain, nothing at all. The information I convey will merely be of use to you, that is all. It appears the goddess has honored you and requires you to carry a grand message outside the bowl, for that is where you will meet her, that bowl that I saw in my dream last night."

"What is this bowl?" Then skeptically, "What is the nature of this message?"

"Ah, Macumazahn, as always you doubt your friend, the Old Cheat. But perhaps this time you are more justified than usual, for I can tell you no more. The fiery stones, the bowl, the queen of the gods, the message . . . these are all that I am allowed to be privy to and no more, no more details at all, for a vast black shield blocks my arts. It is as though something or someone wished to whet both our appetites, and, once having done so, withdrew.

"Now begone with you. Though we are friends of decades, at the moment you tire me, and I want to consider what power it is that can turn the great 'Opener of Roads' into a mere tool."

Shortly thereafter, Hans and I were soon back at the wagons, where my men had made the final preparations. The oxen and the wagons were ready to go, for which I was thankful because I wanted to be away from the Black Kloof as fast as my feet and the feet of our oxen could take me.

I spent the better part of several days trying to understand what had happened. The most amazing thing of all is that, for the first time, I saw the great Zikali seem contrite and not in control. Never in my presence before or after that affair did he seem so *unsure* of the ground on which he stood. I alternated between shaking my head in wonderment at that and trying to make sense of the vision I saw, or thought I saw. It was almost as though the Hebrew God "I am that I am" took a moment off his busy schedule to ask a favor of me!

Dash it all! My head hurt when I pondered all this, so after a while I pushed all else out of my mind except the glorious image of a hot bath in the simple tub in my small home in Durban, the small home I had not seen in nearly a year, for that was the length of Zikali's little grocery trip!

*   *   *

"So, gentlemen, that is merely the beginning of the story. It is but the preamble to a journey that seems in retrospect as unlikely as, say, bumping into the honest-to-goodness Pearly Gates while strolling through London's West End. For myself . . . perhaps I am a doubting Thomas or perhaps I am merely pragmatic . . . . "

[*Watson note: Quatermain did not finish the thought, but instead sighed deeply and said, "But the telling of the rest will take some time. Should I continue?" Well, you (Church) and I were both quite caught up and adamant that it was out of the question that he just stop there. The end of it was that Quatermain asked for more brandy, which request you happily obliged, and there was quiet all around except for the crackling fire in the hearth. Quatermain rolled the amber liquid in his glass, catching the glow of the fire through the glass. In time, he heaved another great sigh and continued his story. —J.H.W.*]

CHAPTER ONE

Allan's Unwanted Guests

As we approached Durban on the very day of Epiphany, January 6, 1872[20] [Quatermain continued], the town had a merry appearance, still in the throes of Christmas celebration. I remember how all this Christmas atmosphere and a generally melancholy mood (somehow imposed on me by that damnable wizard!) put me in mind of the history of the area. Europeans had first troubled themselves to notice the southeastern coast of Africa on a Christmas morning in the fifteenth century and the area had been called Natal ever since as a consequence.[21]

I remember too how I mused that Lieutenant Francis George Farewell would hardly have recognized the trading community he founded in May 1824, which he called Port Natal, but which name was changed a few years later to Durban, after the then new governor of the Cape. Not only had it become a prosperous and bustling town (rather than the half dozen or so poor structures that Farewell's people had thrown up) but, at the moment in question it was so festooned with decorations of the season that it appeared more a carnival than a serious community.

"Baas," Hans said while rubbing his dirty, sparsely stubbled chin, "I hope the Big Baas in the sky can forgive you your sins for which his Son was pinned to a tree, since you don't look like a man who is in the mood to celebrate anything at all, least of all His Son's birthday."

This was only nine years ago—it seems like a lifetime ago, but of course I've done a great deal since then—but I'm never likely to forget the reason for the frown that had so changed my face that it prompted Hans's remark: There in front of my house stood four men, three of whom were very serious, business-like men, which was precisely what I did not want to see at that time. I was tired after a very long trek and only wanted to settle into my little house, but somehow I knew that that particular small reward would be denied me.

"Look yonder, Hans, and tell me what there is to celebrate."

He did as I bade and seemed startled, I presume because he had missed this new circumstance even though it was as evident as the nose on his face, something he subsequently wrote off by saying he was distracted by all the holiday ribbons and festive colors, though I knew he secretly admonished himself about it for days to come.

"Oh, Baas, those four have faces like the Predikant, your reverend father, when he would find me drunk behind the shed—stern and unsmiling—but your father never had a face pale like plaster as these do. All my poor life I have known white men, both high and low, but these men are more white than any of the others, and therefore all the more ugly for it." Then he grinned, "But they also look rich, which can only be good news, as I have heard you mutter to yourself that our purse is poor and even more so since we have used up so much on this journey and gotten no reward for our grocery errand except a pat on the back from The Opener of Roads."

"Hans, I don't care if they offer me a golden platter heaped with diamonds, I intend to rest and intend to do exactly so and nothing more."

By this time, we had arrived at the proximity of my front porch, and the men in question approached. One separated himself from the others and held out his hand to me. "Mr. Quatermain I presume?"

"You are correct," I said as we shook hands.

"Mr. Quatermain, my name is Richard Holmes. I am with the British Museum on some rather urgent business. These are my associates Thomas Huxley, Will Scott, and Sergeant Cuff."

Mr. Holmes looked as though he represented a museum. He was average height—meaning that he was somewhat taller than myself—middle aged and scholarly. His cheeks held thick tufts of graying hair and his hairline receded, but he was otherwise clean shaven.

Huxley would have been tall, if he wasn't so stooped. His face was nearly covered with thick white whiskers, though his chin and cheeks were clean shaven. It seemed to me, too, that Huxley was beginning to grow somewhat stout about the middle. But I remember his eyes especially—so piercing and intense that when he shot a glance at you, some part of your mind had to remind yourself that you had not in fact been shot. This contributed to the great power—almost that of a youth in his prime—that I felt emanating from the man and I decided that he was not a man to be toyed with. Beyond that, I remember thinking that his high forehead and the smooth cut of his exposed cheeks above his beard bore an odd resemblance to those of the young man who had been introduced as Will Scott.*

I said, "Mr. Huxley, your name is familiar, but I fear that I can't immediately place it." But then I remembered, "Oh! I have it now. Aren't you the man who has stood at Mr. Darwin's side through thick and thin?"

---

* Editor's note: William Baring-Gould, who has done much to fill out Sherlock Holmes's life beyond Watson's biographical and anecdotal sketches, tells us in his biography of the sleuth, *Sherlock Holmes on Baker Street*, that Holmes's parents had three boys, Sherrinford in 1845, Mycroft in 1847, and Sherlock seven years later. Holmes's father wished to name their third-born son after the 17th century theologian William Sherlock, but his mother preferred naming the child after her favorite author, Sir Walter Scott. "At last," says Baring-Gould, "a compromise was arrived at. The boy was baptized William Sherlock Scott Holmes." —T.K.M.

Huxley seemed pleased with this perception and my phrasing of it. "Indeed I am," said he. "Though I must admit some surprise that in a spot so remote you would have heard of my humble efforts on behalf of my friend and his conclusions. I suppose, my being a fellow of the Royal Society and all, that my name creeps into public awareness now and again."

To which I responded, "Though I may be a backwoodsman, I've read of your championing Mr. Darwin, sir, and I admire your courage for standing up for what you believe. Though my reading of books is limited mostly to the Old Testament and the Ingoldsby Legends, I have read abstracts of Mr. Darwin's book and have seen enough in Africa to admit that his notions have given me much food for thought, at the least. I have read about you more than once in the various publications that make their way here to Durban. Though I haven't been near a newspaper in almost a year, I recall that 'survival of the fittest' is the phrase that the gentlemen of the press seemed to enjoy trumpeting about."

"Yes, indeed, sir. 'Natural selection' is still quite the topic these days."

My response was to smile politely.

The boy, Will Scott, was hardly more than seventeen or eighteen years and extremely tall and thin. In fact, he was nearly the tallest European I have ever seen, though I have seen some Watuzi of comparable height, if not taller. So thin in fact was he that I feared for his health. His arms, too, seemed unusually long, but his grip was firm, which tells much about a man.[22] Also he stood upright and straight, and with his solid determined chin, he had a singular air of purpose about him.

As for the last member of the party, Sergeant Cuff (and now that I think about it, I don't believe I ever learned the man's Christian name—how odd!), he was of advanced age and average height. But my initial reaction was for this man's health as well, for he was hardly more than skin and bones. Beyond this, it was clear that he had not shaved for several days, his hair was gray and cut extremely short, and his complexion was severely wrinkled and dry.

Just as these thoughts crossed my mind, Hans, who had been able to stealthily come up behind me, whispered in my ear: "Oh, Baas, this one you must be careful with. He is like a dead man who still walks and talks. Do you think he might be one of the spooks who belong to The Opener of Roads?"

"Hush!" I said as unobtrusively as I could. Then to Cuff, "Mr. Holmes introduced you as Sergeant, sir. Are you retired from her majesty's service?"

"Oh, no, Quatermain. I'm a policeman."

"A policeman! What on earth?" I shook my head in confusion. "Gentlemen, gentlemen! I'm afraid I am most perplexed."

"Mr. Quatermain," Cuff rejoined, "it falls upon Mr. Holmes to explain the details at this early juncture."

Holmes opened his mouth and I'm sure would have told me all about it, about Cuff and all the rest of their business, but I would have none of it. Just then, suddenly, I was filled with a sense of defeat and perhaps a little foreboding, and it was all I could do to smile politely. I was not pleased at this uninvited, unwanted attention, but I could see that these were determined men with a mission, though at that moment I had no idea what that mission might be.

"Gentlemen! Not yet!" I said, surrendering to the feeling of fate about to overwhelm me. "I'm sure you have far more to tell me than my poor head can hold for the moment. Please allow me! As you see me this moment, I have not crossed the threshold of my house for nearly a year, and there it is, just a few feet away, beckoning me, and I'm afraid its allure is far more than I can handle."

This statement shocked them all into apoplexies of apologies, and they quickly stood back and let me through.

"You see," I began, actually enjoying the tiny bit of power I was able to assert just then, "I am anxious to take off my boots and sit in my chair. And the last thing I want to hear at the moment is your purpose. I beg you, therefore, to indulge me while I settle back into the domestic life."

With only a little comment, they were kind enough to oblige. I invited them in and they made themselves as comfortable as they could in my modest accommodations.

These, then, were my first impressions of these men with whom I would journey far and share experiences the nature of which it will be extremely difficult to communicate [but for the sake of you two gentlemen, I will try]. Among these impressions was the sense that though Holmes initiated the talking, Huxley was the man in charge. In addition, though Cuff might have looked like a cadaver, I quickly became most impressed with the man's energy, an energy that entirely belied all my first impressions.

*   *   *

After we all shared a simple dinner of buttered rice and mutton, washed down with Kaffir beer, I finally consented to hear out my unwanted guests. Hans, who had disappeared at the start, as he was wont to do when "customers" first made their appeals to me, reemerged and silently settled down onto his haunches unnoticed in a corner.

"Well," I said to Mr. Holmes, "what business does the British Museum have with me, not to mention the police?"

Here, young Will Scott chose to speak. "I'm afraid much of the blame falls on me, sir. I'm sure you don't recall, but we met almost two years ago at Castle Ragnall. It was at a rather large garden party."

He waited for some light of remembrance from me. "I'm sorry, young man, I don't recall having seen you there."

"But of course, since I was only fifteen or sixteen then. I had been invited by my dear friend Luna, Miss Holmes.[23] You may recall that you made quite an impression on her."

"Yes, of course, I do remember that. She pumped me for every detail of every trek I had ever undertaken in southern Africa. A lovely young woman. How is she?"

"Quite fine. She and Lord Ragnall married not so long ago. It was when Richard here mentioned to me his desire to hire the 'best damned guide in Africa' that I remembered you and went so far as to recommend you."

I looked at Richard Holmes and said, "Might you be a relative of Luna?"

"Oh, no. Just a coincidence of names. I have yet to meet this young woman, who one and all refer to in the most reverent tones. But, yes indeed," Holmes added, "after inquiries, I determined that you were just the right man for the job."

"And just what is the job you have in mind?"

"You know of course, just four years ago, Britain sent a large force to Abyssinia for the purpose of rescuing hostages from Emperor Theodore."

"Yes, I was upcountry during those events, but I learned of the Ethiopian campaign belatedly."

"Some 280 ships unloaded 32,000 men and 20,000 mules, and materiel enough to keep them all going. Quite an astonishing expedition. Field-Marshal Lord Napier marched his army into the highlands for some three months. In the end, Theodore took his own life (or seemed to, which is one of the reasons we're here). A certain amount of bounty was acquired for the purpose of paying the men. I can proudly say that I accompanied this expeditionary force and was there when the emperor's treasury was cataloged."

"Plundered is more like it," broke in Huxley. "I hear the soldiers went through the place like mad beasts."

"True enough, I'm afraid," responded Holmes, frowning with the memory. "In the end, however, I was able to retrieve some 900 manuscripts and other historical documents to return to the museum for preservation. It has been my great and fortunate honor during the interim to examine and determine just what we found."

He had paused, for effect, I think, but since he failed to continue, I felt obliged to speak. "And this has to do with me in what way?"

"After the demise of Theodore," Holmes continued, "the three chief contenders to the throne warred amongst themselves, and still are for that matter. Her Majesty's government, for various reasons, supports one by the name of Kasa Mercha, who has been extending his influence for well over a decade. In fact, in about two weeks, it is intended by our government that he ascend to the throne. I believe he has chosen the name Yohannes IV. Naturally, this has been a long time in development.

"But the fact is that in recent months rumors have reached Mercha, and thus to the top levels of the British government, to the effect that Theodore is not dead. That the dead man we came upon on the steps of his fortress Magdala was that of a fanatical look-alike. There is talk amongst Ethiopians that Theodore still lives and rules from some secret location. The talk is that the King of Kings has risen from the dead and rules.

"Mercha, as you can imagine, is a bit nervous about these rumors. His own attempts to send agents to determine the truth have failed. Her Majesty thus feels a responsibility to make the effort to put the lie to the rumors or find Theodore if he lives. We—" he took in the others with a sweep of his arm, "—are her tools in this regard." At that, Holmes ceased to talk and there was silence.

Finally, I said, "This is all well and good, gentleman, but, I repeat, what does it have to do with me? And what does this purely political matter have to do with a noted biological naturalist like Mr. Huxley here? Or a policeman such as Mr. Cuff? Or, for that matter, a museum curator such as yourself?"

All eyes turned to Richard Holmes. He seemed to blush for a moment. He cleared his throat and continued.

"You see, Mr. Quatermain, Napier's expedition had some corollary effects. Several, as a matter of fact. First things first, though. Sergeant Cuff is here in the official capacity of determining whether Theodore is alive or dead. He was chosen because his methods of deduction have proven over and again to be of great service to the Crown. The official determination of Theodore's continued existence or not is in his hands."

Here I looked at Cuff, but he merely rubbed the growth of gray grizzly beard on his chin. As I had nothing to say to the man at that moment, I was about to give my attention back to Holmes, when Cuff addressed me.

"I see that you have climbing roses around your porch, Quatermain."

"Why, yes. I'm afraid I don't have much chance to enjoy them, though."

"Ah. Of course. Perhaps if you were around more, then they would be better cared for. I couldn't help but notice that they're only one step from the wild state."

I was stunned. I had no idea how to take this comment. Was it innocent? Was it meant critically? If so, how dare he, who hardly knew me? Such thoughts filled my brain as I stared astonished and wide-eyed at the man.

It was Will Scott who jumped to the man's rescue. "Quatermain, please understand that beyond police work, Sergeant Cuff's primary passion in life is the cultivation of roses. That is all we heard about on the voyage here."

"I'm sorry if I offended you, Quatermain," said Cuff. "It's just that roses poorly tended rub me the wrong way. A year is a long time to be away, though, to be sure. And, yes, it is my affidavit that may very well put an end to this Theodore affair."

Not quite knowing what to make of all this, I took a long quiet, and what I hoped was an unobtrusive, breath and then slipped on my bartering face, the blank expression I always wore when trading with the various peoples one encounters in Africa. Unfazed by the interruption, Holmes was continuing. "Huxley's role is one of an entirely different character."

Huxley took up the tale: "You can imagine what it must have been like, 32,000 men and tens of thousands of animals crossing the desert and thence into the highlands. Though I was not there, I can see in my mind the cloud of dust. Richard was there, however, and he has described the scene. No matter the details. You see, once the army had accomplished its goals and marched back through the village of Zula to Annesley Bay, the harbor from which the expedition had been mounted, one soldier, Corporal Saint James by name, knowing it would take several days to dismantle the camp, decided to do a bit of sightseeing. You understand, his activities at that time were strictly contrary to orders, but he rationalized that he would never be in Ethiopia again and that he had a small boy back home in India for whom he wanted to find a proper souvenir. His route took him into some barren, terrible areas, as he describes them. At one point he found something of particular interest. Not being an ignorant man, he knew he had found something of interest to more than just his young son."

Huxley slowly reached into his inside coat pocket and removed a leather pouch. He opened it, extracted some wadding, which he unfolded, and produced a piece of bone, which he then held out to me. Taking note of the wadding and extreme care with which it had been packaged, I took hold of it very gingerly and held it up into the light from a beam that poured through the window into the room from the setting sun. I turned the bone every which way, showed it to Hans, and so on. But in fact, it wasn't bone at all but rock in the shape of a bone, so I knew it to be some sort of fossil.

Huxley continued, "He spotted a dozen or so pieces just such as you have there just lying on the desert floor, exposed to the elements. He picked them up, protected them, and, of course, intended to get them aboard ship without anyone noticing."

I examined the piece closer, saying, "It looks to be the forearm bone from a monkey of some sort." I looked at Hans, who was nodding his head vigorously. "Fossilized," I added, "which implies great age. However, aside from that, I am not clear as to its significance."

"Ah, you are quite right, Quatermain," said Huxley. "It does in fact originate from a primate of some sort. You see this is but one of the several pieces that Saint James found. It is a convoluted story, but Saint James's escapade did not go unnoticed and his souvenirs were commandeered. Fortunately, they made their way into my hands. I shudder when I imagine what could have happened to them if they had been the responsibility of less learned men. Suspecting an unusual provenance, I brought them to the attention of Darwin. He and I have spent days, weeks, with the bones, measuring, weighing, comparing, conjecturing, mulling over the whole set. The upshot is that we are convinced that these bones belong to a primitive ancestor of Man—perhaps as old as a million years.[24] The very sort of creature Darwin hypothesizes about in *The Descent of Man*, which in fact was being printed in February just as these fragments came to our attention."

I must say that this new information made me look anew and with greater admiration at the odd bit of bone in my hand.

"However, our conjectures are meaningless with so little to go on, so it quickly became imperative that a team be assembled to go to Ethiopia and more closely investigate the region Corporal Saint James stumbled upon. Through official channels, it was determined that both the needs of the British government, as relayed by Mr. Holmes, and that of Mr. Darwin and myself intersected and that it would be mutually beneficial if we teamed together. Feeling grateful that there was a chance to hastily join an expedition of an official nature that was in itself being hastily prepared, I, as Mr. Darwin's representative, became part of the group you see before you today. In fact, as I had pressing responsibilities, it was necessary that I feign illness from overwork." Here he grinned. "I was so successful that my doctor prescribed therapeutic travel. Only Darwin and a few others in the government know where I truly am. To the rest of the world, I'm on holiday in France and Germany. In addition, young Will Scott, here, has agreed to accompany me as my assistant since a fair amount of tedious digging and methodical record keeping will no doubt be necessary, regardless of the outcome. And let me say that he volunteered to do this at no small inconvenience to himself, as he was about to take up residence at Christ Church, where he will begin his first year at Oxford in a few months, when these circumstances became known to him." Huxley looked over at Scott and fairly burst with pride and affection.

Scott blushed at the mention of his name and said quickly, "Yes, I'm Mr. Huxley's assistant." He smiled broadly. Then he opened his mouth again as though to say something, but Huxley's demeanor instantly changed and he gave Scott a quick look, at which the young man snapped his mouth shut. This, of course, aroused my interest and I remember thinking that under different circumstances I would have determined what exactly the boy had wanted to say. As it happened, though, I was simply tired and really did not care.

During this entire conference, I was sitting in my rocker, one of the items I missed the most while traveling. I rocked. And I rocked. I must tell you, there was a profound silence in the room. I rocked because I was thinking.

Eventually, I looked again at the group's spokesman and said, "Mr. Holmes, I must admit that these various tales I'm hearing are interesting. Though, as I said, the notions of Mr. Huxley here and Mr. Darwin have given me pause, actually, I tend to lean toward the Old Testament in such matters, and besides, it seems to me that a monkey bone is merely a monkey bone. And that is the end of it. As I said, this is all very interesting, but it doesn't explain your presence, Mr. Holmes."

The face of the museum curator suddenly glowed; his eyes grew wide and he exclaimed, "Mr. Quatermain, I am present for no less reason than a miracle . . . . "

"My dear Mr. Holmes!" I exclaimed, for I was not used to being associated with such terminology.

"Mr. Quatermain, are you familiar with the Great Library of Alexandria?"

I'm afraid that my education, being rough and administered in the wilds of what is now the Cradock district of the Cape Colony, lacked some subtlety and the particular institution to which Holmes referred meant little to me. I said as much.

"Indeed, the Great Library of Alexandria was planned by the first Ptolemy and developed in the third century B.C. by Ptolemy II. Its goal was no less than the accumulation of all knowledge, and it seemed to have succeeded in that regard. Within its walls were some 700,000 papyrus scrolls containing the wisdom of the Macedonians, Romans, Egyptians, Jews, Indians, Persians, and Phoenicians, all their religion, science, and history. Over six centuries, this library evolved into the intellectual core and splendor of civilization, the crowning achievement of human life on earth. But, at the end of the fourth century A.D., the Christian Emperor Theodosius ordered it all burned."

"My word! What on earth for?"

"Well, Christianity was so sufficiently new that Theodosius was fearful of anything pagan, which is how he thought of the library and its contents. It was not one of the prouder moments of the Christian era, to be sure." Here he paused. "Yet, as I studied in the British Museum the hundreds of volumes from Theodore's treasury, I found several references, delicious hints, if you will, that inferred that a portion of the library, or at least many of its important scrolls, were secretly packed up, removed to Abyssinia, and hidden from the book burners. Preserved, in other words. And there is every reason to believe that that remnant of the library has not been touched since, that it is waiting to be rediscovered . . . perhaps to help humankind enter a new renaissance."

Holmes then pulled a paper from an inside coat pocket. "Quatermain, let me give you one small example of the nature of the sorts of things this library may hold for us. What I have here is a translation from a fragment of a scroll I found in Theodore's treasury. It, in turn, is a copy of a scroll far older that was part of the Alexandrian Library. Now, please indulge me and read this."

Reluctantly, for I knew that by doing so I was enmeshing myself further than I desired into this venture, I reached for the paper.

Yet, before I was able to touch it, Holmes drew his hand back, saying, "Quatermain, have you not heard of the Synoptic Problem?"

"The what problem?"

"In the Bible, man! Mark, Matthew, and Luke are called the Synoptic Gospels because they have such similar elements. Of Mark's 661 verses, more than 600 of Matthew's and 350 of Luke's are the same. But Matthew and Luke have 200 other verses that are the same but that do not appear in Mark."

"I'm afraid I had no idea," I said.

"For years, scholars have hypothesized that Matthew and Luke were independently compiled, or drawn, from Mark and from *another* and *unknown* source document. This would be an entirely new gospel."[25]

"Yes . . . I can see that," I said noncommittally.

"What you are about to read could well be a fragment from that new gospel. The author purports to be one Gaspar, which is the name tradition has given to one of the three Wise Men. Many scholars believe that if the Magi existed at all, they were probably Zoroastrian priests from somewhere in Asia Minor. It is also claimed in tradition that Gaspar was the youngest of the Wise Men and that he was Ethiopian."

He handed me the paper, his eyes wide with expectation, and I began to read [*Watson note: Here Quatermain closed his eyes and, struggling only a little, recalled from memory the gist of the document. —J.H.W*]:

"Thus Gaspar says:

"These are the words of Gaspar the Ethiopian.[26]

"I am dismayed. A significant portion of my life has been given to the study of one man, and more and more frequently I hear reports concerning him that are blatantly false or twisted far beyond the simple truths.

"Why is this? Can there be so many whose self-interest out-weighs the simple truth?

"In all things, Jesus the Nazarene said, 'Treat others as you would have them treat you. Do good and give as you can with-out expecting a thing in return. Your reward will be great, and God will call you his children. Show mercy even as your Father shows mercy. Do not judge, for how can you judge? What right do you have to judge when you have no understanding why a person is the way that person is? Remember, the standard you use will be the standard used toward you.'

"The one God is real, a spirit that is at the core of everything and everyone. God is always observing how you treat and judge others and how your actions and words, or inaction for that matter, affect others. This spirit doles out according to your actions. Hurt and you will be hurt, love and you will be loved, cause someone to cry in suffering and you will be made to cry with your own suffering. This circle of doing followed by God's response may be experienced immediately or may be held off for a future lifetime, according to the will of God for his own reasons.

"Jesus explained the way of the world in a simple manner, with parables that even children can understand. He was proud of his ability in this respect. He told his followers and all those who would listen, 'Blessed are the eyes that see the things that you see, for I tell you that many prophets and kings have desired to see those things that you see and have not seen them, and to hear those things that you hear and have not heard them.'

"And yet I, Gaspar, mourn, as none of this do I hear from the caravans. Instead I hear about magical wine and multiplying loaves and fishes. Where is the word of Jesus the Naserene, who told us not to worry about our lives, what we will eat, about our bodies, or what we will wear, for isn't life more than food, and the body more than flesh? Did he not remind us of the way lilies grow, that they do not work or spin, but that even Solomon, in all his splendor, was not as glorious?"

And thus the document ended. [Gentlemen, don't look at me so. There is no trick, I assure you. I had many an opportunity to study it in the weeks to come and I can recall it quite easily.] When I had finished reading, I looked at the men grouped in my house. I wasn't sure what they expected me to say or do. I wanted to say something like, "Mr. Holmes, surely you have better things to do with your time than to dabble in romance writing of this inferior sort" but I thought better of it. Instead, I looked at them all and said, "I don't understand."

Holmes looked exasperated. I must chuckle to myself when I think back on it. He took the sheet back, neatly folded it, and returned it to his pocket. Then he continued as though I had said nothing. "This is only a fragment. If the full Gaspar document had been in circulation about 50 A.D.—which is when we believe it was written—then it would certainly have become part of the Alexandrian Library. Alternatively, if Gaspar was Ethiopian, then it's not entirely unlikely that a copy of his writings would have found its way into the library of an Ethiopian 'king of kings.' In either case, the full document, if we considered it and nothing else at all, would be priceless beyond discussion. And if it turns out to be the lost source document of which I was speaking, decades of arguing would be put to rest." Holmes let that sink in for a moment, then said, "But that could all be moot because we are not looking for one document but a library, or at least a significant portion of one."

As preposterous as all this sounded, I was beginning to realize that these important people hadn't come all the way from England to test my patience. "I repeat for the *third* time," said I, "what does all this have to do with me?"

"We want you to help us find the surviving remnants of the great Library of Alexandria," said Holmes.

"To help locate King Theodore II, if he still exists," broke in Sergeant Cuff.

"And to help locate the region where I can find more primitive bones," said Huxley.

I took a deep breath, calmed down. When next I spoke it was some minutes later. "Gentlemen, I assume your passage from London to Durban was done at the expense of the British government. That is all to the good. Because what you are proposing is lunacy—pure lunacy on a grand scale on a myriad of levels. I would have thought that men of your backgrounds would have realized the total futility of these sundry ventures, not to mention the cumulative lot, and would have given it up no sooner had the thought entered your collective minds.

"It would be one thing if you had maps or directions—though heaven knows I have seen enough suspect maps in my day!"[27]

Holmes then muttered something, a characteristic that did not seem to become the man, though I had only just met him.

"I beg your pardon," I asked.

"Quatermain," he began again, but with less conviction, "we

did bring some statements that might be of navigational assis-
tance." He drew some more papers out of his coat pocket. He
shuffled through them a moment, settled on one, and continued,
"Corporal Saint James described his journey as well as he could.
Let me read some extracts from his account [*Watson note: Here
Quatermain again closed his eyes, remembering. —J.H.W*]:

"Our thousands had been steering down from the highlands into the base camp. I was near the end of that long column, a fact that allowed me to move around somewhat more
than others without being observed. At an opportune time,
when the front of the column arrived in the vicinity of the bay, I
took off at dusk heading at first due south into the desert, then
following the easiest path, which turned me a bit to the east. I
didn't know what I was looking for, only that my boy would
like a fine souvenir. But the further away from the column I got,
a kind of giddiness took over. I felt a kind of freedom I hadn't
known since I was a boy myself. I kept telling myself I'd best be
going back, but my body would not obey my mind. The funny
thing is that I didn't feel at all worried at being found out. Instead I felt more like a kid at play. Anyway, seeing that you
want to know my route, after some time the moon came up and
I could see my surroundings pretty clearly. I'd say it was about
twenty miles from the start that a range of mountains kind of
popped up on my left. Even though I could see, on account of
the moon, I couldn't see much. I just knew they were there . . .
how far away I couldn't be certain. So far my path presented little more than broken rock and sand from the start. Then I saw
something that chilled my soul. In the distance, southwest of
my position, the sky was glowing with redness, I couldn't help
but aim toward the spot and after several miles I could see what
looked like a boiling cauldron at the top of a large hill. "I'll be
daft," I thought, "a volcano!" That I wasn't expecting! I looked
around at the ground thinking a volcanic stone or two would
suit my purposes, and indeed I did grab a couple, like chunks of

black glass. I stared at the fiery sight for a time, then, instead of turning back, which would have been the sensible thing to do, I decided to see what other wonders this strange land might reveal. Before long the cauldron had turned back into a glow on my rear horizon. Everything I've been describing took up most of the night, and as the sun rose, I felt like an egg in a pan. It was well over 100 degrees it was, maybe 120, 130, something like that. I found some shelter in a sort of cave formed by two boulders and was properly grateful for it, to be sure, and here I rested till night again, using my water sparingly. When I started up again, I continued on in more or less the same direction, that is to say south, southeast. I think that I forgot to say that the range of mountains I'd seen to the east did nothing but grow during my entire journey. All the while, I could see those mountains, sometimes dipping toward the horizon, sometimes looming so close it seemed like they were the whole world, if you catch my drift. And the volcano that I had left behind had merged into another, lower range of mountains off to the west, so that I was making my way through a sort of valley, I guess."

Here Holmes looked up at me. "And he goes on like this describing what he saw. He was asked some pointedly specific questions having to do with the kinds of rocks he noticed, type and degree of vegetation, etc. Unfortunately, he wasn't able to provide more than a middling amount of specific information, not being a naturalist of any sort. But in broad outlines, his expedition has been documented up to the point he found the fossil bones, which is the point at which he finally determined he should return. Now it is fairly certain that the volcano he encountered was Mt. Erta Ale, the location of which, obviously, is well known and mapped. The point is that his journey can be extrapolated and his probable positions placed on a map. So you see, in effect, we do have a map of sort leading to the general vicinity of his wonderful find."

I opened my mouth to express my incredulity, since the "vicinity" he so blithely spoke of was no doubt equivalent to hundreds of square miles, but I was cut short. "But there's more, Quatermain." Here he shuffled more of his papers. "Those rumors about Theodore still being alive include some geographical detail, namely that his (if it is his) base camp is probably near a ridge that is approachable from the east on a path that leads between two volcanoes. The entrance point of this path is about three days northwest by horse from the tip of the peninsula that is the African side of the Strait of Bab el Mandeb. Once again, extrapolating from the available information, we have reason to believe that the volcanoes in question are the Dama'Ali and the Kurub Koma, two of a complex chain of mountains and volcanoes that dot that country. The camp itself is on the western side of the volcanoes. And here it gets a little tricky. No one can say if the camp is approachable from the west."

Abruptly, young Will Scott broke in. "It is very exciting actually. If the camp is approachable from the west, then it would be in a spot just about due south of the fossil find, perhaps fifty or seventy-five miles. Our proposal then is to use Saint James's information to locate the fossil beds, and then we turn south and try to approach the camp from the west, and if we can, determine if Theodore is still with us or not. If that proves impossible, then we merely circle toward the south and east to find the path between the volcanoes."

To say I was dumbfounded would be an understatement. Tomfoolery, tommyrot, suicide, the whole venture was. And I said as much. "Young man, I have heard nothing but a lot of very vague terms in the last few minutes, words like *might provide, middling information, broad outlines, fairly certain*—you see, I have been listening!—*extrapolated, in effect, general vicinity, rumors, reason to believe*, and now you just uttered the most foolhardy of them all. One does not *merely* circle around a pair of volcanic mountains in singularly unknown territory."

Young Scott seemed abashed and his face flushed red, but this lasted but a moment, for he cleared his throat and launched right back into his justification for the expedition, "You see, it is perfectly obvious that there are some correspondences here that may be of use. The map extrapolated from Saint James's account seems to fit nicely into the particulars of the camp location, which are more than rumors, I believe, being actually the intelligence appropriated by spies, and, therefore, that much more credible. So you see, there is some sense to this enterprise. We only need to put all this disparate information into focus."

I looked helplessly at these unwanted guests of mine. I looked at each face in turn, at once trying, I suppose, to communicate with my eyes the hopelessness of this plan, and at the same time gain some sense of their degree of purpose. Indeed, all I saw was their passion and determination.

I looked at the papers still in Holmes's hands that told of two completely unrelated aspects of terrain in a part of the world of which I knew precisely nothing and uttered my exact sentiments.

"Gentlemen," I said testily, "I don't see how these fool scribblings will help one bit. Furthermore, what on earth do either of these sets of directions have to do with your great library or a new gospel? What is the connection?"

Holmes was the one who spoke. "Quatermain, this base camp we have been speaking of . . . Theodore's hideout . . . we think it is one and the same place where the remnants of Alexandria's library were sequestered. At least, that is the working theory of some who are positioned in the government just to make such informed conjectures. The reasoning goes thus: if thousands of books could exist there safely for almost fifteen hundred years, why not one man for four years?"

*   *   *

I was already so numb from this veritable landslide of nonsense that this new pebble hardly affected me at all.

Here Holmes looked pointedly at Lieutenant Cuff. "It is Cuff's job to officially put the lie to this whole untidy affair, or, if true, give Theodore certain communications and promises. The problem is," he continued, "that so little is known about Abyssinia in Europe. We have the limited knowledge derived from the Napier expedition, of course, but they pursued a course into the highlands and stuck to it, while ours will lie in the other direction into the desert. Ideally, we need the services of someone with perfect knowledge of the country's geology, climate, peoples, and natural history."

"I hope you don't think I'm such a person."

"No, of course not," Holmes said. "However, we do think you are the next best thing. You, Quatermain, as very few others, are intimately acquainted with Africa, its moods, its pulse, and its people and cultures. We need you to help us in our endeavor to navigate its exotic and strange nature."

I was quiet for a time, then I said, "I'm flattered your opinion of me is so high, and I must admit that I am familiar with the geographical region of southern Africa and some of the adjacent country, for of course that is how I earn my keep. But Ethiopia is an entirely different matter. As I have said, gentlemen, it's out of the question. Admittedly, I would not ordinarily refuse a commission, but I'm tired and want nothing more than to spend some time quietly in my home."

During this discussion, Hans had maneuvered himself closer to me so that now he was just below my ear.

"Whoa, Baas!" he whispered in Zulu, "We were only a little while ago talking about the Big Baas in the sky, and I see that he certainly knows more than you about your own pocketbook for he is sending you even now that big gold plate full of pretty rocks of which you were also talking so recently."

And the truth of it was that Hans was correct. Our financial situation was sad indeed. The long trek into Heu-Heu land may have provided Zikali with his great medicine, which Hans was pleased to call "groceries"—by the way, did I explain that this medicine consisted of leaves from a grand old tree called the Tree of Illusions, which Zikali required for his black arts?—but all I profited was memories, most of which I would have just as soon done without, for there was much fighting involved and death and much sorrow . . . but that is a whole 'nother tale.[28]

Anyway, Hans's talk had a sobering effect on me, and I found myself saying, "Gentlemen, let me try to summarize. You, Mr. Holmes, have found evidence that at least a portion of the Alexandrian Library may still exist in Ethiopia and possibly a fifth gospel, as well. Also as a result of the same expedition of 1868, evidence has surfaced that the earliest ancestors of Man may have once lived in Ethiopia, and Mr. Huxley and Mr. Scott are determined to return to the scene of Corporal Saint James's explorations to seek more such fossils. And over and beyond that, there is the hope to determine that King Theodore did in fact "go to the spirits," as the Zulus say, or not, as the case may be, and this is Sergeant Cuff's role."

Holmes grinned. "Yes, yes, to kill three birds with one stone so to speak!"

"And you have come to me to be your guide, despite my never having been to that region and having no familiarity with it or its people at all."

"Mr. Quatermain, the British Museum, indeed, the British government—Her Majesty herself, I might add," said Holmes, "as well as others—have every reason to believe that if anyone in Africa can help us, it is you, sir! They have the greatest faith in you!"

"I am indeed flattered," I said, looking at young Will Scott. "What on earth did you tell these people?"

He grinned and said, "Though I might have brought you up, it was Lady Luna and Lord Ragnall who convinced the authorities that you were the most practical man for the job."

"But what if I hadn't just arrived back to Durban, not to return for a year or more, as I am wont to do in my business—as I have just done?

"But that isn't the case—is it?—we are happy to say," Holmes responded. "But now that you have a notion of what we want to do, shall we discuss terms? For your services, to begin in due course after you have had an opportunity to rest for a time, the British authorities will pay you—" whereupon he mentioned a sum so prodigiously ample with terms so fair that I would have been a fool to have turned it down.

Hans, who had been watching and listening the whole time, took this opportunity to whisper to me, "Whoa! Baas, such a pretty number I have never heard. Yes, our trek has been long and my feet need to rest, but perhaps our feet only need a very little rest after all."

Frankly, I was beginning to think along those very lines myself, and the end of it was that I agreed to attempt what seemed at the time to be the most ridiculous proposal I had ever heard in my entire life.

CHAPTER TWO

Allan's Headache Grows

Within twelve days I was able to settle my affairs and was readying my house once again for an extended absence and preparing to board the *H.M.S. Deborah*, the British Navy vessel that had brought my clients. With Hans, I was returning from town with an armload of supplies, my home being on the outskirts of Durban, when I became aware that someone was sitting on my porch. A giant of a Zulu had made himself comfortable on the little swing that I had there for decorative purposes. I don't know what possessed me to buy and install the thing except that it reminded me of similar device that hung from a certain other porch that I knew well in my youth, being part of a home and farm called Maraisfontein. This farm belonged to a Boer named Henri Marais[29] who was our closest neighbor in the Cradock district of the Cape Colony, being only fifteen miles distant from the station where my father had established himself as a Church of England clergyman. I never used the thing, that is to say the swing, first of all since I was seldom home but more so because the act of swinging seemed somehow frivolous, while I am at heart a practical man.

But I don't know why I am getting off the subject. I was speaking of the Zulu. The man jumped up when he saw me. He was naked, of course, except for an animal skin about his middle and various ceremonial accouterments that hung from his neck, ears, and ankles. He held up his *assegai*, or short stabbing spear, in royal salute, greeting me by my native name.

"Macumazana, I am Bayushtiak. The Great One has sent me to protect you."

By "Great One," I knew he was referring to Zikali, but I had no idea what he was talking about otherwise.

"Bayushtiak, thank you for your diligence," I responded in the Zulu tongue, "but please return to your master and tell him 'no thank you' as I am in no need for a bodyguard."

"Oh, that is not possible, Macumazahn, for he told me that if you were to start your expedition without me as part of your party, then I would die in a dishonorable fashion and that my spirit would live forever trapped in a turtle shell without hope of escape. So you see, Macumazahn, that, unless you wish me thus, which, as you well know, would be far worse than even wandering forever in the featureless underworld, you must allow me to take care of you as a wet nurse would her mistress's baby."

Now, clearly I was offended by this analogy, but beyond that I was confused. "Bayushtiak, did your master say why I would need a bodyguard?"

"He showed me some signs and whispered secrets into my ear, but there is nothing that he gave me leave to share—not even with you."

Now, I was in an untenable position. On one hand, I had no need for protection. It was my job, in fact, to protect the others in my charge. But if I refused the man, I knew full well that the hideous black dwarf would cause the man grief somehow, and I didn't want to be responsible for that. What matter if we had an extra member in our party, and the man looked capable enough, strong, self-confident—no doubt a good man to have with you when trouble arose.

"Well, Bayushtiak, it appears that I don't have much of a say in the matter as I well understand how Zikali keeps his word. Welcome, then. But I would appreciate a word of warning when you see this mysterious danger approaching."

"Oh, Macumazahn, do not fear on that account. The Great One heightened my sight and gave me wondrous charms and medicines that will allow me to see forward when the time comes."

"Well, then," I said, feeling manipulated, "it's all settled."

*   *   *

The next morning, Holmes, Scott, Huxley, Cuff, Hans, Bayushtiak, and myself boarded the *Deborah*. The ship weighed anchor, and off we headed north up the east coast of Africa.

I had a time of it explaining to the others about our new compatriot, for he was not the sort of companion that any one of them was used to, but, in the end, they all accepted this unexpected turn of events, since they, just as myself, had no real control of the situation. Thus, you are beginning to understand the power of Zikali.

The master of the ship was one Captain Endfield, and he took full and instant umbrage at having Bayushtiak come aboard. It offended his sensibilities to have a "savage" on the ship. Bayushtiak, for his part, took no notice of the man, occupying his time, once we had set sail, observing the world from the standpoint of the bow of the ship.

"Macumazahn," he would say to me, "little did I know that the world was so wet and big. I see that it goes on seemingly forever, and no matter how fast or far this vessel moves, even as day turns to night and night becomes day, over and again, there is still more water ahead, with no end in sight."

"Yes, Bayushtiak, such is the way of the world, or rather the planet, for they say the earth is a round ball. Naturally then, you can travel around it forever, and they also say that it is mainly covered with water, so you could travel thus forever surrounded by water." I noticed that whereas a civilized man would soon become bored with the monotony of the endless sea, Bayushtiak's demeanor was never less than sheer wonder. Many a time I would see him there rooted at the ship's bow, and I would think how much like a child he was.

Without prolonging this narrative longer than necessary, let me just say that we sailed up the coast—a journey of some three thousand miles and nearly two weeks time—then eventually around the Horn into the Gulf of Aden, through the narrow Strait of Bab el Mandeb comprising Yemen on the east and Somaliland on the west, thus into the Red Sea. Within a few more days, we turned hard south into Annesley Bay and finally came within sight of the two wonderful piers tipped with lighthouses that the English army engineers had built four years previously in preparation for receiving Napier's armada. These piers—marvels of engineering both—extended 900 and 700 yards into the sea from the desert shore. Beyond them, a few hundred yards further up on the shore, was the strange and anomalous sight of several derelict and rusted locomotives, which had been left behind by the army as it hurriedly left. Beyond these, some thirteen miles away due west, the Ethiopian highlands began their precipitous climb high into green mist.

As cool and refreshing a sight as the highlands struck me just then, I knew that we would be headed south into the desert.

As we approached the piers from the east, we were very surprised to see another vessel approaching from the north. Captain Endfield was not expecting this and, as was his nature, became quite flustered. As it would have proven fruitless to even discuss or guess about the nature of this "intrusion" or "crossing of paths" or however it should be phrased, we passengers simply watched and waited. It seemed certain, though, that the other was also a British naval vessel, for we could see the colors flying in the wind through the spy glass that the captain made available to us.

The *Deborah* landed at the end of the longer of the two piers. As we unloaded our supplies, Holmes described to us what he had seen there before, comparatively recently.

"Gentlemen, just imagine four years ago, at this very spot, utilizing these very piers that he had built for the purpose, Field-Marshal Napier gathered together all his men, animals, and materiel, which included fifty elephants with which to carry the heavy guns. Once the shorter pier had been constructed, a tramway was laid along it, and the fleet began to unload.

"Can you imagine, all along the shore there was a city of tents. Thousands of Indians, Egyptians, Persians, and Ethiopians hauling supplies from the ships. Over there was the native bazaar, over there the hospital, along there the storehouses, beyond those the animal compounds with over 20,000 mules alone. Right here on this very spot on this pier and yonder on the other as well were the two condensers that produced almost 200 tons of potable water each day. You can see there where they were fastened down.

"The heat was appalling, and the flies a veritable plague. Dust stirred up by all the feet, both human and animal, billowed in the air constantly. A city popped up in the desert almost overnight. The logistics of it all were inconceivably awesome, at least to one inexperienced in such matters such as myself. The army assembled, then marched and conquered. It was hardly more complicated than that, given the anachronistic, almost barbaric, nature of the enemy. On our return, it was all dismantled and loaded back onto the ships, everything, that is, except these piers and those locomotives. The whole affair was quite remarkable."

Hans, of course, took all of this in and then offered his own brand of wisdom. "Baas, even if the Baas with the shiny chin had not said so, I could tell he spoke truly from the tent pole holes, the droppings, and all the rest of the spoor. Even four years has not been enough to make all these things new again. Just think, Baas, it would be like all of Durban here one moment and gone the next!"

It was about this time that the other vessel reached the piers and secured itself. Captain Endfield, my clients, and myself, all stood by, our curiosity at a peak.

It was not long before some people disembarked and approached us. Of course, there were among them sundry mariners, but the central group comprised four men and a woman. One of the men was obviously the captain of the other vessel and he broke off from the group and approached our captain. He seemed quite happy. They greeted one another precisely and the new man introduced himself to Captain Endfield as Baker by name, Captain Joshua Baker.

"Captain Endfield," said Baker, "We were beginning to wonder if you would ever show up," which was an interesting manner to start the conversation. Thereafter, the two discussed numerous matters of consequence to the navy. In the end we learned that, for its own reasons, the British Admiralty had required Baker to catch up with the *Deborah,* and that Baker had found that using the new Suez Canal—which had connected the Mediterranean Sea with the Red Sea just two-years before—made this feat simplicity itself. It made entirely moot the necessity of circumnavigating the entire continent of Africa, which is precisely what the *Deborah* had been required to do, first to pick me up at Durban, and then to continue on up the east coast of Africa. The sailing of the *Granger*, which was the name of the other vessel, had been smooth and without incident. In fact, they had been waiting for us for six days, using the time to take depth measurements off the Abyssinian coast and other assorted matters of marine research.

Now it was that Huxley stepped up to Captain Baker in a not altogether cheerful mood. "Huxley's my name, sir, and I would greatly appreciate knowing the meaning of this. Leaving Britain, as we did under the strictest orders and secrecy, nothing was mentioned of collateral matters."

At that moment, the rest of Captain Baker's group joined us. It was the older of the three other men who approached Huxley. He was a man in his fifties. From his upper lip and chin grew a prodigious growth of facial hair that was part mustache and part goatee, while his cheeks and temples were smoothly shaven. He was about five inches taller than myself, seemed strong and fit, at least it appeared so due to the girth of his chest and shoulders, and subsequent events would prove me correct.

This fellow held out his hand and said, "My good man, I gather you must be Huxley, Thomas Huxley. And these others are—" At which point he nimbly attached the names of Holmes, Scott, Cuff, and myself to their correct owners while briskly shaking each of our hands in turn. When he was quite done, he said, "Now, please let me introduce myself. I am Richard Burton."

He said that in a simple manner, but I couldn't help but notice a bit of a gleam in the man's eyes.

Indeed, he no doubt had good reason for his mirth, for the umbrage that had seemed to fill Huxley now suddenly dissipated just as abruptly. There was a profound silence among our group that was broken only by the cries of the sea birds. The silence became prolonged and a kind of amazement overtook my Europeans, myself included, I must admit. Finally, like a dam bursting, we all began to talk at once. Realizing the futility of this, we all stopped and Huxley took over again.

"Mr. Richard Burton of Meccah, Harar, and Tanganyika fame?" inquired Huxley.

"I suppose that would be one way to describe me. Yes, I have visited those places and made a bit of a stir in the process."[30]

Huxley swallowed and bowed. "Please, Burton, I offer my apology. Perhaps my manner was a bit impudent, but I'm not very good at surprises. I can only assume that there is an excellent reason for all this."

"You're right there. At least the Crown seems to think so. But let me introduce the rest of my party. This charming lady is Professor Maria* Mitchell, and these two chaps are Gunnery Sergeants Daniel Dravot and Peachy Carnehan."

They both saluted smartly at the sound of their names and the one called Dravot stepped forward. "Of the Queen's own royal infantry, Indian Army under Field-Marshal Lord Napier, SIR!" he added forthrightly. An immense man with a full flaming red beard, he reminded me rather of a Viking of old. He stepped back and

* Editor's note: Pronounced Ma-RYE-ah.—T.K.M.

joined his mate Carnehan, whose own distinguishing character-
istics were his bushy dark eyebrows that went clear across his
forehead without a break and shoulders that were as broad as
Dravot's beard was red.

Burton went on, "The Crown has loaned us these two fellows
because of special knowledge that is theirs. Since the four of us are
embarking on a sort of quest that was instigated at the request of
Professor Mitchell, I'll let her explain."

Maria Mitchell smiled at my group and spoke with a clear
American accent. "I should be happy to, but shall we first retire out
of the sun to a more comfortable situation with plenty of room to
spread out."

The two captains graciously offered accommodations on their
respective vessels, and finally we were led to the officer's briefing
room aboard the *Granger*. We were quite a group, I must say. When
we were all settled—Bayushtiak choosing to stay on deck to continue his examination of the world's girth, and Hans as usual,
crouching unobtrusively in a corner—there were Captains
Endfield and Baker, myself, Holmes, Huxley, Cuff, Scott, Burton,
Dravot, Carnehan, and, of course, Professor Mitchell. Eleven men
and a woman who had mysteriously come together and assembled
in this simple room on the edge of the closest thing to the middle of
nowhere that I could imagine, all by the will of the British government.

Except for Professor Mitchell, who stood, and Hans, we all
somehow fit around an oblong table. She appeared to be in her
fifties. Her countenance was expressive but entirely severe. Her
hair, which was dark and beginning to gray, was pulled back into a
tight knot. Her clothing matched her countenance in both tone and
style, being dark and severe with only a white lace collar to add a
little diversion to the whole.

"My name, as you know, is Maria Mitchell. Some of you
perhaps have heard of me. Certainly my name doesn't have the

cachet of Mr. Burton's, nonetheless, in some scientific circles, my name has some meaning. For instance, Mr. Huxley and Mr. Holmes, I would be very surprised if neither of you knew of me."

The two men thus addressed rose to the occasion. Huxley cleared his throat and sat rather more tall in his chair. "Certainly, Professor Mitchell," he began, "I have the pleasure of addressing the eminent professor of astronomy at Vassar College in New York State. I believe it was in 1847 that you discovered a comet, a fact that remained newsworthy for nearly a year. I was but a lad at the time, but I remember it well."

Miss Mitchell smiled and was about to open her mouth when Holmes also took up the challenge as well. "If I recall correctly, professor," he began, "your particular fields of interest are sunspots, the surfaces of Jupiter and Saturn, and meteorites."

"Indeed," she responded, seeming pleased, "correct on every point, and it is the latter interest, that of meteorites, that brings me to Africa and to this very spot conferring with you gentlemen at this very moment. I've come in search of a phenomenon unheard of thus far in the study of meteorites. This phenomenon came to light in 1868 here in Ethiopia and was witnessed by these two men," indicating Dravot and Carnehan. "Gentlemen, please do me the honor of taking up the tale from the beginning."

The two men stood and snapped to attention just as though an officer had barked an order. It was Dravot who started.

"At the beginning, all right. Well there we were, Peachy and me, happy as could be. Stationed in Bombay we were and glad of it. We were gunnery sergeants, we were, under Field-Marshal Lord Napier in the Queen's own Indian Army. Well, next thing we know we were boarding a ship and weeks later landed at the very same God-forsaken spot where we are right now, pardon my language, Ma'am. And soon, in a matter of mere days, as I live and breathe, a whole town popped up . . . . "

Holmes took this opportunity to interrupt, a bit impatiently. "Dravot, my man, the details of the camp are well known to us and not important at the moment."

Dravot looked a little abashed as though the wind had been socked right out of his sails.

Seeing that reinforcements were required, Carnehan stepped in. "Be that as it may, Danny here and me at some point considered all the problems and difficulties that lay in the direction of the general march, which was northwest up into those very mountains outside there, but which wouldn't seriously start moving for several days, and we decided to explore a bit in the opposite direction, to the south it was, which we found was truly horrible desert country, as you will soon see."

Dravot took it up. "And it was when we were out there in the desert several days, glad to be away from the hubbub yonder in the mountains—a lot of bloody shooting and such—that the miracle happened."

"Not that it was rightly a true miracle," interrupted Carnehan, "but it came with all the accessories, a great light in the sky and loud noises from heaven, as God is my witness! But I suppose it was really that we just happened to be in the right place at the right time. It was about midnight, we were bivouacked in a dry riverbed where we were toasting the Queen, bless her heart, when it exploded out of the sky, it did, and streaked toward us, scaring the stuffings out of us."

Dravot took it up. "It was a meteor, as you live and breath, a real spectacular rock shooting from the sky. What with all the blazing and crashing and whistling and all, it was quite a show it was. Well, it hit off to the east of where we were, and not too far. So in the morning we went looking for it, and blimey, what we found was queer enough to get the whole ever-lovin' government to wondering, which explains just why Peachy and me are right back here."

"And just what did you find?" I asked, by now bursting with curiosity.

"Why a graveyard of meteorites, of course! Have you ever heard of the graveyard of the elephants or of the whales, well this is much the same thing, hundreds of craters each with a bit of charred rock half buried. We found the new one, all right. It was still red hot from its plunge, but otherwise it didn't seem any different than the others. They all seemed part of a family if you don't mind my conjecturing. Well, we scraped around a little and found some interesting pieces, having no notion as to the value of the things, and pocketed them."

"The wonder of it," Peachy continued, "was that when we went back the way we came and merged into the tail end of that long column the front of which was days ahead high up into those mountains, no one seems to have noticed that we'd been missing."

Dravot interrupted in a precisely timed manner. "My thinking, y' see, was that they were glad to be rid of us! After all, it wasn't as though Peachy and me didn't have a pretty thorough reputation!"

"So there we were, possessors of this most arcane knowledge," Carnehan continued. "'Danny,' I said, "'what are we to do now? You and me, we've been bloomin' witnesses to a true-blue wonder of nature. So what's next?'

"Well, there was nothing next. At least immediately. That was four years ago, and we gave up trying to figure out how to make a profit, so to speak, from our discovery, but tongues being what they are, word got 'round and bits of our rock got 'round, too, and lo! some months ago, this lovely lady here communicated with us. We've never asked for details, but it must have been a pretty picture, she digging through those layers and layers of government bureaucracies in order to find the likes of us. But bless it! She did, and here we are, loaned out by the Queen herself to help this here lady seek that very exact same spot of our bloomin' miracle."

"Thank you, gentlemen," Maria Mitchell said, continuing.

"Naturally, one of the first things we attempted to do was to contact Mr. Holmes here to request his guidance and aid due to his previous experience in the area. It was then we discovered we had missed him by a matter of only a few weeks. With the aid of the Museum authorities, we were able to contact Mr. Burton, who, auspiciously for us, had only just then rejoined the world, having been entrenched for months focusing on his Zanzibar project. We caught up with him just as he was preparing to retire to Trieste and proposed that, given his background in east Africa and gift of languages,[31] his companionship and guidance would be of great service, to which he kindly agreed. We, nonetheless, were firm in our belief that Mr. Holmes's services would be invaluable. In due course, we were able to compute the probable course and timing of your northerly expedition from Mr. Quatermain's home and realized it was highly likely to rendezvous with you via the Suez Canal. And, at long last, here we are, all together, by the grace of the great God Himself."

CHAPTER THREE

And Then There Were Twelve

Dravot and Carnehan told us that their "graveyard" was three or four days forced march south-south-east, which was in the same direction that Saint James had indicated he had gone, though the two adventures had been separated by some weeks, one at the beginning of the army's expedition and one at the end.

"Like it as not," Dravot volunteered, "seeing that it was just the two of us, Peachy and me made good time. We wanted to do our sightseein' and be back before we was noticed missing and in short enough a time that we could come up with a sensible excuse. But with the likes of this crowd, with a lady and without a gun in our back, so to speak, it's probable to take twice as long, at least. Six, maybe seven days." Dravot shrugged, looking for all the world like a man who, for the moment, had no control at all over his destiny.

Well, there was nothing for it now. Once the direction of travel was made clear, as well the terrain and climate we would encounter, taking into account that we wouldn't have bearers, we spent the next day choosing and packing our kit, which consisted of the following items:[32]

Nine express rifles and six hundred rounds of ammunition.

Two Winchester repeating rifles (for Hans and Maria) with two hundred rounds of cartridge.

Ten Colt revolvers and two hundred rounds of cartridge.

Eleven Cochrane's water bottles, each holding four pints.

Ten blankets (Bayushtiak eschewing such frivolities).

Ninety pounds of biltong (sun-dried game flesh).

A couple hundred small dry biscuits.

A selection of medicines and a few small surgical instruments.

Our knives, compasses, matches, a pocket-filter, some tobacco, a trowel, sundry digging tools, and the clothes we stood in completed our supplies. Later, too, I discovered that Burton had brought along his surveying equipment to which he was much attached.

In my experience, which in many African matters is substantial, this allotment of equipment was modest for the desert adventure we proposed. These were the bare necessities. Nevertheless, every ounce, I knew, would seem to double as the trek lengthened, especially when crossing a scorching desert. Even still, it was a heavy load per person. Obviously we would not allow Miss Mitchell to carry a full load, as she did not seem by nature to be an outdoors woman, and so approximately half of her kit was distributed among the others. She protested vehemently about this, but soon gave up as we men were not about to give in.

What I had no way of telling at that time was what a *vital* woman she could be when her back was against a wall. In a few days her mettle would be tested and she would prove to be much more than she seemed.

As we were all making these final preparations, double-checking our supplies, etc., Hans stepped up to my side. "Baas, tell me again why it is here I am going to die, cooked like an ostrich in an oven," he queried in his insolent tone. "I don't understand why these old books and old bones and rocks from the sky are worth all these fine men and that lady turning themselves into hyena food. Of course I don't count myself amongst those fine men, but unless I am mistaken, I too will join them in the hyena's belly."

"You silly fool," I whispered harshly. "If worse comes to worse, I would grab the hyena's throat and eat him, and thus we would all live."

"Baas, the Kaffirs here call you Macumazahn, which means 'Watcher by Night,' not Uhlanya Ngokweqile, which means 'Mad Beyond All Reason.' I beg you to remember that if you were to grab the hyena's throat, he would try to tear out yours and in all like-lihood would succeed."

Naturally I was not about to take such language, even from Hans, so it was that I said not too kindly, "How dare you waste my time with your silly nonsense," all the while as the toe of my boot strove to encounter the seat of his filthy pants, but he was too quick and jumped liked a startled rabbit. But this was more of a long-standing and time-honored ritual between us than anything else and the next time I saw him, neither of us thought to mention the matter.

We had become quite a swollen group to be sure. At first, I thought I would have to fight with Burton for my rights as safari leader, but he was perfectly happy for me to take the lead, which I was grateful for insofar as I wasn't in the mood for political non-sense at that time.

I remember that about this time I began to think wistfully about the locomotives that were just sitting there. If only one of the things would come to life and haul us away wherever we wanted to go . . . .

To the northwest, thirteen miles away, the fertile slopes of the highlands began to rise, but to the south, the desert was boundless. From the Red Sea water's edge, as with most shores, sand ruled. The difference was that the sand continued on indefinitely.

Thus, we made arrangements with the captain of the *Deborah* to return to this spot beginning in three weeks, wait a week, then return after another three weeks, and so on for four months. During the extended intervals, the vessel would be performing mapping and surveying duties for the British government. The *Granger*, we all agreed, had concluded the business that it had with its four passengers, and we discharged her Captain Baker to con-tinue on whatever other Queen's business he was obliged to pursue.

We decided to avoid the heat of the day and to travel by moonlight. And so it was in the late afternoon, deep in shadow since the sun had dropped behind the mountains on our right, we headed directly into the heart of one of the loneliest, bleakest spots on the face of the earth, a vast area of barren wastes, broken lava flows, crumbling rock, and salt flats known as the Danakil Desert—a truly hellish place, arid, monstrously hot, torn by volcanoes, and prone to earthquakes.[33]

That first night we passed over patches of uneven gravel and greenish sand rich in copper and through fields of broken and jagged black obsidian. As hard to traverse as it was, it did have the advantage of being relatively flat.

At dawn, we entered a different realm altogether, one of torturous, steep gullies that rolled away from us like endless waves to the horizon. One notable feature of these gullies was the vibrant colors they presented—deep reds, bright yellows, translucent greens, browns and blacks, and aquatic blues, all arrayed in pleasant stripes along the gully walls. I assumed this was due to the fact that, as in many deserts, it seldom rained here, but when it did or if there was a heavy rain, however short in duration, in the mountains to the north or west, the water would rush in torrents that funneled into these gullies, vanishing afterward into shallow salt lakes that, in turn, soon evaporated. But in the wake of these floods, the sides of the gullies and ravines would appear riven, as though a giant's axe had cleaved asunder the old tired and worn walls of rock, revealing shiny new, thick layers of rock of distinctly different colors and character, minerals from distant eras, from epochs unimaginable.

Yet as fearsome as these gullies seemed at the time, it turns out they were relatively shallow and nondescript compared to the region we would soon encounter—but I'm getting ahead of myself.

We halted on the south side of an east-west oriented gully that was deep enough that it could almost be called a shallow canyon. There was some discussion that perhaps it would be better to make camp on the bluff above, for in the event of a flash flood, the water could roar down on us with the speed of an express locomotive, and also because, typically, gullies and canyons in this climate tended to be hot and stifling. But due to some trick of nature, that gully at that time enjoyed a steady and comfortable breeze coursing along its length, and, added to the relief afforded by the shady side, in the end gully won out over bluff and we settled into our first camp, which was plain and practical.

We supped on some of the provisions we'd brought, drank warm water sparingly, and fell into conversation. This was the first opportunity we'd had to actually get to know one another, and I was rather curious about this assorted lot that it was my fate to have fallen in with.

As happens when several people who are mostly strangers to one another are thrown together by chance, our group had naturally broken into little groups. Huxley and young Will Scott sat conferring quietly. Richard Holmes and Miss Mitchell were as well. Dravot and Carnehan were prowling together around the edges of the gully. Detective Cuff, Hans, and Bayushtiak stayed more or less off to themselves. So it was that Burton and I gravitated to one another, as our backgrounds had points in common.

"Quatermain, I say, I've been wanting to meet you for years," said the famous explorer.

"Well, sir, it appears that your wish has finally come true. I, too, have heard much of you. I'm actually surprised that our paths haven't crossed before."

"I believe that you haven't come this far north before now, and I haven't had the opportunity to visit your home country and in between, as they say, is the 'Dark Continent.'"

"Yes," I responded, for some accountable reason feeling chastened. "But, of course, that region is not so dark now that you have explored and surveyed so much of the central lake region. I must say that I feel I already know you through the stories passed on by travelers I've encountered and from the newspapers."

"Yes. That is the way of it, isn't it," Burton said philosophically.

Thus we chatted, neither feeling particularly comfortable, I suppose. Eventually, knowing that rest was more important than talk, I went about the posting of a guard, Dravot I believe, and the rest of us settled in, preparing as best as we could for the heat of the coming day. In my own fashion, I was asleep before you know it, it being my nature to be able to sleep under any circumstance, hard or soft, wet or dry, hot or cold, imminent danger or not.

*　　*　　*

In the late afternoon, we ate, broke camp, and set out once more. Before two hours were up, we came to some of the most desolate and forbidding territory I had ever encountered or could imagine. Suddenly, we could see in the bright moonlight a vast and frightening region comprising wide gorges and ravines and hills cut into the wasteland by wind and the action of prehistoric rivers. It was truly astonishing to see these nearly vertical five-hundred foot dips and rises, one following another like wrinkles in a titanic rumpled blanket out to the horizon as far as the eye could see.

We consulted Dravot and Carnehan and they were adamant that they had, in fact, encountered this very same landscape and had not found it necessary to traverse it. Those four years before, they veered further south and had succeeded in circumnavigating the gorges. Indeed, as we marched through the night, the treacherous terrain smoothed out somewhat.

Needless to say, from the start of our journey, Huxley and young Scott had their eyes riveted to the ground at all times—both as we marched, of course, and particularly when we stopped—searching for the bones of the human ancestors they coveted. Obviously, proof of the continued existence of neither Emperor Theodore nor of millennia-old scrolls was forthcoming quite yet, as we had only just started.

At dawn we settled into the second camp of our expedition. It was as we were preparing to sleep that detective Cuff spoke to Professor Mitchell. "Perhaps you can explain to those of us not acquainted with meteors, falling stars, and such, just what you are seeking and why. Please understand that this whole detour, so to speak, was not part of my charter, and I need to come to terms with it." Well, I must tell you that that appeared to be just the right question, for, just as though a coin had been inserted into a player piano, the lady then almost gleefully launched into what amounted to a lecture.

"Well," she began, "let's define our terms at the outset. If you see a streak of light in the sky, what you are seeing is a bit of material from outer space possibly no bigger than a grain of sand entering our atmosphere at a tremendous speed, possibly around 20,000 miles per hour. Its substance encounters the particles of air in our atmosphere, and at such a high speed, the pure friction caused by the encounter burns the material, vaporizing it out of existence. This bright streak in the sky is called a 'meteor' or, less accurately, a 'shooting star.' These flaming bits of sand constitute the vast majority of the meteors that we see.

"Larger chunks of material can also be seen as meteors as they plummet through the atmosphere, but these are far fewer than their smaller brethren. Many of these are sufficiently big that only the outermost layer burns, then some part of the original material survives the superheated furnace as they enter the atmosphere and crash to the ground. Once the surviving material hits the ground, that material is called a 'meteorite.'

"Virtually all meteorites to the naked eye of laymen look no different than ordinary rocks. Nonetheless, they can be categorized into three groups—stones, irons, and stony irons, with the stones being by far the most common."

It was left to Hans to ask the most obvious question and, of course, he directed his query to me. "But, Baas, in my head I can see a picture of rocks falling out of the sky, some burning all up, some not, but where do they come from?"

Miss Mitchell was quick to reply, "My good man, meteors and meteorites can originate almost anywhere beyond the earth—the Moon, perhaps, or the other planets, comets, asteroids. Over time, these bodies tend to jostle about and shake off the stones and irons that hurl through space for millions of years. Some eventually reach earth and, well, now you know what happens."

Hans lifted his filthy hat and scratched his scalp, his perplexed countenance not having changed. I knew that later I would need to concoct an analogy that he could understand, seeing that matters of even the simplest astronomy were excluded from his world. Dear me, in fact, I could only just grasp some of the concepts that the woman was tossing around so blithely. Twenty thousand miles an hour, indeed. Just what does "outer space" mean anyway? Then it was that I asked something that tugged at my mind.

"Professor Mitchell, just why aren't we beaned by these falling rocks on a regular basis?" The funny thing is that just at that same moment, I noticed that Huxley seemed to want to say something, but then he caught himself and continued to bite his tongue, restraining himself from saying whatever it was that was on his mind. I bring this up because a few minutes later an explanation for this odd moment presented itself.

Professor Mitchell smiled. "That is a wonderful question, Mr. Quatermain. Actually, it is estimated that only a few dozen meteors per year survive the journey. And the earth is so vast that the majority of these fall into the ocean or into the ice of the poles or into virgin territory of one sort or another. The chance of being struck by a meteorite is astronomically small." She smiled again, perhaps at her play on words.

"And now that we have the benefit of this explanation," I went on, "please tell me again why we are searching for this graveyard of yours, or rather that of our two imaginative soldiers yonder."

"That can be simply stated," she replied. "The examples of the rock that Mr. Dravot and Mr. Carnehan brought out of this desert were of the iron variety. The description of the region the men provided leads me to believe that most, if not all, of the meteorites they've seen are irons. So the principal question arises: Why do so many of these iron rocks from outer space come to earth in such a concentrated manner? Is it the region that somehow attracts them? Or is it their timing and trajectories that somehow cause their falls to be focused?"

There was a lull in the conversation, and I was about to suggest that sleep was most important just then, when Huxley chose this moment to break his silence.

"Before retiring, my dear, I must tell you that I have been most anxious to discuss with you an avocational interest of mine. You see, beyond the fields of biology and anthropology in which I have some notoriety, I also have an interest in astronomy. My particular passion is for the myriad of asteroids. I have spent much time studying their dynamics relative to the orbits of Mars and Jupiter."

"Well, that is wonderful, Mr. Huxley. Then you must be familiar with the work of my colleague Daniel Kirkwood."

"Naturally. Naturally. His demonstration of the existence of the so-called Kirkwood gaps—just six years ago, wasn't it?—has proven consequential in my own research."

"May I ask what the nature of that research is?"

"It is a qualitative mathematical analysis of various permutations of the Olbers hypothesis."

" . . . That between Mars and Jupiter there once was a planet that exploded, thereby forming the debris that we call the asteroids."

"Yes, precisely . . . . "

The two of them had been walking to the edge of the camp during this discussion and I heard no more. I could see that they would be animatedly discussing their mutual interest for a while, and that it would be pointless to try to persuade them just then to rest.

And I must tell you, personally, I wished Cuff had kept his question to himself, as I didn't like the aching in my head that followed this discourse on subjects utterly foreign to me. As I have said, I am a simple man with simple needs, and the notions that were being thrown about that dawn were such that I would have been very pleased to have avoided them altogether.

*   *   *

Thereafter, we left the land of gullies and canyons behind and the volcano—Mt. Erta Ale, if I haven't mentioned the name already—grew steadily more prominent in the west. Nevertheless, despite the proximity of an active volcano, the terrain became less rocky and more sandy. Indeed, most of that night the going was made all the more difficult due to the fineness of the sand and the fact that our progress was intermittently blocked by vast sand dunes. The next morning, we had again set up in the pitiful shade of one of the few prominences of solid rock still available to us. I was checking our water supply and lecturing on the subject of water rationing when suddenly we heard a distinct cry in the distance.

"What was that?" said Cuff, startled.

"It sounded like a cry for help," ventured Miss Mitchell.

"Rather like a lost soul," said Richard Holmes.

Even as we were making such queries, the cries continued unabated. The whole group—save Burton—became agitated. Even implacable Bayushtiak seemed over-awed by the sounds.

Hans plucked at my sleeve. When I looked down at him I saw a sight I have rarely seen, that of Hans with huge eyes and an expression on his face that was not insolent. He said ever so carefully in Portuguese so that no one of our party could understand,

"Baas, I think that spirit is calling my name. Don't you hear it? 'Haaannnsszzz . . . Haaannsssszzz . . . Haaaannnsszzz." I was filled with mixed emotions. I wanted to tell him that he was being ridiculous, but the look of fear on his face quelled that first instinct, and also, the sound *did* sound like a voice protractedly crying my servant's name.

For myself, I doubted that the sound was human. I had begun to formulate a theory—wagering silently to myself that gas vents from the volcano were doubtlessly nearby and that the sound was some sort of escaping steam—though I had to admit I had seen nothing to back up my idea and, furthermore, I really had no idea if such a thing was possible.

In the meantime, Holmes and Miss Mitchell were walking toward the edge of camp and were continuing on. Holmes was saying, "We must help the poor wretch. I hope we make it in time" and such when Burton spoke up.

"I wouldn't bother if I were you," he said.

The two erstwhile saviors looked indignant and demanded to know if he were so unchristian as to not care when confronted with such a plaintive cry for succor.

His response was, "Of course I would . . . if the cry was genuine. But what you are hearing is not emanating from a person, or from spirits (as your manservant assumes, Quatermain [a pronouncement that startled Hans as much as I, for we both thought our conversation private]), or from jinns as the Bedouin believe. This sound is merely a variation of El Bromador, a geological condition that has been observed in the deserts of Spain (and Chile, as well, if I'm not mistaken). The distinct cries you hear are the consequence of shifting sands in large dunes such as we have been seeing. Some call them 'the singing sands.' There are even cases of brave folk who have been lured to their own deaths trying to rescue will-o-wisps. In my wanderings in Arabia, I have had the opportunity to become acquainted with the phenomenon, but only occasionally I assure you since it is really quite rare that the sound should occur when there happen to be human ears about. We should consider ourselves blessed by Allah that he has allowed us this privilege. Sit back and enjoy."

Holmes and Miss Mitchell returned to their places reluctantly. And indeed, as we sat and listened, the wailing quickly grew in intensity and then changed pitch, metamorphosing into the high notes of camel bells, then still later we could make out mournful violins and gleefully plucked harps, then the roar of a mighty organ, and the roll of drums. This turned into a successions of explosions, as though someone in the distance was setting off canon blasts. The finale was volleys of what seemed like thunder. It was really quite amazing and we all loitered around the camp in awe of the sounds and quite unable to rest. Around noon, in the absolute heat of the day, it all stopped suddenly—as inexplicably as it had begun. All at once we were left in silence and the normal quiet of the desert returned. Gratefully, we started to snatch what rest we could.

As I have explained, I have no trouble sleeping, but neither do I have trouble coming instantly awake and fully alert when necessary. The sun was still up when I woke to another sound of moaning, another cry in the wilderness. I was about to dismiss this, as I was learning much about the strange way of deserts, when something about this cry seemed distinctly different than that which we had heard earlier.

Hans, Bayushtiak, and myself were up and running toward the sound before anyone else was awake. We flew around a dip in the nearest shallow dune and there found not more singing sands, but a desiccated and dying man.

He didn't seem to have any wounds or even broken bones, so we picked up the poor fellow and brought him into camp. To say that my group was surprised would be an understatement. It wasn't long before some rather harsh words dealing with priorities were exchanged with Holmes and Miss Mitchell on one side and Burton on the other, but this blew over quickly. We spent the rest of the day and half of the next night nursing the man. He was resilient, there can be no doubt. Once we were able to finally persuade him that he had in fact been rescued and that we were not a troop of angels come to escort him to St. Peter, he was wonderfully grateful.

His name was Axel Lidenbrock, who we learned was a German geologist whose field was volcano research. Physically there was nothing about him that stood out, except perhaps that I could see that before his travails, his face and complexion must have been what you would call "cherubic," which lent him a far younger appearance than the middle age he declared himself to be.

"It has been a goal of mine for years to explore Mt. Erta Ale." he said. "My team is on the other side of the mountain. I went off on the trail of an elusive basalt when I was tempted first by this stratum and then by that metamorphic intrusion. Perhaps I was foolish to set out on my own, for soon I had no idea where I was. I think the heat affected me more adversely than I was prepared for."

By the middle of the night, he understood clearly enough that we were on our own journey and couldn't very well leave him there to die. But neither could we take the time to seek his companions. He really had no choice but to join us. By the time the moon rose over the dunes, he had gained enough strength so that we were ready to continue on our astonishing hodgepodge of missions.

Though somewhat chastened and upset by the occurrences of the day, my party mustered its will and forged ahead. In fact, nothing much had really changed, except that now our ranks had been swollen by yet one more, so that now there were twelve of us.

Before dawn, the vast quantities of sand began to dwindle and we came to an area where a series of cliffs rose steeply on our right and where the gorges had reappeared, dipping in and up and curving around randomly on our left, that is to the east, with only a barely distinguishable path between these two obstacles. We hated to have so little choice, still it was good to have any kind of path to follow in that wilderness, though I suspected that at any time the path might run into a blank wall or take us to the edge of a precipice.

Then, as the sun rose over that far off but ever-present eastward mountain range, the same that dogged Saint James's heels, as you may recall, we began our search, as we did each morning, for an appropriate place to settle for the day. At that point, Hans drew my attention southward.

"Baas, I think we had better hurry and find a roof for our poor heads, for, if I'm not mistaken, this oven of a desert has cooked up a new surprise, one that will tear the skin and flesh from our bones, then chew up the bones for good measure."

Indeed, there between us and the horizon, a great mottled sickly yellow and brown haze with swirling wispy edges had formed. You didn't need to be a true-born Bedouin to see that some sort of sirocco was fast approaching. Then it was that I heard Burton barking orders, to which I added my refrain. In a short while, we found shelter under a low rock overhang, and, piling our bags, sacks, and whatnot between ourselves and the open desert, we dug in for the duration. It didn't take long for that burning, furious wind to hit. It was fearful. It howled and bellowed around us for hours, sometimes sucking the very air out of the little makeshift cave and other times finding the gaps in our redoubt, blasting needles and knives of sand at our hunched-together bodies.

When finally it was over, providence proved to be on our side for we were unscathed for the most part. And insofar as there were a few hours of scorching daylight left, we made ourselves as comfortable as we could right where we were.

When the moon rose, we roused ourselves stiffly and slowly

moved about gathering our things. I remember that I was over-seeing these preparations when one of the two soldiers, Carnehan I think [as the two of them have tended to blend in my mind], began to curse, and when I went to investigate, Hans with me, the man thrust his rifle out so that both Hans and I could see it clearly.

"Whoa, Baas! What did I say of late about this desert eating first your flesh and then your bones? Oh! I must learn to keep such things to myself, as the spirits might sometimes like what they hear!"

Certainly, Hans had good reason to want to eat his words. Apparently the rifle had been protruding out from the barrier that we had hurriedly constructed and, as such, caught the full power of the wind. Its wooden stock had been sandblasted clean off! Only pitted metal remained!

The three of us, and also Dravot, who had been attracted by the cries of his comrade, could do nothing more than shake our heads at the wonder of it. Then we went about our business packing our kits and such, so that within an hour, we were off again.

Can you just picture us? Ten able men, one invalid, and a woman wandering in the desert, in the dark, at the mercy of one of the most horrible climates on earth, with no clear idea what our destination was, with only the vague hopes of a few academicians and politicians and only some uncorrelated scribblings and unau-thenticated statements [probably made under duress, now that I think about it] to guide us! My poor mind boggled that I ever let myself be talked into this foolhardy venture.

*   *   *

Our trek for the next day and night meandered across a sere land-scape not remarkably different from the drab, blistering desert we had been traversing all along. Just as we were setting up yet another camp, Huxley approached me and asked my opinion of a certain geological feature that he had noticed on a rise a bit to our south. I peered at it through my glass and offered my opinion that it seemed to be a small cave. He and Scott then determined to explore it, and I admit my curiosity was piqued so I went along. The ground there was particularly broken, not sand at all but shattered sandstone. The rise was steep and the three of us climbed hard as we aimed for the cave. Then Huxley noticed something partway up the slope. He stopped and peered at it without touching it. Scott did the same.

"That's a bit of arm from a sub-man . . . a troglodyte perhaps," Scott said.

"I think not," I said. "It's too small. It must be a monkey of some kind."

All three of us knelt to examine it. Huxley said, "I believe you're right, Will. It is nearly human, but not quite."

I looked again. "Monkey," I said with conviction.

Huxley ignored me and pointed beside my foot. "What is that, Will?" Scott carefully picked up a scrap of material and announced, "Why, it's the back of a small skull."

A few feet away was part of a femur, a thigh bone. We stood up and began to see other bits of bone on the slope: a couple of vertebrae, part of a pelvis, all of which Huxley announced were sub-human.

Scott picked up a bit of bone and stood quite still for a moment then said, "Thomas, do you think these are all part of one individual, parts of a single primitive skeleton?"

Huxley grew so excited, I was frightened for him. "I can't believe it!" he cried. "I can't believe it."

The two of them began to howl with joy, jumping up and down. They hugged one another in the hundred degree heat, but as I looked at the heat-shimmering gravel, I could see many more of the small brown fragments.

"Gentlemen," I said quietly, "don't you think that caution

would be more appropriate here since that which you are cele-
brating is still on the ground and quite vulnerable. You may step on
something."

Hans, who had been attracted by the din, came up quietly
behind me and asked, "Baas, why are these grown and plainly
sober men behaving like drunkards, even as I myself have been
known to do, or so you tell me and I would never disbelieve anything you would have to say, even though I happen to know that it
would have been quite impossible for them to have drunk anything
at all because if there had been something, you know I would have
sniffed it out." He said this last with a grin that exposed all of the
coarse stumps that were left of his teeth and I had to wonder what
his skeleton would look like if it was dried and scattered about the
rocks as this other one had been.

"But, Baas," Hans added after a few moments more of wit-
nessing the odd scene playing out before us, "watch the older one,
the one with the hairy face. Does he really seem so filled with joy, or
does he seem more like a man jumping up and down to impress
another man's wife?"

I told him I had no idea what he was talking about. He
shrugged, then grinned and shuffled off, commenting that it was
none of his affair anyway.

Well the end of it was that Huxley and Scott very carefully
packed up the various pieces of the skeleton in cotton and small
sacks brought for the purpose. As they took measurements of the
spot where they had found the bones, Burton indicated that he had
with him (indeed never went anywhere without) chronometers,
prismatic compasses, thermometers, a telescope, a portable
sundial, sextants, barometers, and a box of mathematical instruments, the services of which he offered. Thus, with Burton's aid
and his surveying instruments, the precise location of the bones
was determined, the better to guide future naturalists should they
wish to follow in our footsteps.

Once all had been measured and packed, young Scott remembered the cave, which had been our destination prior to their discovery. He chose to return alone up the slope and investigate its interior and, except for one small incident of the type that you would expect from exploring a new cave, he exited it before long, and thus we rested until nightfall.

CHAPTER FOUR

The Abyssinian Enterprise
(Being the First Digression)★

[Sherlock] Holmes threw down the news section of the *Daily Tele-graph* in disgust and paced the floor. I looked up from the novel I was reading, it not being necessary for me to utter the obvious question that paused at my lips.

"Once again, the deficiencies of the journalistic method become only too clear," Holmes ranted. "There is an item today about a journalist in Burma who claims to have endured, and to have been rescued from, quicksand. Nonsense! The man is clearly a fraud!"

This was too much for me, and my impatience showed, I fear. "Holmes, you have no right to accuse another man of lying until you have 'walked in his shoes,' so to speak."

"But I have, Watson!"

Then I thought I understood. "Of course, Holmes, you are

★ Editor's note: Being curious as to the nature of the "small incident of the type you would expect from exploring a new cave" that Quatermain refers to, and finding no further reference to it in the manuscript, this editor made inquiries. In time, Mr. Gary von Tersch of Belmont, California, contacted me, confirming himself as a distant relative of Dr. Watson. He sent me a photocopy of the astonishing item included here, found amongst a trunk full of miscellany that he had acquired ("inherited" being too strong and specific a word) from a spinster aunt (whom he asked not be identified) upon her passing. The piece appears to have been Watson's first attempt at writing up Sherlock Holmes's "Adventure of the Copper Beeches," which was written at a much later date than the transcription of Quatermain's Ethiopian adventure. That the following passage was excised from the final published version of "Beeches" was an obvious editorial decision as it is totally irrelevant to the main narrative. That Holmes's telling of the adventure in fact happened at the precise chronological point just prior to the arrival of Violet Hunter, I believe can be taken for granted as accurate. I reprint this material here in the belief that it will shed light onto a number of different aspects of the narrative presented in this book. —T.K.M.

referring to that horrible moment last October during the Basker-ville investigation when Mrs. Stapleton and I pulled you out bodily from the great Grimpen Mire."

"Ah, my dear Watson, I commend you for your excellent recall. Indeed, sinking to my waist in that green-scummed, foul quagmire did include some moments of concern, of that there can be no doubt! Yet I speak of another incident altogether, one of a different sort, I must say, since I can testify firsthand that the sensation of being pulled down by slimy miasmatic mud is, on the whole, a different one from being consumed alive by talcum-fine sand. Another point of rather important difference, for the record, is that for the former my trusted Boswell was there, for which I will always by eternally grateful, but for the latter, I was totally alone!"

To say I was aghast by this pronouncement does not give justice to my feelings. "You were? What on earth do you mean? Where were you?"

"I can see I piqued your interest, Watson, and I suppose it would be foolish of me to hope that you could merely return to your novel without an explanation."

"That is most certainly true," I said.

"Well then, once in a foreign land, when I was a lad still in university but traveling, I had some ignominious ill-fortune. It is an embarrassing episode in its own right and is nothing I very much like to remember let alone discuss."

"Pray do nonetheless."

"Only to put the lie to this scoundrel newspaperman who is presenting fiction as fact."

Here, Holmes sat in his favorite chair, steepled his hands under his chin, closed his eyes, and reflected for several moments. I was under the distinct impression that he was putting himself into a self-induced hypnotic state. When next he spoke again, his voice was, remarkably, a higher pitch!—the voice of a mere youth! Here are his exact words as I jotted them down:

*   *   *

"I opened my eyes [said Holmes] and was instantly aware of many impressions simultaneously. Foremost among these was the lack of sensation in my limbs. By this I mean that, with regaining consciousness, I attempted to move my arms, but found it impossible to do so. In a moment I deliberately made the effort to move my legs, with the same result. It was at this point—being totally disoriented, not remembering where I was or what I was doing there—that the seed of panic was born within me.

"I found that I could manipulate my head, twisting it around, and blink my eyes at will. Yet it had not occurred to me yet, so great was my disorientation, that perhaps the better part of valor at that time would be to vocalize my concerns, that is, to speak up or call out, but I suppose one reason the thought had not as yet occurred to me was because there was nobody to be seen and, therefore, presumably, no one to hear my outcries.

"But it was the lack of sensation in my limbs that concerned me the most. At first I thought it was merely a case of common numbness, that my muscles had deadened for some good but temporary reason, as when circulation is restricted for a time and your leg falls asleep.

"It was then I began to fully take into account my surroundings . . . and was horrified for the effort. Once I attempted to maximize my acuity and make sense of what my limited senses perceived, the impression came to mind that I was completely within some sort of giant mouth, for I could plainly see a patch of dim light to my left around the interior perimeter of which I could see equally plainly rows of teeth, inhuman, monstrously long and malformed, but teeth nonetheless and not to be doubted with regard to their material existence.

"I suppose that everything I have so far described took place within a time span of, say, ninety seconds. For all the world I was like a disembodied head floating in the dim cavern of a gigantic maw. *And I had no idea how it happened that I had arrived at such a fate.*

"Realizing that I had best focus my energies elsewhere, I regained possession of some of my faculties—taking the tiger by the tail, so to speak—and decided to concentrate on the immediate problems. I decided that my primary concern, and the one that needed to be dealt with first and foremost, was the problem of not being able to move my limbs. I tried to ignore all sensations but the acceptance of my physical surroundings—to better understand my predicament. But the light was so dim that this availed me little. Then I tried to list that which I *did* know.

"Now let's see . . . who am I . . . ? I asked myself. And no sooner had I framed the question . . . I felt myself move *down*. Oh, my good Lord! What was happening? Then I felt a curious sensation, and experienced a plethora of emotions. For the first time I actually *felt* my body. But I felt it because there was some enormous suction pulling at it. Pulling my torso down from below. I flailed. As you can imagine, out of some pure instinct I flailed wildly and then I saw my arms and from them flew mounds of sand, and suddenly it came to me that I was buried up to my neck in sand.

"But it further came to me that I wasn't merely buried. I was being pulled down into some sort of desert quicksand. Then I remembered. It came to me that I had bogged down in the stuff and, out of pure horror, I had passed out . . . not a proud moment to be sure, but a useful one, for apparently my suddenly quiescent body attained some sort of stasis or equilibrium and the process stopped with my head still above the sand. So great had been the shock that I had lapsed into a momentary amnesia, but it all came back to me now. Just then some sensibility pierced through the panic, and I fully realized that it had been my cessation of movement that caused the descent to stop in the first place . . . and that my only hope lay in the possibility that it might work again. So I sputtered a curse, for the sand was already up to the top of my lower lip, held my breath, and resisted all instinct to move.

"And, my good man, it worked! In a moment, the suction stopped all at once with only my nose just above the level of the sand. I waited a while, breathing fitfully through my nose, as I can assume you appreciate, and slowly forced my head back to try and get my mouth clear, succeeded to some limited extent, and waited.

"For an eternity I waited thus. Able to do nothing but breathe, sort through my fears, and hope for deliverance. Of course, I dared not cry out for fear of upsetting the balance of things. My only chance lay in my mates coming back to look for me, which I knew they must, for they were one and all honorable men, and they wouldn't tolerate my absence for long.

"And, indeed, presently I heard Quatermain's voice. 'Will! Will Scott! Will!' Yet he did not as yet appear at the opening of the gallery—for that is what the giant mouth in fact was, of course, the opening to one of the lesser caves within a cavern—and I hesitated a few moments before responding. But then I saw his silhouette and that of Richard Holmes, and I whispered, 'Here, Quatermain.' But of course it wasn't nearly forceful enough, and neither could they see me with only my face protruding above the sand. 'Quatermain, over here,' I said a bit louder. But it was no use. In a moment they disappeared from my perspective, and then I heard my brother, 'Will, are you playing some sort of game? You are much too old for that sort of thing, you know.' Then I heard Holmes's voice respond, even as it faded behind a bend in the tunnel, 'My dear Huxley, I rather doubt that your assistant would stoop to mischief under the circumstances. That would be a serious matter indeed. But there is some sort of mischief afoot; of that there can be no doubt.'

"Well then, you can imagine my circumstances. I had to make a quick decision as to whether to cry out at that moment or bide my time till they returned. Heaven only knew, however, how far down the passage they would go before retracing their steps and how long it would be before they returned. I decided that I had not a moment to lose, and I cried out, while trying to summarize my situation as succinctly as I could: 'Hallo, over here! Just past chamber. Quicksand! Quickly!' At least the last word I had intended to be 'quickly,' but the sand had covered my mouth by that point and I knew I was gone. By some survival instinct, I held my breath, shut my eyes an instant before the grit pored over them, thanked God for what modest success I had had in life up to that point, and waited to die."

*　　　*　　　*

Holmes roused himself and after a few moments wherein he seemed to regain his orientation, he said, "And it came to pass that my cries were heard, a strong tether touched my hand, which I had somehow forced over my head. I clung to the rope with a strength seemingly independent of my own will, grasping it with all my might, and by heavens, here I am to tell you the tale and give the lie to this infernal journalistic fool, Watson. You may title your notes of this affair 'The Abyssinian Enterprise' if you wish."

Whereupon he snatched up the *Daily Telegraph* again and turned to the advertisement sheet. He perused that section for some time, then let out a great sigh. I expected the worst and he did not disappoint me.

"My dear doctor," said he, "I fear I must ask for your most profound forgiveness. The cup of my patience is so low today as to be virtually dry and my mind is awash."

Here he seemed again to contemplate the vicissitudes and pointlessness of existence. I was beginning to believe that his general displeasure had finally vented itself, when he tossed aside the advertisement sheet and remarked, "To the man who loves art for its own sake . . . . "*

---

* Editor's note: From here on out the narrative is identical to "The Adventure of the Copper Beeches," which is readily available. However, at the end of Mr. von Tersch's photocopy, there was an additional note, a mere penciled jotting that was pregnant with possibilities, and one can only wonder if Watson ever pursued this last vagrant thought, and if he did, how Holmes responded, and, if Holmes responded candidly, how Watson would have responded in turn! The scrawl at the end of the manuscript, clearly in Watson's hand, read:

"*Scott, Richard Holmes, Huxley . . . and Quatermain! I have heard these names in juxtaposition before! I would ask my dear friend Q, but he has been lost to us for a half decade now. I must confront H when he is in a more amiable mood.*"—T.K.M.

CHAPTER FIVE

The Truth Be Told

So it was on the following morning that we gathered around a fire made of ancient camel dung we had collected near camp and conversed about our successes and our general situation.

I said, "Well, we've found Professor Huxley's bones, which proves, I suppose, that Saint James's directions were accurate enough. We've also found a stray German geologist to boot. Now all we need to do is find some meteorites, a library, a sort of new Bible, and a monarch." When I said that, I noticed that Huxley, Holmes, Scott, and Cuff exchanged glances. Unexpectedly, it was Cuff who spoke up. He had been the most taciturn of the four during the entire trip, except, as it happened, when the subject of roses came up, at which time we would all be instructed at length on the details of their cultivation, care, and feeding.

"Mr. Quatermain," began Cuff, "I'm afraid that we—that is to say Huxley, Holmes, Scott, and myself—have rather an embarrassing admission to make, an admission that will prove that we have been doing you an ill turn."

I was not exactly caught off guard by this surprising statement because my suspicions, and Hans's, had been growing for days. My response was no response at all, for I had no idea how to respond. I just stared at him.

Eventually he continued, "The problem is that this business about finding Theodore—determining if he is dead or not for the benefit of Yohannes IV, which I'm sure he is called now since the coronation was scheduled for some days ago—was pure fiction. We invented that particular goal hoping that it would give this expedition some credibility, just the sort of practical turn that it is so well known you prefer, not being one who goes off willy nilly on adventures for reasons that you perceive as impractical.

"Her Majesty's government finds that there is sufficient interest in our other goals to have sanctioned this expedition. You were an essential element, so we chose to prevaricate a bit to get our way. I hope you are not too upset."

Actually, I'm proud to say, looking back on it, that I behaved quite rationally. I said, "Let me get this straight, gentlemen, putting the ruse aside for the moment, the Crown saw political potential in Mr. Huxley's locating fossil evidence establishing the existence of some intermediary form between ape and humans, a discovery that would certainly be a boon to Mr. Charles Darwin. Is that right?"

"Quite."

"And, the government also would benefit by locating whatever surviving books may exist from the Alexandria Library, and if you were to happen to locate the adjunct volume to the synoptic gospels, as I believe you called them, that would be icing on the cake."

"Yes, again, my dear Quatermain." Cuff looked positively beatific.

I thought this over for a full minute, then said, "If this is all true, Sergeant, suddenly your role in this charade seems to have evaporated. No Theodore, then no official determination, thus your presence here is a mystery."

"Ah, but that is easily explained. I still have legal authority vested in me by our government and I possess certain important papers from the P.M. that are intended to smooth over awkward situations, should we run into that sort of trouble."

It was this moment that Hans tugged on my shirt sleeve and whispered to me in Zulu. "Baas," he said, "I have known in my life a few fellows who make their livelihoods from the sea, and who, as a result of working around fish all day, smell like fish more than the fish do themselves because the smell clings not only to their garments, but to their spirits, those very same spirits that your Predikant father never ceased speaking of. So, I tell you this man smells like fish," and here he chose to plug his nose and wave his hand in front of his face.

I responded with, "Hans, I quite agree. Your cunning has seen through the lie and through the still deeper lie."

Then I said to Cuff and the other three in his group, "Gentlemen, I am ashamed that it must certainly be true that I appear to be such a thoroughly gullible man. In fact, though, I am not stupid. There is clearly something else—so far unmentioned—that you are after. And I am here to say that I for one will not lead you another inch until I am told the whole truth."

The faces of the four of them screwed into a perfect rhapsody of guilt. They conferred in quiet tones, after which Holmes took up the narrative. "Quatermain, you are both right and wrong. Though our little group did in fact come together initially for all the reasons already discussed—independent of the meteorite cache, which is Professor Mitchell's affair—word of our venture became common currency to those high up in our government who need to know such things (and not only ours but in other governments, as well). Very discreetly, then, representatives of the Vatican at the request of the pope himself, asked a special favor." I must have appeared as though I intended to say something because Holmes continued brusquely, "Yes, yes, I know that the British government and the papacy haven't got on so well since the time of Henry II and Becket and all, but the Romans explained that they had reason to believe from recently unearthed evidence that somewhere near or along our path we might stumble upon a particular Christian artifact, a relic I suppose one could say, the true and material vessel . . . that object that we have come to call the Holy Grail. They said that if we should happen to run across it, they would appreciate it if we brought it back 'home' to Saint Peters."

*　　　*　　　*

I was so taken aback that I was unable to talk for quite some time, and when I did it was more akin to undiluted and incoherent blustering than any sort of common communication. It was not one of my better times, that is certain.

Just then, Richard Holmes rummaged through his rucksack and withdrew a bundle that he presented to me. "This is to substantiate what Cuff is saying," he said. "Almost two years ago some documents came to light that Church officials acquired. They tell quite an astounding tale that laid the ground for our own present quest. The manuscript in your hand is a summarization of the catalyst event. It was drawn up by His Eminence, Alberto Cardinal Cigliutti, Prefect of the Holy Office and Vatican Secretary of State. What you have there is a translation from his Italian and, though it is told in a rather reflective tone with perhaps more assumptions and leaps of faith than historians care for, it is nonetheless the reason we are where we are, sitting around a pitiful excuse for a fire in the most God-forsaken desert on the planet."

I quickly scanned the manuscript and my primary reaction was pure wonderment that such distinguished men of the realm could be so ready to believe a word of it (and I thought *I* was gullible!).

[Quatermain note: As it happened, Mr. Church, because the manuscript was somewhat complex, I asked to keep it so I could take my time studying it. Thereafter circumstances changed so quickly

and with such astonishing force, that I never had an opportunity to return the document. As I still possess it, I am asking Dr. Watson to have it copied as well and to attach it to the narrative he is preparing for your enjoyment. —A.Q.]

[Watson note: I have done as Mr. Quatermain requested and inserted Cardinal Cigliutti's document at this point in the story so as to maintain the continuity of the tale. —J.H.W.]

CHAPTER SIX

The Reflection

(Being the Second Digression)*

A Reflection into the Final Moments of Piero Lorenzina's Earthly Life

By His Eminence, Alberto Cardinal Cigliutti

Dearest God the Eternal and All-Knowing, please forgive me my presumptuousness. If I seem to be consciously taking upon myself that divinely prescient quality that you hold so close to your own breast and only share with the greatest of your prophets, I ask that you understand. I am doing so only because of my urgent need to understand better the man named Piero Lorenzina. Unknowingly, except perhaps for a moment at the very end, he was clearly the

---

* Editor's note: When I, the modern editor, finished reading the manuscript that Mr. Quatermain says was presented to him at this juncture, it occurred to me that some sort of corroborative evidence would save me and other readers the necessity of taking this most unusual narrative at face value—despite my temptation to do so. As it happens, my wife's mother has an influential lay position in an important California Diocese of the Roman Catholic Church, and I was able to persuade her to field some inquiries for me. In about six months her efforts bore fruit in the information that the Vatican Secretary of State during the time frame in question, Alberto Cardinal Cigliutti, had living relatives who retained some of his personal possessions. For reasons of privacy, I am unable to divulge the names or even the nationality of these fine people. Let it only be said that they were kind enough to allow me to explore the cardinal's papers, where I discovered in a yellowed heavy envelope in a dusty trunk a hand-written manuscript. Though I don't read Italian, my Romance language background being French, I could see certain words that seemed to be appropriate. Indeed, when that manuscript was translated, the tale it told—while obviously not word-for-word identical due to the vicissitudes that lead different translators in different eras to different decisions and interpretations of abstractions—was the same story, point for point, as the one contained within the Watson/Quatermain manuscript, the original of which had been in the possession of Jim Turner, then editor of Arkham House.[34] The version here is based on the Watson/Quatermain manuscript. —T.K.M.

vehicle of your purpose, a tool that you wielded. In a way, he was your messenger, meant to bring back to the world the supreme joy, the ultimate wonderment, that has been lost for so many ages. I feel compelled to understand the man; I need to understand why this man was special to you. I have studied the man and his life for many weeks and have assembled a complete historical and bio-graphical dossier that includes interviews with his few living friends and many of his students, as well as the testimony of those individuals he encountered on his last journey and who witnessed his outward behaviors. I believe I have enough now to begin the—perhaps impossible, perhaps impudent—task I have set upon myself, namely to reconstruct the last hour of his life, his thoughts, his emotions, the essence that was Piero Lorenzina those moments before you gathered him to your infinitely merciful breast.

Remember, most loving and compassionate virgin Mary, it has never been said or heard that anyone who turned to you for help was left unaided. Inspired with this conviction, I run to your pro-tection and stand before you penitent of my wrong doings, for you are my mother and the mother of all. O Mother of the Word of God, neglect not my prayers, despise not my words of pleading, but in your mercy, please hear and answer me.

Divine Mother, I ask that you please guide my thoughts, my imagination, my assumptions, to be worthy of you. Amen.*

March 10, 1870

★ Editor's note: The majority of the cardinal's manuscript, which follows, was written in the grammatical form called the perfect conditional tense. In this tense, in the English version, most predicates include the qualifying verb combination "would have." So, rather than writing "Piero threw out some corn," the cardinal wrote "Piero would have thrown out some corn." Instead of writing "In its place, fear arose" he wrote "In its place, fear would have arisen." The purpose clearly was to unequivocally qualify each and every one of his extrapolated statements. Since he didn't know Piero Lorenzina and was not witness to the scenario described, he felt incumbent to write no statement at all as fact but as speculation. As the entire manu-

A score of pigeons dived and whirled around Piero Lorenzina. He scattered another handful of dried corn over the dewy pavement. In front of him, across the piazza, a rosy opalescence fanned through the thinly clouded sky over the silhouetted face of Santa Croce. With east at its back, the basilica often took on a fiery, sanctified cast as the swollen sun rose over Florence's sea of ancient, red tile housetops.

Piero studied the pigeons intently. As they bickered and pecked at the corn, a worn smile of indulgence moved across his smooth, age-spotted face. For eight years he had shared his early morning hours with Florence's pigeons—since his beloved Maria Grazia had passed on. Now, it was only a week to his eighty-seventh birthday and nearly all his friends had gone, too, each funeral giving him progressively more reason to attend to his birds.

During these last years, he had disciplined himself to rise each morning before dawn, spruce up, put on a clean suit, and patiently walk to either the open-air restaurant in the Piazza della Repubblica or to the Caffe Campana d'Oro where he liked to sip a coffee with milk and read. But he always stopped at Piazza Santa Croce, for the church had been Maria Grazia's.

Somewhere distant a horse squealed. All at once the pigeons took off with a half-hearted flapping, describing a wide half-circle above Piero's head, and fluttered back down some distance in front of him.

Come back, my fidgety little friends, thought Piero. He made a motion with his arm as though tossing a handful of corn to the ground. Instantly, the pigeons were airborne, and in one low hop were back at Piero's feet. A few pecked at the remaining kernels

script is couched in this stilted manner, I have taken the liberty of removing the awkwardness. Though causing the cardinal's manuscript to be somewhat less precise, this has had the corollary effect of making Piero's presumed last hour eminently more readable. —T.K.M.

and crumbs, but most peered at the ground and cocked their heads up at the old man questioningly.

"Ah, my little children are not so very smart," he said. "You are always fooled so easily by Piero's little game."

He threw out another handful, and the birds flapped around, jostling one another for the corn treats. A dusty-white dove lighted on Piero's right shoulder, cooing gently. The old man said, "So, *piccino mio*, you think to thank me." He placed a morsel between his wrinkled lips and puckered. Without hesitation, the bird snatched the tidbit, lifted its beak, and swallowed imperially.

At that instant, the entire flock, including his small companion, took off furiously. Piero followed their flight into the pale-blue sky. In a moment, he was surprised to see the sky fill with birds, countless throngs rising high from the four corners of the city, circling and converging—thousands of pigeons peppering the vault.

After the initial wonder of the spectacle, Piero's surprise quickly fled. In its place, fear arose. Living over eight decades had taught him something: animals have an unaccountable prescience about disturbances of nature. Some evil was impending. In this light, the sky full of circling specks abruptly took on the likeness of a routed army—legions running pell-mell from a marauding enemy.

But whatever the evil, Piero knew that it would be useless to run and hide from a force that frightened the pigeons from an entire city. To rush around seeking shelter from some vague terror could only be in vain.

Besides, he thought he knew what to expect.

He started to walk slowly away from the church, using his treasured Ethiopian ebony cane—an anniversary gift from Maria—as though it were a third leg. Methodically, childishly placing its tip where the cracks in the pavement intersected, he came to the fountain at the Palazzo Ferristori end of the piazza. Sitting on the ledge of the pool, he planted the cane in front of him and rested his small, weathered hands on the head. In a few moments, he felt the soothing effect of the gently splashing arcing twin streams of water. His gaze took in everything around him.

It was still too early for the morning throngs and bustle. The vias were quiet, the piazza all but deserted. He spotted a young couple slowly walking toward the basilica, and he thought of Maria Grazia. *How many times would we have walked around the earth if all our walks were added together?*

Santa Croce stood firm and spiring like a mountain. Its gray and white marble face had emerged from shadow and had begun to gleam milkily in the morning light. Piero made out, beyond and to the right of the church, the massive stone bulk of the Biblioteca Nazionale.

As always, Piero was impressed with the fact that from this one spot on the ledge of the fountain he could take in at one glance the houses of both God and the cumulative knowledge of mankind. There, in one eyeful, were two veritable vaults, one housing the classic art treasures of several centuries honoring God and His own, the other guarding some of Western Civilization's most priceless manuscripts and incunabula.

I am Alpha and Omega, the beginning and the ending, he thought. *Behold! The Father and the fruit of His children!*

He glanced again at the couple—tiny in the distance—walking arm in arm toward Santa Croce. They were very young, no more than fifteen, surely.

At that moment, all at once, he greatly longed to be fifteen again himself. The feeling lasted only seconds. He could not let himself be seduced by thoughts of the poignant impossible. Not at his age! Then, stretching his legs out, he thought of his many children. *Santa patata! The children!*

Piero and his wife had never had children of their own; nor had they adopted. Instead, they were satisfied to devote their lives to *challenging* the minds of children. Maria Grazia, through her strength of character and pure determination, had been taken on as editor of children's books for Giuseppe Berini, Publisher, and Piero had been a teacher.

Piero loved teaching. He had taught ten and eleven year olds, for *their* minds, he believed, were especially bright, inquisitive and open to new experiences. There had been nearly a thousand of them during the twenty years he had taught *scuola elementare*.

Then he left municipal education for the more lucrative private sector. During the next twenty-four years he had tutored boys and girls of substance, opening up the cosmos for them, being always conscious that he was crafting them into the kind of men and women he believed should properly populate the earth. Maria Grazia had delighted teasing him, calling him her little Dr. Frankenstein.

Piero had loved her. He had loved all the children. He had loved his work.

Now, he watched the couple stroll toward Santa Croce and sighed.

His attention was again drawn to the swarming birds ominously circling high overhead. He waited for what he knew must come.

In another minute it came.

Gently, as though a small sleeping child had rolled over, the ground shook. Some cigarette butts and a lone scrap of paper bobbed placidly in the calm at the edge of the pool. No wrenching. No thunderous tumult.

A reply to Piero's sigh.

Piero heard a dull, thudding crash behind him. He turned and saw a cloud of dust rising from the wide sidewalk across the via. A pile of broken brick and mortar lay near the corner of the old apartments adjacent to the fifteenth century Palazzo Ferristori, the "Poorman's Palace" as it was called.

Piero's curiosity was piqued, but he assumed the tremor was only a precursor of worse to come. He sat and waited, watching. He spotted the couple rushing up the church stairs, then lost them in a shadow. An ornate carriage rounded a corner behind him and ventured down Via de Benci, its single passenger engrossed in a newspaper, apparently oblivious to the geological shiftings transpiring beneath Florence.

He waited for more shocks, but there were none, and after awhile he saw that the city was coming alive. Some shopkeepers arrived at their kiosks in the piazza, flinging open plank shutters. Other merchants began opening up their shops and stalls. Cabs and carriages became more numerous. It seemed as though no one else had noticed the tremor or, for that matter, the pile of brick by the corner of the apartment. Looking up, he saw that the pigeons were descending again.

Then he spotted a knot of book-toting youths walking toward him—toward the mound. They were still two blocks away, talking among themselves, in no great hurry. Quickly, with some pain, Piero stood up and crossed the via. He peered down at the crumbled bricks. He looked up at the corner of the apartment. At first, he could make out nothing. Then, squinting, he saw the gash in the wall near the corner of the second floor.

Santa patata! A thought struck him with a weight it never had before: these buildings around the piazza were well over four hundred years old. Santa Croce itself was over six hundred years old. No wonder the building would begin to fall apart at the slightest jolt. With this last thought, Piero's first inclination was to draw back away from the moldering building, for he still feared aftershocks.

But before he could put action to the thought, he spotted a

tiny anomaly. He pushed aside a piece of a brick with his cane. He thought he saw a bit of brown paper. He bent down and tried to pull it from the debris, but the piece broke off into his fingers. His breath caught. It was very old, brown and brittle. One was not born a Florentine without having an inborn sense for priceless things. He achingly got down on his knees and brushed aside some of the dust and crumbly mortar with his handkerchief. Carefully he moved some of the smaller bricks by hand and pried away the larger ones with his cane until he exposed a thick folio. Part of it looked damaged, but the cracked leather binding appeared to have protected most of it from major loss. Carefully, piece by piece, he picked up the tiny fragments of broken paper; then he warily lifted the cover slightly and inserted the pieces between the folded leaves.

The group of boys passed him by now, hardly giving him a second glance. Just another old beggar rummaging through the city's refuse. Eagerly, gently, he pulled the volume out of the pile. It was heavy. With his cane he probed the rubble. When he was sure he had picked up every scrap, he held the folio tightly against his chest with his free arm and crossed back to the piazza.

Breathing excitedly, Piero sat on the fountain ledge, carefully centering his find on his lap. He used the handkerchief to wipe away the dust from the decaying, grainy leather. Whatever else the book might be, it was certainly ancient. Piero guessed it could have been hidden in a niche in the apartment wall centuries before, then plastered or bricked over, much as it was suspected must have happened to Leonardo da Vinci's vanished wall painting *The Battle of Anghiari*. Given the age of the building, the volume could well prove to be fifteenth century. The binding appeared to be leather, perhaps pigskin, but Piero did not pretend to know much about such matters.

Set into the center of the cover was a circular, tarnished

bronze medallion. He spread open his hand to measure the medallion. It was not quite as wide as the distance between the tips of his thumb and little finger. Squinting, Piero could just make out the design, for the green tarnish and the embedded dust of centuries combined to dull the image—a dish or bowl of some sort over which floated an eight-pointed sun; the sun's beams were triangles with their tips truncated, the lower one of which poured into the bowl; a ring of intertwining snakes and vines encircled the whole image, breaking wherever the open beams met it; a Latin legend—VIVERE EST QUAERERE QUAERERE EST INVENIRE PRAEMIUM EST VITA IN PECTO DEI MD—surrounded the wreath and formed the circumference of the medallion. Piero translated the legend: "To live is to seek; to seek is to find; the reward is life in God's breast," followed by the year, 1500. Piero smiled, for the maxim could easily have been one of his own.

An emblem with this sort of design, he knew, was related to alchemy. More than likely this was an old alchemist's text. When he realized this, he flushed with excitement. Slowly, carefully, he opened it as much as he dared and studied what he saw. The rag paper was thick, brown with age, and fragile. He ran his fingers over it. It felt coarse. A line of faded, black ink proclaimed in Latin that this was the workbook of Tomasso Masini da Peretola[35], dated in Roman numerals from 1496 through 1500. He turned slowly one by one through the pages.

Steadily, his ecstasy was joined by the rage of helplessness.

Though he had never heard of Tomasso Masini, the volume he held in his hands was clearly a work of art, a creation of genius. That filled him with joy for his good fortune at finding this masterwork. Yet, the irreparable damage done by the long fall from the second story made his heart ache. His fury ranged out, irrationally cursing Masini for not taking proper precautions, at the uncounted tenants of the apartment for being so abysmally blind and ignorant, at the inept mechanism of pitiable Fate for delivering up a prize of this magnitude in such a manner!

He barely noticed as a breeze came up, widening the spray of mist from the sparkling arc of the fountain.

Despite this great rush of conflicting emotions, he continued to turn each leaf gingerly, allowing each page a brief inspection. Surprisingly, he found that much of the writing was intact. It was a veritable hodgepodge of Latin, Greek, Hebrew, medieval Italian, and some sort of incomprehensible cipher, all interspersed with a potpourri of ornately drawn symbols, part mythical, part mathematical. As he leafed through, Piero read many disjointed phrases, but they seemed meaninglessly jumbled. Most pages were richly illuminated with serpents, trees, and nude men and women reminiscent of Eden; or with exquisite, richly colored mandalas; or with moons, flowering plants, pointed stars, towers, and all manner of archetypal images. There were also frequent woodcuts and engravings so bizarre and grotesque that, in Piero's estimation, they rivaled Hieronymus Bosch.

The book was a colossal find! At the very least, it was an orgy of medieval design and color. And that was an assessment based solely on its visual power. There was no guessing what marvelous insights Tomasso Masini da Peretola could now share with the world.

Then turning over a page, Piero was surprised to find a ragged scrap of parchment covered with clumsy Black-Letter Latin. It was immediately plain that the parchment was centuries older than the rest of the book and had been sewn in separately. The writing was faded and filled the page into the corners so that Piero had a difficult time trying to make any of it out. Indeed, parts of it were blackened, possibly scorched. He ran his fingers over the page. It was crisp and full of what he supposed were wormholes.

Quickly, Piero flipped the parchment to see if there were any more like it. The shock of what he saw petrified him. Disbelief and wonder snapped his vision out of focus. He fought to sharpen it. This had to be a dream! Not in his wildest imaginings could he have foreseen this! He quickly looked ahead to see how many of these new sheets there were: fourteen leaves of vellum, yellow with age but of a much finer quality than the parchment. They, too, were sewn separately into the book. Piero's gaze lingered over the *familiar* style of the precision sketches, over the eccentric, backward script that only one man could have achieved so effortlessly. He touched the pages gently, reverently.

It was unbelievable, yet there could be no doubt. Whatever else this book might be, he knew that these fourteen leaves, filled on both sides with drawings and annotation, were priceless beyond knowing. He held in his hands actual pages of a Leonardo da Vinci notebook! A lost treasure of untold consequence! A new codex!

Santa Maria, Madre di Dio! What have you led me to?

Carefully, he closed the folio. A wind came up, spraying him with moisture from the splashing fountain. Suddenly afraid, he pulled off his coat and wrapped it around his find.

He must think. What should he do? Should he take it home to his little apartment and study it to his heart's content? Should he sequester it somewhere, keeping it for himself? The temptation was tremendous. At length he looked up and his eyes rested on the imposing stone vault that was the Biblioteca Nazionale. But, of course, there was only one thing he could do. The book must be put into the hands of proper scholars—authorities who *could* study it and disseminate their findings. He had been foolish to even consider keeping it for himself.

The excitement made him feel weak. *Maria Grazia, what*

should I do? If only you were alive and here to share this with me. How would you want me to handle it? The thought of his long dead wife suddenly filled his mind. It turned his thoughts forcibly to Santa Croce, towering so grandly before him. She had been the religious one, a good Catholic attending Mass every morning. He had not thought it necessary for himself. He felt comfortable with his God and didn't feel that a daily pilgrimage would improve things any. It had hurt her at the start of their marriage and was the cause of many arguments, but Piero's temple was the human brain, where God resided at all times. He considered all works of both nature and man to be God's works. Though he thought of Santa Croce as monumental, awesome architecture; as a measure of the skill of his species; as a reflection of both the magnificence and delicacy of God; he doubted that God was any more there than He was in the cobblestones below Piero's feet or in the pigeons that were now tentatively returning to the piazza.

Nevertheless, he had often accompanied Maria Grazia to church, and many times he felt a distinct warmth rush through him as he knelt beside her and received the Sacrament. But he had always attributed this more to being close to Maria, loving her, and sharing with her something that was important to her, than to the powers of Christ.

Then, when she died, he could not bring himself to attend church alone except sometimes on their anniversary, or when he was caught up in the Christmas or Easter spirit, and even then it was only a hollow gesture. The trouble was that Maria Grazia was his only link to the Church.

And now, feeling the weight of the incalculably valuable volume on his lap and wishing that Maria Grazia was there so that he could relish the wonder on her face, that old warmth rushed over him again.

Piero Lorenzina began to sob. The memories of fifty-six

years of marriage, of true love and companionship, flooded in on him.

* * *

He remembered the task ahead of him and wiped his face dry with his hands. With a fraction of his attention, he noticed that a crowd had gathered curiously around the heap of bricks behind him on the sidewalk. He stood awkwardly and began to walk the length of the piazza toward the biblioteca, clinging to the tome that somehow had opened up a link to his dead wife.

The square was buzzing with activity now. Piero, blinded to all but his self-imposed duty, was oblivious to the leatherware shops and the kiosks displaying plaster Madonnas and the maniacally hawking merchants and all the rest whose lifework was the waylaying of insatiable tourists.

As he drew near the basilica, the wind came up and Piero felt the morning chill bite through his shirt. He was not used to going without a coat at this hour. The book was heavy and bulky and he needed both hands to hold onto it. It was difficult walking with a load and not being able to use his cane, which dangled uselessly from his left hand.

He turned south onto the via toward the Piazza dei Cavalleggeri. Across from that piazza was the main entrance of the library. Suddenly, a blast of cold wind shot clear to his bones. He stopped in front of Santa Croce, trembling. He tried to get a better hold on the book. The wind blew steadily down from the dark, shop-lined via behind him. He shivered violently, grimacing. He took a few more steps, but stopped again, suddenly dizzy. He tottered, feeling a tremendous pressure push down on him. He felt as though he were carrying the world.

Abruptly, he made up his mind. The burden and the cold were unendurable, and the open doors of the vast church were too inviting. The shelter inside would rejuvenate him. Though it was critical to get his amazing find into proper hands, if he were to collapse from exhaustion halfway there, someone else finding the tome might not know what must be done.

As fast as he was able, he mounted the church stairs and, passing through the cloisters, entered the nave. Though not strictly warm, the dusty air was considerably more comfortable than the chill outside. It had been almost a year since he had entered Santa Croce, but it appeared not to have changed at all. That somehow made him feel more comfortable.

As he stood just within the cavernous Florentine-Gothic interior of the basilica, he was struck as he had always been by the wholly different quality of the sound within. Somehow, the resonance or the air pressure or both caused a definite physical sensation, contributing to a feeling of other-worldliness. Oddly, this sensation, too, was a distinct comfort to him now.

Piero moved to the right side of the church and slowly made his way down the aisle past Michelangelo's tomb and the tomb of the composer Rossini, past monuments to Dante and Macchiavelli, by a bas-relief of the *Annunciation* by Donatello, and turned into the right transept. His movements were automatic, as though time had erased nothing.

At the end of the transept, he walked straight into the Baroncelli Chapel, which had been Maria Grazia's favorite, and was grateful that it was warmer still than the nave. Nothing had changed here either. The Giotto fresco of the *Coronation of the Virgin* still watched over the chapel from above the altar exactly as it had when Maria came here every morning. He moved to the front pew, genuflected, and sat thankfully on the plain bench, placing the book carefully beside him. He made the sign of the cross and knelt painfully in the exact spot where Maria had put her knees so many times. He gazed up at the ghostly outlines that were all that remained of the Coronation after the fresco was inexcusably covered with whitewash some centuries before, and he considered the frailty of mankind. He was terribly tired; yet, in this setting he found himself waxing contemplative, weighing human artistry against human perversity. He laughed at his foolishness, then prayed for strength enough to take the fabulous volume to the biblioteca. He sighed deeply; closing his eyes, he asked, too, that Maria Grazia was well and happy. He breathed quietly, savoring his immense good fortune, feeling thoroughly content, remembering . . . .

All at once, a chill ran through him despite the comparative warmth of the chapel, and he had a strong craving for a steaming coffee. He was still on his knees and wanted to sit because his knees ached, but he couldn't summon the strength to move his legs. He tried very hard, but he only succeeded in making himself more tired. The physical exhaustion turned to sleepiness. He rested his head on the support in front of him. He closed his eyes and saw a vision of Maria as she had appeared on their wedding day, so young and dark and slender, dressed in white and blushing behind her veil. He felt his heart fill with her. The fullness pushed on his chest. He opened his eyes and the vision did not fade. She was still there holding her hands out to him. She moved into the pew and sat beside him. He was very cold, yet he knew only gladness that his Maria Grazia was beside him again. He took her outstretched hand. It, too, was cold, as though she'd just come in from the out-of-doors.

A tingle of joy swept through his body, cresting along his spine. He couldn't keep his eyes off her.

Maria, the book, the great book—it must be put into proper hands. The scholars must get it. Please, help me. I cannot tell you how important this is! It must not fall into the hands of the callous or the careless or the unthinking. It must not!

Don't worry, my Piero. It will turn out well, he heard her say;

then all faded except for Maria Grazia, his cherished wife for eternity.

*   *   *

Thus ends, Heavenly Father, Holy Mother, my reflection on the last hour of Piero Lorenzina's life on earth. However, there is great—without doubt inspired and divine—irony here. Be it noted that I have assumed in the preceding that Piero took absolutely for granted, perfectly naturally so, that the earthquake had dropped into his safekeeping an authentic Leonardo da Vinci codex. I made this assumption because my in-depth study of this otherwise learned man has shown no strong inclination toward art history or comparative scholarship. Otherwise he would have seen what our Vatican art historians and textural scholars easily observed, namely that the journal was another of the many extant works by the able hand of Gian Giacomo Caprotti. Leonardo adopted the ten-year-old Gian, nicknamed Salai, which sobriquet underscored his devilish nature, into his household in 1490 where he seemed to have fulfilled many roles, part apprentice, part servant, part devoted companion.* In any event, it has been shown that Salai is the artist responsible for numerous paintings and drawings done in Leonardo's style, but not done by the great artist himself. In addition, and therefore conclusively, once the reverse script on the fourteen pages of vellum had been read and much of its oblique meaning deciphered, it became obvious that it was no less than Salai's own journal of his long, taxing journey in search of the ultimate wonderment. That he mimicked here his master's frequent

---

* Editor's note: Salai stayed by the artist's side for 26 years until the great master's death.—T.K.M.

tendency to secretiveness is only natural given the nature of his quest.*

Alberto Cardinal Cigliutti

---

* Editor's note: The cardinal made these statements about 1870 at a time when over-enthusiastic scholars were seeing evidence of Gian Giacomo Caprotti's work everywhere. More recent scholarship has thrown into doubt many of those findings.—T.K.M.

CHAPTER SEVEN

Bayushtiak Intervenes

"Twaddle," I said, thinking that Hans and I had been thrown into the company of lunatics. Or at least some of them were.

I quickly pulled aside Miss Mitchell and asked if she had had any notion of the true goal of Holmes, Huxley, Cuff, and Scott.

"Why no, I didn't, Mr. Quatermain. I'm as appalled as you, you can count on that. Why, the Grail is merely a Celtic myth. And I cannot account for the behavior of these otherwise notable men."

Burton, of her party, volunteered much of the same, as did Dravot and Carnehan.

Nonetheless, their falseness aside, these people had hired me, and they were dependent on me. "There's nothing for it," I said to them all, "but to turn around and return the way we came. I vow to continue to the best of my ability."

"But Quatermain," Holmes was quite firm. "I haven't shown you the final proof yet. Remember, you just read that embedded in the book Piero Lorenzina found there was a vellum notebook. That notebook tells how Leonardo da Vinci's friend Tomasso had stumbled across the final written words of a dying eleventh century crusader and that the crusader's words gave detailed directions on how to find the Holy Grail. Furthermore, because he determined to his own satisfaction that the writing was both sincere and authentic, in the year 1500, Leonardo dispatched Tomasso and another close companion named Salai off in search of the Grail. That notebook was in fact Salai's journal and describes how they traveled for months in extreme climates, all the while following the route laid out by the crusader. And according to Salai, and later vouched for by Leonardo, who added copious notes in the margins of the journal, they did in fact find the Grail. However, they chose to leave it right where they found it. Salai wrote, I'm sure parroting Leonardo's wishes, that he couldn't see any good bringing it back. It was better off where it was—away from the greed of men. And so they returned home, richer only for the experience.

"Unfortunately, just as was typical of Leonardo when he wanted to be either discreet or abstruse, his compatriot Salai did an excellent job expressing himself in an entirely oblique and cryptic manner. Much of his 'travelogue,' if you will, is meaningless to anyone but Leonardo and himself. All our attempts to glean something instructive and geographically useful from the notebook have thus far failed."

So it was only natural for me to ask, "So what good is it?"

Here Holmes positively gloated. "Don't you see. Leonardo da Vinci *said* Tomasso and Salai found the Holy Grail. If Leonardo said it, then it must be *true*. The man was a paragon and his word is *not* to be doubted."

Well, in fact, I didn't see. I didn't see it at all. My patience with these people had reached its uttermost limit. I remember vividly letting out an enormous sigh of helplessness. I remember this particularly because such a reaction is not typical of me. I was half embarrassed when I'd realized what I had done and was immediately grateful that nobody seemed to have noticed.

But nothing really had changed. Thus, I went on explaining things as I saw them. "Twaddle is what I said, and twaddle is what I meant. To get back to what I was saying, there's nothing for it but to turn around and return the way we came. I will do my utmost to fulfill my end of the bargain and return you all safely to our point of departure. I can do no more."

But Holmes was rushing on headlong and was not to be stopped. I'm quite sure he hadn't heard a thing that I'd said. "You just read in that manuscript about a parchment with Black-Letter writing," said he. "Well, I have the translation of that parchment here, as well." At which point, he thrust another batch of papers into my hands. "It tells the story of certain knights during the period of the First Crusade," said Holmes. "Indeed, it contains the original geographical statements that were written by an eleventh century knight and which we misstated to you, saying they derived from Yohannes IV's spies about Theodore's location."

You've heard the expression, that a last straw can break a camel's back. Well, Holmes's last remark was frankly that last straw. I took hold of this new sheaf of papers while in a sort of daze, the feeling of betrayal and violation now so vast that it was like part of me suddenly and violently separated itself from my body and looked at the whole scene with complete objectivity, finding it all vastly comic. This separate and new me laughed and laughed, then got control of itself and harshly whispered in my ear. "Allan," it said, "what is the use of continuing this charade that life holds any value? What more could life hold for thee beyond more heartbreak and faithlessness? Leave them to die. They are not worth your succor." And the fearful thing was that I was not able to distinguish my true thoughts from those of this shadow version of me. It was like I had to struggle to breathe and I could see dimly that survival lay only in my total abandonment of these four European devils and the others as well. Let them fend for themselves. Let them know firsthand what it is like to be brutally betrayed . . . . And that was the tenor of my thoughts as I stared at these men whose lies had led me so far away from my comfortable little home in Durban. My hatred was black indeed.

And I am here to tell you, gentlemen, that, looking back on it, I truly believe I was on the precarious edge of insanity at that moment. No doubt I was exhausted having only just concluded one arduous journey—that being to Heu-Heu land and back—and then starting another right away. No matter the cause, I could see myself truly tossing away forever all notions of empathy and compassion and thereafter living solely for my own selfish betterment, or perhaps, as the voice suggested, giving up on life altogether.

What saved me was at once obvious and unexpected. The warrior Bayushtiak had crept up behind me and touched my arm. He tells me that I reacted by snarling like a wolf. Though, clearly there would have been many witnesses, I was never able to glean from anyone other than the Zulu, not even Hans, whether my reaction was really such.

"Macumazana, come back," he whispered to me in Zulu. "It is I, Bayushtiak. I am here to save you just as the Great One has directed me to do. The portents and signs he shared and caused me to remember are now coming to pass, even this very moment. The world of true men is losing you and the foul witches are claiming you . . . unless you can find the fire within you to return to the surface world that is real."

I can tell you quite frankly that this ugly (and quite frightening . . . to this day I fear its return) side of me did not give up lightly. It fought Bayushtiak's ministrations for what seemed like hours, and all another part of me could do was watch and bear witness. I suppose it was because this drama was being played out on a stage far removed from our real world that the time seemed stretched.

Imagine the scene! Holmes had just handed me the new set of papers, and I was holding them in the air in my fist just as a kind of fearsome mask passed over my face and a kind of paralysis possessed me, only to then have the savage Zulu approach me and whisper in my ear. What could these calculating, deceitful Europeans (as I thought of them then) have thought by this little scene that was playing out before them?

Of course, I never told them what really happened, for what would they have thought?

[Quatermain note: Indeed, now that I think of it, I have never told a soul of this incident before now! —A.Q.]

[Watson note: Here, as you may recall, Church, Quatermain became very thoughtful and quiet as he stared for a time into the fire blazing in your hearth. And then he said he was in need of fresh air, thus we all moved out to that elaborate patio (I believe you called it your "Court Hall") that looked out upon the Hudson River and the Catskill Mountains beyond—at least during the day it did, as I could see for myself come the dawn. The air was fragrant and not at all uncomfortable, and so we made ourselves comfortable on the benches there and Quatermain continued, first taking a slow sip from his brandy glass. —J.H.W.]

They tell me the pause in my conversation and Bayushtiak's subsequent interruption lasted only a few minutes. Be that as it may, in a moment, thanks to Zikali's foresight and the proud presence of Bayushtiak, all was back to normal. I do admit to then upbraiding with a certain forcefulness the four men who had hired me, but that is long past, and is water under the bridge now.

I then turned my attention to the papers that were still in my hand and began to read . . . .

[Quatermain note: Now, Church, though I gave you that night the essence of the knight's story that I read then, insofar as I also retained that translation of the knight's parchment, along with Cardinal Cigliutti's document, I am asking Dr. Watson to include this material as well. —A.Q.]

[Watson note: Which I have done at this point. —J.H.W.]

CHAPTER EIGHT

The Parchment
(Being the Third and Last Digression)

THE WRITING ON THE BLACK-LETTER PARCHMENT

Duke Stephen is dead, as are Count Albert of Clermont, William of Saint-Giles, and Fulcher of Tyre. So too 9 and 40 other fine and noble knights. By God's grace, I live. I am the last of the 50 brave men chosen by God to carry out His will. For by following his signs, Duke Stephen led us and we found the sacred vessel that was touched by the lips of our Lord Jesus Christ. We knew this was so for the archangel Gabriel, in the form of St. Andrew, came to Stephen in his sleep and made known this fact. Now this holy relic is truly safe, no longer soiled by any that is not also holy. So now I can die in peace.

This is my story: I am Bors, Count of Mainz. Following the Christmas fest of 1096 and taking to heart the spirited words of His Holiness Pope Urban, I and my comrades in arms joined Godfrey of Bouillon on the Danube at Worms, and by ways small and great passed through Hungary and Bulgaria to Constantinople at the bidding of Emperor Alexius. Here we joined with Raymond of Toulouse, Prince Bohemond of Tarentum, Hugh of Vermandois and others.

Soon we crossed the Bosphorus and laid siege for 7 weeks on Nicaea, a capital of the enemies of Christ. Our army was 600,000 strong and we marched in God's name. Following the surrender of Nicaea, we set out toward distant Antioch. Soon we who were with Godfrey heard that Bohemond's men were in need of succor, so we came to their aid and slew the Saracens all the whole day long.

Then came 500 miles of blistering, terrible desert, but finally we of Godfrey came to Antioch and laid siege for 7 months, nearly starving ourselves, but in the end, Emir Firuz betrayed his city and opened the gates. However, no sooner had our force entered the city, then we were surrounded by Keborgn of Mosul and 200,000 heathens. So we the besiegers were suddenly the besieged and what little food we found was soon consumed. After a month we despaired, and all may have been lost but for the dream of young Peter Bartholomew in which St. Bartholomew came to him and revealed the sacred, secret spot in which was buried the Lance that pierced our Lord's side, and Lo! It was Duke Stephen himself who recovered the holy blade, inspiring us with new hope. The lance was carried aloft by our mighty host and we left the city gate and vanquished the foe. It was a great and divine victory.

But I must now tell of the dream of Duke Stephen. This day alone Stephen had slew a score of Saracens in his own right. In the night, St. Andrew came to him, he who was exhausted and sleeping deeply, and said that it was he, Stephen, who was chosen by the Lord our God to recover the Holy Vessel and then revealed its location.

Duke Stephen gathered about him 9 and 40 of his most trustworthy liegemen—including I, Bors—and gathering what supplies that could be spared, we set off. Ere long, riding eastward, our journey took us to Sarras, a small village of heathens and it was there that we found the Holy Cup sequestered in a finely wrought box of ebony that was set in a vault buried under the floor tiles in the heathen mosque. Who put it there, how or why, we never learned.

That it was the Graal, there could be no doubt because upon seeing it, our entire party to the last knight beheld a vision of the archangel exclaiming with words that hung in the air and shown with gold that before us, forsooth, was the most holy of treasures.

Now, it is true that it was only at this juncture that there was disagreement among the knights. William of Saint-Giles led the faction that believed the Graal must come to Gaul, the only land with sufficient sanctity in their view. Others, led by Albert of Clermont wished the Graal taken to Rome.

But it was Stephen who, of course, won the day. It was his idea not to ride north as would seem natural, but to go south through the Holy Land into Arabia. He said he would know where the Graal belonged when he saw it. Insofar as it was our duty to follow our liege, our small party rode hard through the sandy wastes, keeping to the eastern shore of the Red Sea. In time we ran out of land at the southern tip of Yemen, but Stephen was intent on going further. We were able to cross the Strait of Babel el Mandeb on a barge that was used by the local villages for trading purposes. Once upon the land of Africa in the southern regions of the Axumite state, we found that the terrain and climate were much the same from whence we came on the farther side of the Red Sea, by which I mean the worst kind of desert and hot.

Stephen continued to lead us as a man obsessed. We knights, who had seen the angel ourselves and understood the notion of a task undertaken for God, of course, followed his lead without question. We began what would be three days of travel by horseback in a northwest direction and thence came to the twin flaming mountains. Stephen led us between these hellish—

[Watson note: Here the translation stops mid-sentence. A marginal note, perhaps scribbled by Richard Holmes, indicates that the writing of the original Black-Letter document had been deliberately and irretrievably scraped away beginning at this point, continuing for approximately thirty-five lines. The author of the note poses the likelihood that some combination of Salai or Leonardo or Tomasso were the guilty parties and that their intent was to obliterate the detailed instructions that led them to their destination. —J.H.W.]

—rode right up to a high, vertical cliff where he looked disappointed. He ordered us to spread out and look for a way beyond the cliff. It was Thomas of Arc who spotted the cleft, which was forever in shadow and darkness and hidden from view due to the arrangement of the terrain there. We quickly entered and came out the other side of the cliff—

[Watson note: Here the translation again stops mid-sentence. Another note explains that the parchment had been exposed to fire at some point centuries past and that the writing for several inches was scorched and hopelessly lost. Nevertheless, the ending of Bors's tale remained. —J.H.W.]

—we all then were intent on returning home to our families and homes. Crossing back to Yemen we rode north and soon enough recrossed the Bosphorus with the intent of making our way to our Holy Roman Emperor to tell of our deeds waged against the heathen Saracens and also of our sacred charge fulfilled. Riding hard through Hungary, our small band, which, praise God, still numbered 50, found that the way west was blocked by furious bands of murdering peasants determined to destroy any man who wore the red cross.

We headed north with the hope of by-passing these misguided peasants and passed through the Transylvanian Alps, whereupon we stumbled unknowingly onto a great plain on either side of which thousands of men had gathered in preparation for war. We soon garnered that these were yet more of those mad Hungarians in a dispute with the local Poles, and seeing that there was no passing through or around these great armies, Duke Stephen prayed on it and in the end chose to lend our swords on the Polish side, believing their Christianity to be the stronger of the two. Soon the two armies were in pitched battle and we fought well, dying one by one for the greater glory of God so that at the battle's end, only I am left, but it is clear not for long.

I have, therefore, taken up the quill and feel the responsibility to record these events for all time so that those who follow will know the Graal is safe in Ethiopia.

In God's name.

Bors, Count of Mainz

CHAPTER NINE

The Gathering of Heaven's Dead

By the time I had finished this fairy tale for children, I felt so
abused, so exhausted, and so terribly out of control, that I did what
I always do in such situations. I excused myself and went to sleep.

*　　*　　*

The next evening, we found that the natural path we were following led to the base of an exceedingly steep but not unclimbable
hill.

Carnehan suddenly got excited. "I know this place," he said.
"We're very close. Danny, what do you think? Ain't we made a
bulls-eye? The devil take it if we didn't."

Dravot looked about and said, "I believe you're right, Peachy,
my man. I'd venture that it was at the top of this hill and yonder a
bit."

Naturally, at this news Professor Mitchell became quite ani-
mated and attacked the hill, Holmes with her, only to find that
more was required than just spirit and enthusiasm. Undaunted,
most of my party all began to claw up the side of what was a monstrous drift. Cuff and I hung back to help Lidenbrock up the slope.
He seemed depressed that he could not manage on his own and I
needed to encourage him repeatedly to keep him moving. In the
end, whether burdened with an injured man or not, we Europeans
had to rest several times. On the other hand, Hans and Bayushtiak
were waiting for us at the top when we arrived and had been for
quite some time.

The moon had just set and there was nothing at all to see, as
excited as we were to see something of this particular goal after

having given so much of ourselves to the quest these last days. But, nonetheless, there was something about that particular night, I remember. The sky was the deepest black with the stars shining particularly bright, sharp, and unwavering—a sight even unusual for one who has spent the better part of his career out in the open on the deserts, savannas, and veldts of southern Africa.

Hans, who was never far from me, was even prompted to whisper in my ear, "Baas, the sky is ablaze as though Shaka's battalions were cooking a wedding feast over fires covering a field stretching from one horizon to the other."

Frankly this observation was quite accurate and I responded with, "Let's hope it is the fires of a happy wedding rather than the blazes of warriors tempering and sharpening their blades in preparation for a glorious battle, which, frankly, doesn't interest me overly much at the moment."

"No, Baas! Don't mention such battles, lest you put a curse on us all." And he made the Hottentot sign that was meant to ward off evil. Unfortunately, his effort was in vain, as will soon be seen.

Not being able to proceed further, we set up camp rather precariously on the hill's summit and slept an unsound sleep.

That morning we awoke and saw that we had, in fact, climbed to the top of a rolling plateau constituting a mixture of sand and broken volcanic rock, and from our vantage point we could see miles in every direction. As would be expected, the entire face of the desert to our left was a rolling profusion of gullies and ugly ravines. Ahead of us, along the horizon, a series of massive symmetrical cones were lined up like titanic cauldrons simmering some monstrous witches brew, proving that we were still in the midst of volcano country.

It was here, and it was only natural, I suppose, that Lidenbrock rallied somewhat, bearing in mind that the man was never totally coherent during the brief time we knew him. One glance at those blackened and eerie mounds, and he found strength from who knows where, pulled away from our group with the intent, I suppose, of marching across the desert to investigate those mounds more closely. He was muttering something about "tuffs this" and "igneous that," and "plugs and dikes," and heaven knows what else, which I assumed were all related to volcanism. There was one particular thing he said, though, that has stuck in my mind all these years. Perhaps that is because he slipped into his native German just then, and Burton who happened to be near, translated for me. As Lidenbrock went stumbling ahead of us, he cried out, "See, the shadow of Scartaris, it moves slowly with the radiant star of day." And then he started calling out for his uncle. I was never able to make anything out of it because we had enough to do without being diverted and had to keep the poor raving man from chasing his beloved and, admittedly, awesome cinder cones.

I felt it was necessary to take advantage of the cool of the morning and I insisted we continue steadfastly on. Within an hour, we heard Dravot shouting, "I see it! There, beyond that rise. Do you see the black patch. That's the beginning of it."

He and Carnehan threw down their gear and loped ahead to the spot Dravot had indicated. They were quickly at the top of that rise jumping and waving their arms and shouting.

Well, the end of it was that soon our entire party had joined them, and there below us was one of the most astonishing sights I had ever seen, notwithstanding several days of concentrated astounding sights.

The two soldiers had not been making up a story, as I had more than half believed. The proof was before me—a veritable blasted valley, a scorched bowl about as wide as a racetrack and as big around. And the whole of it was filled with craters, some new, some old, most overlapping older ones, and older ones still, and each crater awash in shattered black stone.

"Baas!" cried Hans. "Am I dead that I have come here to the gates of that very underworld that your Predikant father so often warned me about when he caught me sampling square face."

The poor fellow was clearly upset. But who could blame him really, for this description was certainly quite accurate, just as his description the previous night of the stars had been. I bethought me that Hans was developing a poetic, or perhaps "dramatic" would be a better word, streak that I had not experienced before.

Still, call it the gates of underworld, or a graveyard of meteorites, or the very pit of Hell itself, whatever it was, there it was before us . . . daring us to stay away.

*   *   *

There was no rhyme or reason to how we behaved. We all dispersed at random through that amazing field of mysterious stones from the starry reaches outside and above the earth and we wandered aimlessly as though through a maze, around the bigger stones, stepping over the smaller ones, circling the craters, kneeling and stooping and behaving like tourists at Kensington Gardens.

I heard Professor Mitchell exclaim, "Why, just as I suspected, they're almost all irons and some stony-irons, but I can't see any stones—none at all!" Then a little later I heard Holmes exclaim, "My word! There are some green ones and some with shiny bubbles that shine with miniature rainbows!"[36]

Bayushtiak approached me then and asked, "What is this place, Macumazahn? It is like a dream world. Such rocks I've never seen in my life and have never been told about by my fathers or my fathers's fathers." You see, in the course of Maria Mitchell explaining to us the scientific background that underlay her quest, I saw no reason to translate her lecture for Bayushtiak's benefit. So, of all of us, he was the only one who arrived at this place with no preconceptions at all.

I then took a few moments to condense for him what little I understood. When I was done, his face was stern and his eyes hard as ebony crystal. He swept his arm around in a wide gesture and said, "Then these are the corpses of the stars. As I think you know now, The Great One warned me of conditions for which I must be wary. One such event has in fact happened just as he said." Here he looked at me with wide open eyes, indicating I suppose, secret knowledge, but I was too proud to respond in kind. He ignored my stubbornness and continued. "Yet here is another. 'Beware,' he said, 'of the gathering of heaven's dead.'"

My response was calculated, of course. "Bayushtiak, my new friend, I have known you only for a few days but already I know that you are strong and stalwart and would be a great ally in time of trouble, but I don't anticipate—regardless of what your master says—that I will have much to fear from a pile of blasted rocks strewn across the plain."

His response came slowly. "Macumazahn, I don't believe that is what The Great One meant." At that, he only stood tall and proud, gazing at the cosmic field and said nothing more for a time.

When we were all sated with this new experience and Professor Mitchell had collected a number of canvas sacks full of samples, we set up camp before the sun beat down too harshly. We started a fire to heat water and prepare our meals. After we had all settled down, naturally we began to speak of what we had just seen.

Richard Burton seemed to be bursting with his desire to share his thoughts. "It occurs to me that this spot is not that far distant from Mecca, where, of course, can be found the Black Stone embedded in the north-east corner of the Kaaba. Now this stone is thought to be the only remaining relic of the shrine used by Abraham and his son Ishmael for the worship of God, and is, therefore, considered to be the very right hand of God. But in actuality it is a common enough metallic aerolite—a meteorite. I know because I have studied it with my own eyes and touched it with my own hands, and even have kissed it, all this for a full ten minutes, more than most Muslims (who are typically pressed from behind by thousands of their brethren wishing likewise to venerate it) and certainly more than any European. As most of you know, I am one of the few Europeans who have entered Mecca in the last half of a millennium—and lived!"

As Burton spoke, his eyes shown, and his chest puffed out. He was definitely a man of accomplishments, I will say that for him.

"In fact, Dr. Wilson, of Bombay showed me a similar specimen which externally appeared to be a black slag but the interior of which was a bright, sparkling grayish-white which he assured me was the result of combining nickel with iron. The point I'm trying to make here is that it is possible that the Black Stone was no different from one of those yonder and that it merely missed the mark, so to speak, and fell in Arabia, which is only a bit north of here."

Burton stopped speaking, and I have to admit that this information of his gave me much food for thought, and perhaps it did the same for the others, for we were all quiet for a time.

Richard Holmes then spoke. "You know, it is sometimes said that the Grail we are after is actually a fantastic black stone, possibly a meteorite . . . at least that's the way von Eschenbach would have it."[37] He looked around expectantly at each of us, but as no one seemed inclined to pursue this line of thinking, he let it drop, I believe a little disgruntled if I read him right.

Professor Mitchell chose that moment to offer us some of her thoughts. "My theory is that this spot is particularly magnetic, in fact possibly a titanic lodestone if you like. If that can be proven, then the research possibilities are almost endless—between the region's natural magnetic quality and the nature of the meteorites themselves!"

Holmes spoke next. "Do you mean that as debris enters the atmosphere, those stones that are chiefly iron would have a tendency to be deflected to this spot due to the presumed extraordinary magnetism here?"

"Yes, that's precisely what I mean. Mr. Quatermain, do you

have your compass available?"

Within moments, we were all peering at our assorted compasses. None of them were pointing north. They all behaved strangely. Mine, in particular, moved around in circles. Burton's merely wobbled up and down like a seesaw.

At this point Holmes and Miss Mitchell conferred, then announced that, as Miss Mitchell had indicated, this was an unprecedented phenomenon and that this area required a team of specialists to follow and take detailed readings. What was required were trained mineralogists, chemists, physicists, and the like. Burton then lent a hand surveying the place with his instruments and nailing its precise location for any future visit.

Then Miss Mitchell opened her mouth to say her peace, stopped in mid-utterance, and, to my surprise, peered at each and every one of us minutely, and even looked over her shoulder! When she was apparently satisfied, she voiced her thought: "There are even those naturalists who wonder quietly if life itself may have arisen not on earth as we all suppose, but was translated to the earth via a meteoric infection, if you will."[38]

I believe she intended to elaborate on this notion, but I'm afraid we never heard her ideas because at that moment we were attacked.

CHAPTER TEN

Attacked!

But at this point, I must get off the subject for just a moment. The native inhabitants of the area we were traversing are a tough, hostile people that the Arabs called the Danakil. Indeed, the very desert we were crossing was known as the Danakil Desert.[39] These people are all muscle and unusually thin and tall. Their faces are hard and chiseled, and they keep their wiry mops of black hair groomed with melted butter. Strength and courage are all important to them. There is nothing more prestigious than for a man to kill his enemy, who he then castrates for the grisly trophy. For each man and boy a Danakil has killed, he adds a leather thong to the large, curved blade that he wears forever across his stomach. They even castrate the dead, dying, and prisoners as proof of strength, which prizes are then offered to their women. Indeed, a Danakil woman would not even consider marrying a man who had not proven his mettle, so to speak, by killing at least one man and harvesting the appropriate trophy.

I can say all this with confidence because since the events I am about to describe, I have looked into the history of these people, which accounts record several incidents where they massacred armed parties of explorers.

To get back, then, our group, that is, my charges, were discussing the ramifications of the meteorites and had just heard Miss Mitchell's pregnant pronouncement—when Danakil tribesmen intent on butchering us swooped into the graveyard. We were rushed on all sides. With banshee screams, they pounced on us with their spears, daggers, and occasional guns.

I am quite certain that we would all have been killed in short order if it had not been for the instant leopard-like reaction of

Bayushtiak, who, if I haven't mentioned it before, was also called "Umoya Oshisayo Womphefumulo Wengwe Emnyama Elindile," which means, in fact, "The Steaming Breath of the Crouching Black Leopard" and was a special title of nobility—hence, invincibility—amongst his people.

Two questions begged to be answered: Why were Hans and Bayushtiak not aware of the presence of the attackers? Also, given the latter's clearly stated concern about the area, how on earth did Bayushtiak fail to see them coming? I've thought about this often and my only explanation is that though my two friends were wise in the ways and particulars of southern Africa, the Danakil had the advantage, for we were smack in the middle of their home desert and also, we were jubilant and naturally distracted. For his part, Hans refused to accept this and insisted ever after that their approach must have been camouflaged by some sort of supernatural agent. "Baas, how could it be otherwise?" was his defense. "How could thirty or forty men sneak up on us, with me by your side—with me whose eyes are like the eagle's and whose nose and ears are like the wolf's, and who swore an oath to your Predikant father as he died that I would care for you always, as long as I lived."

In any case, though Bayushtiak had been unaware of their coming, the very instant of the Danakil attack he was suddenly everywhere at once slashing and stabbing with his *assegai*, eerily silent as he went about his bloody business. His instant single-handed defense so confused the attackers that they retreated, giving me time to disperse our guns and form the group into a defensive circle behind Bayushtiak. This had hardly been completed when the Danakil, who must have realized the error of their strategy, rushed back with murderous intent. The next few minutes were a blur of anguished screams, of dodging and thrusting, punctuated by explosions of scarlet. And in the mad confusion, somehow Hans, Sergeant Cuff, and I got separated from the others and found ourselves backing deeper into the meteorite graveyard where Bayushtiak had already led many of his attackers.

At some point, I looked and saw Bayushtiak atop a huge pointed, obsidian-like meteorite chopping and slicing at what seemed a never-ending torrent of Danakil savages. Hans was to my right and Cuff was at my back, and the three of us moved to protect Bayushtiak's rear. It was fearsome, finding ourselves surrounded by savages, dodging whirling daggers and razor-like spears.

It was deadly clear that our small defending force was severely outmanned, and I had already given up hope, I must admit. I knew as clearly as I have ever known anything that I was about to die. While one part of me mechanically continued to blast and chop at the enemy, another part was preparing to meet my Maker, listing my many transgressions over the years and hoping I could talk my way past the Pearly Gates.

Then it was that something like a miracle happened that turned the tide permanently. At one point, two warriors broke through the circle that some of our men had formed around Miss Mitchell. But she was not a woman to be intimidated or killed so easily. She had somehow grabbed a long dagger, almost a sword, from one of the warriors and at once stepped into the fray unmindful of danger and with a perfunctory hacking of the blade sent the head of one of the Danakil rolling. Ten yards along the ground it rolled and off the edge of a nearby gully, falling fifteen feet or so into the sand below.

At this, the fellow's confederates ceased fighting to a man, turned on their heels, and retreated. So startled was Cuff by this rapid turnabout that for one instant he was caught off guard—time enough for one quick-witted tribesman to thrust his jagged dagger deep into Cuff's loins. The next instant the Danakil was shot dead by a bullet from Hans's Winchester.

A good shot, but too late, for the damage had been done. I dashed to where Cuff had fallen, ripped open his shirt, and evaluated his wound. When I had determined that he was alive, Dravot and Carnehan lifted him and carried him back to our camp.

Of course, our first reaction was to feel confusion mingled with relief. We were not then, or ever to be made, certain as to why the attack turned so fast. Hans, I think, had the best thought on the subject. He said, "Baas, what I think happened is that the warriors saw a woman behave like a man and not only defend but attack and kill. After all, it is their job to impress the women. I think that the lady's attack was something they could not understand and therefore they grew afraid, perhaps of witchcraft for all I know, and left as quickly as they had arrived."

As he happened to say this in English, he was overheard by Miss Mitchell, who, though exhausted, laughed heartily. She said, "Mr. Quatermain, your man may have a point. All I can say for certain is that I may be a woman who men are inclined to coddle and protect, but I'm not about to stand back and let myself be killed when there is still so much to learn. The stars in the heavens above and all their brethren in all the spaces in between are my domain and I have promised the almighty God himself that I will not die until I chart their courses and know their secrets to the very best of my ability." She became thoughtful for a moment, then declared, "But all that notwithstanding, there was something else. During that time when I was so surrounded, I felt infused with some special power, something radiating from within and from without . . . something I've never felt—"

But just then, there came a yell. It was Carnehan. He was waving his arms some distance off. "Over here!" he called out. We rushed over to where he was standing over Lidenbrock, who was crumpled on the ground. I was the first to arrive, rolled the geologist on his back, and could see easily enough that the poor fellow had been killed. Blood was oozing from a long wide slash across his breast easily seen through his sliced shirt.

"He's dead," I said. But then I added, half to myself, "But this isn't right." I motioned Holmes to my side. "Look at this wound. It wasn't made by a savage's blade. It's much too clean a job. This was done with a precision instrument . . . like a doctor's scalpel, say, or a keen blade, even a razor."

Huxley ventured, "Perhaps it was an obsidian blade finer than the others."

"Perhaps," I replied, "but compare it to Cuff's. This is undeniably different. I've seen many a blade wound, and this one seems more 'civilized,' if that isn't an odd word to use, than anything any native could have accomplished."

Then there began a discussion between Burton and myself where the tribesmen could have acquired such a blade, deciding that it was probably from a looted caravan.

Obviously all the others reacted in manners according to their personalities. After all, we hardly knew the man. His exposure and exhaustion prevented him from communicating much, and what little he did say was mostly ravings of one sort or another. Holmes, Miss Mitchell, and Huxley were, for example, solicitous, worried about his next of kin, what to do with his mortal remains, etc., while the two soldiers seemed stoic enough or even unconcerned.

It was young Will Scott who had the most interesting reaction. As I was hovering over Lidenbrock's body, Scott forcefully injected himself into the scene, nearly pushing me to the side. He pulled a magnifying glass from out of a pocket, fell to his knees and began examining the ground, all the while grumbling. I would have been appalled, but the oddness of his subsequent behaviors quickly eclipsed all else. As far as I could make out, his grumbles seemed to consist mainly of the words "trampling" and "fools" in all sorts of permutations. When he was finished with the ground, he held his glass close to poor Lidenbrock and looked minutely at every aspect of the body, in particular the wound. When this had been going on for some little while, the novelty had worn off enough that the attention of the others wandered, and eventually only myself,

Hans, and Huxley seemed to pay him any mind.

"Baas," Hans spoke quietly without taking his eyes off Scott, "what is this pup doing? What is so interesting about a man's bones and dead flesh. I have never heard that you can flush out a witch with a glass, but maybe I am wrong . . . or perhaps the pup is a witch."

"I think he is trying to find out how the man died."

"But that is clear enough. One of those savages was handed a kill on a platter and he didn't ask any questions."

All I could do was shrug for Scott's behavior was peculiar to be sure. Then all at once, he saw something that seemed to startle him. He glanced over at Huxley, then redoubled his observations over a certain area. Finally he stood tall, pocketed the glass, and strode with purpose to his mentor. They moved apart and spoke far enough away that I could not hear them. In a few moments, Scott became agitated at Huxley, who seemed completely unperturbed. Then in another moment Scott came close to shouting. But he was able to restrain himself and neither Hans nor I could ever piece together the fragments that we could make out. I heard individual words that sounded like "university" and "saber." Hans thought he heard "brother" and "villain." The oddest thing is that, more than any other reaction, Huxley seemed almost amused by all the fuss Scott was making, going so far as to break into a broad grin.

In the end, I decided it was nothing of my concern, but the upshot of the affair was that beginning then the easy rapport the two had shared—of wise teacher and willing student—vanished completely, and for the duration of our expedition, they avoided one another—as much as one could in our circumstances.

I then began to assess our condition. Aside from Lidenbrock and Cuff, my group had accounted for themselves well, and by the grace of God, we were largely unharmed.

We buried Lidenbrock in view of his beloved volcanoes and Burton took exact bearings to provide to the next of kin. In addition, we fashioned a sort of stretcher for Cuff that we would take turns carrying, then gathered our supplies and marched on despite the heat of the day with the purpose of finding some spot where we could find shelter and which we could defend in the event of a renewed attack.

But that was easier said than done in that hellish landscape. We left behind the meteorite field and all the rest of that day dragged ourselves across the shifting, whispering sands. Slowly, the undulating crevasses and washes flattened out and we found ourselves on flat desert again, which just as abruptly ended at the vertical edge of a plateau. We saw that the cliff ran to both our left and right for as far as we could see. The descent was at least two hundred feet, and not even Hans was disposed to attempt the climb down.

Despairingly, we headed southwest along the edge of the plateau, all the time keeping an eye over our shoulders, half expecting the Danakil to strike again, and also looking ahead for a passage down. Our march was made a little easier at this point because the plateau sloped gently in our direction of travel with the result that the vertical drop to the desert floor steadily lessened.

It was toward nightfall, then, that we saw a tiny gleam of light ahead of us. It was the setting sun reflecting off a polished surface such as metal or glass.

Hans, who tended to act as our scout and was some distance ahead of us, saw it too. He ran ahead and investigated, peering over the edge of the cliff. Then all at once, he began to shout for our attention and jump around like a monkey, pointing down and jabbing with a finger. When we arrived by him and looked down where he pointed, we were amazed by the most incongruous and oddest of sights. Down below, out there in the middle of the desert, built on the edge of a wind-swept ravine, there was a sort of church or monastery mounted with a lacy delicate-looking orthodox Christian cross, the point of which rose just far enough above the cliff to catch the sun and thus attract our attention.

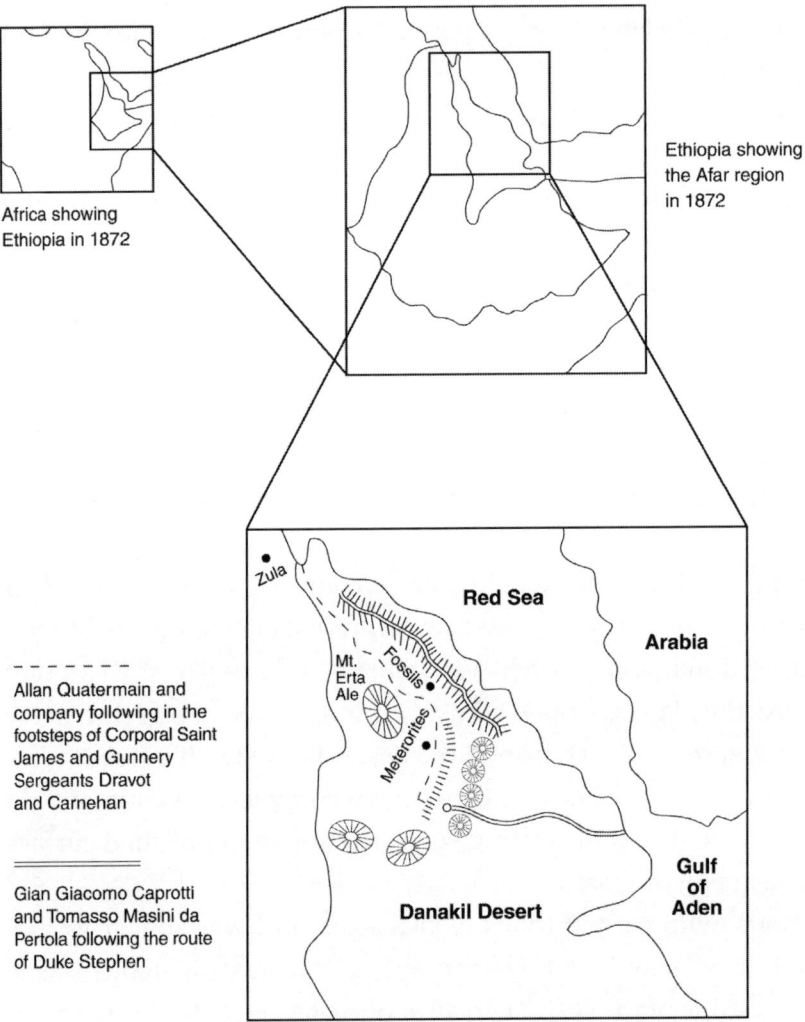

Africa showing
Ethiopia in 1872

Ethiopia showing
the Afar region
in 1872

– – – – – –
Allan Quatermain and
company following in the
footsteps of Corporal Saint
James and Gunnery
Sergeants Dravot
and Carnehan

Gian Giacomo Caprotti
and Tomasso Masini da
Pertola following the route
of Duke Stephen

Zula

Mt.
Erta
Ale

Fossils

Meteorites

Red Sea

Arabia

Gulf
of
Aden

Danakil Desert

This simplified map is the result of analyzing data derived from
the Black-Letter parchment of Bors, Count of Mainz; fragments
gleaned from Tomasso's Zoroastro Codex; the account of Corporal
Saint James; the accounts of Gunnery Sergeants Dravot and
Carnehan; and the verbal record of events as set down by Dr.
John Watson.

TKM 2005

CHAPTER ELEVEN

The Chapel

There were steep stairs—about ten feet wide from edge to edge—hewn into the yellow sandstone cliff face. I noticed that they were smooth and worn down in the center, as though they had been in use for centuries. Having no choice, we clambered down. The reasons were simple enough: first of all because there was no where else to go, and second, Sergeant Cuff was clearly in need of more medical attention than we could provide in the wild, and perhaps this place would be able to help. Indeed, perhaps the residents of this place would know something of the other matters we sought. Also, to be honest, we went because we were all, every one of us, full of curiosity. I suppose we made a great deal of noise as we descended. Certainly, it was a cumbersome business hauling Cuff's stretcher down.

It was only natural then that when we touched the floor of the ravine, there were waiting for us four very formal looking fellows. All were quite black, but three were older, sporting trimmed beards like white, curly wool, wearing long purple robes and matching caps that were perfectly flat on top. The younger, but nonetheless middle-aged, man was beardless but otherwise dressed the same. They all grinned from ear to ear and seemed quite happy to see us. They were standing before the gate of a tall wall that enclosed the monastery.

As our two groups stood facing one another, taking stock of one another, I could see inside through the gate, that is to say into the further side of the wall, a most wonderful little garden filled with roses of every imaginable color.

"Well, Quatermain, aren't you going to speak to them," Richard Holmes ventured in a manner that I considered brusque.

In fact, though, at that very moment I was wondering to myself which language would be best suited when the younger man spoke first. He held out his hand to me in the Western fashion and spoke in English. Utterly amazed, I took his hand, and he said, "Gentlemen, welcome to the Chapel of the Immaculate Heart. I am Tabot Haile Mariam, and these are my brother priests. We are of the Order of Sainte Mariam the Divine. We have been aware of your coming for some days and are full of questions as to what would bring you here to us in the desert, which I daresay is, and I can say this with some authority, without doubt the most terrible spot on earth. Welcome."

"You are most kind," I responded, seeing that the Englishmen and the American woman in my party were all grinning with relief (as I myself felt, though mystified) at hearing our own language spoken.

"Ah, you are wondering how it is that I speak English well. That is simple. When I was a child, some other Englishmen much like yourselves were seeking the source of the Nile and stumbled on my village, which was on the northern shore of Lake Tana. They tarried there for two years studying our way of life and religion and, being a quick study and nimble, I became their go-between or messenger."

This exchange had taken only a moment, and I thought that his explanation seemed reasonable enough. He was about to say something more when it seemed they all noticed the wounded Cuff on the stretcher for the first time. Two of the older men suddenly became totally solicitous and began to minister to him at once without saying a word. Cuff, who was conscious, tried to say something, but one of these priests hushed him by placing a finger over his parched lips. They lifted the stretcher and gingerly carried Cuff through the gate.

It was then that a most unexpected and, thinking back on it, a most wondrous, though predictable, thing happened. The two priests had only gotten about halfway across the rose garden, when suddenly their patient managed to cry out. "Stop!" he called. "Stop, I say. I must see this place!" You can imagine how startled the priests were. In fact, they almost dropped the stretcher, I think. But Tabot quickly translated, and they set the stretcher gently enough on a sort of rock bench that happened to be there.

Cuff was struggling to lift his head and look all around. His face seemed to glow, which was odd given the circumstances, and then he started to rave: "What a rosery! *[Editor's note: i.e., a rose garden.]* A rosery fit for a god. Just the right exposure, yes, south and sou'-west. How do you achieve adequate water in this hellish place? I must commend the gardener." He craned his head up and around, and even though the struggle was apparent and you could almost feel his pain, he ignored all protestations and peered around in as much of a circle as he could. "Ah. Even here, there is clear sign of advanced civilization. See the shape of this rosery—it's a circle set in a square. That is a fine design. And the paths between the beds . . . . Oh, I see they are crushed rock . . . well, I suppose that must do in this region, but beware! Roses do not like being surrounded by rock. It is hard on them."

Thus he waxed about the infrastructure of the rosery for a time, and then fell silent. It was just as the priests were about to pick up his stretcher again that he blurted out once more. "See the colors, whites and reds and yellows. And, oh, there are the blush roses. They mix so well together, don't they?"

At that he seemed to drift off, and the priests were able to continue with their task of moving Sergeant Cuff indoors.

My emotions were many, I must say. Perhaps it was not too late to save the man. But I put all that aside for the time being and turned my attention to Tabot. "Yes, Tabot, your desert does test the most hardened and intrepid. Of that there can be no doubt. In fact, we have only a few hours ago been battling for our lives, even burying one of our own, and some of us have wounds that need to be tended to, though I daresay that the one you have already taken in, Sergeant Cuff by name, is already being helped by your doctors."

"True enough," said Tabot. "We will help him as well as we can, though I cannot promise anything. Now, tell me. What on earth brings you here?"

"That is a very long story, I fear," was my reply. "I don't mean to seem rude, but the telling of it should wait until we are rested. For now, let me just say that we are explorers seeking knowledge."

Tabot chuckled at this and said, "There is a saying in your world, I think, something about getting blood from a turnip. That, I think, is the amount of knowledge you can get from these sands," gesturing out across the desert. He said something to the remaining priest and they shared a good laugh. "Do come in and refresh yourselves, rest from your weariness. Our water is your water. I can't speak for turnips and blood—" (here he broke into a wide smile) "—but, by the grace of God, water is abundant here in this spot—a true miracle from the Blessed Mother. You will find that we are rich, therefore, rich with fruitful crops and numerous sheep and goats."

Hans had skulked up during this interchange and he whispered to in my ear in the Dutch-based Afrikaner language. "Baas, remember the story of the spider and the fly. This is a pretty mirage complete with four smiling spiders."

Really, I was becoming impatient with his ceaseless negativity, but I said, "And what do you propose I do, be still more rude and refuse their hospitality? Besides, we are grown men and well armed and we will be able to protect ourselves if there is trouble."

"Baas, you are no doubt right and far be it from me to suspect your judgment, but still a little voice inside me worries that our gateway to the Big Baas's house in the sky may be through the belly of a cannibal."

At this point I chose to ignore my servant, whose protestations had attracted the curiosity of our hosts. I sidestepped the issue by happily accepting the invitation to enter and refresh ourselves.

The priests turned and entered their grounds, and the ten of us gratefully followed, though I must admit that a verse from the Scriptures popped into my brain at that moment, "Enter ye in at the strait gate: For wide is the gate, and broad is the way, that leadeth to destruction . . . . "[40]

In any event, of course, having no foreknowledge of the astonishing things that would befall us, we entered and found that the rosery included a most delightful well, from which we drank our fill of clean, fresh water. Thus we rested for a while longer in that wonderful little garden with the fragrance of roses filling the air.

Once situated thus, I noticed that the monastery structure was actually two structures. The building to the left as we faced them was the smaller and was in fact the priests's living quarters. The larger, on the right, was the chapel, or church.

Eventually we were led into the spare interior of the former, where we gratefully doffed our kits and sat on the crude benches that surrounded an equally crude table.

Young Will Scott then asked Tabot a question: "Sir, when was this church constructed? It seems so odd to have a church isolated so, in the middle of the desert."

"As a matter of fact, construction began in the year 1500—a nice round year, don't you think? Our order is one that sought isolation, the better to meditate and seek revelations from God—away from the distractions of the world."

Huxley spoke: "My good man, if that is the case, we are sorry that we have arrived on the scene and disrupted your meditative way of life."

"Think nothing of it. We also consider ourselves a holy oasis for weary travelers. Though, of course, we have few enough of those!"

"Tabot," I inquired. "You said that you were informed of our arrival. By whom?"

"Oh! By the Afar—or the Danakil, as they are known outside this land, but Afar is what they call themselves. They have been monitoring your movements since your ship arrived at Annesley Bay. A hardy but terribly mean-spirited people, as I'm afraid you have found out the hard way. They had promised us that they would leave you undisturbed, but I suppose the temptation to raid and perhaps acquire a few trophies—" here he couldn't help but smile sardonically "—were more than they could bear."

"I suppose entertainment options are limited here," Huxley responded. "Still, we did lose a man, as Quatermain said, and had to bury him yonder."

"We regret their behavior terribly and apologize most profusely," Tabot went on. "I am glad that there was no other loss of life among your party." Then he hesitated. "I fear for your friend Cuff, though."

Richard Burton ventured a question at that time. "Tabot, how do you and your priest colleagues manage to avoid becoming, yourselves, souvenirs of your spies?"

"For centuries there has been an agreement, a time-honored agreement. They serve as our eyes and ears and we pave the way for them to a higher world, as we have touched some of them a bit with matters of the spirit. But, I'm afraid that this breach in our agreement causes us some concern. My brothers and I will deliberate on that and decide how we will respond." Whereupon he left us to ourselves for a time.

Then young Scott, who, if I haven't said so already, was by far the most restless of our party, stood and paced about the table. All the while he was muttering to himself, then finally he left, nearly launching himself out of the room, in the direction that Tabot had gone.

Before long he returned with the priest in tow. I was frankly amazed that young Scott would have the gall to behave in such a manner in the establishment of those who were even then giving us succor. Nevertheless, he spoke, "I'm sorry, but I am filled to the brim with curiosity about the chapel and I have asked Tabot to allow us to enter it and observe its special features."

For his part, Tabot seemed unperturbed about this further imposition into his life and life style. He began to lead us to the chapel, or church, proper, and suddenly all seven of my charges rose at once and all but marched after the priest, with Hans, Bayushtiak, and myself following. How and when, I wondered, had I lost control?

The church was circular, and in a moment we found ourselves on a walkway that circled it. This walkway was open at the sides but covered by an awning of thatch. Tabot walked us around this path explaining that he and his brother priests used this area in particular to sing hymns to God as they walked in endless circles around the building. We came to an opening in the outside wall and entered. For a brief moment I became disoriented. It was as though I had stepped into an art gallery of the British Museum. This was an enclosed inner circuit or walkway (the k'ane mahlet), which in turn circled an interior chamber. What had taken me aback was that the walls of the k'ane mahlet were literally covered with paintings of the Virgin Mary in every conceivable pose. There she was alone in the desert, alone in the jungle, surrounded by handmaidens in the desert, surrounded by handmaidens in the jungle, adored in the city, adored by animals, bathing under waterfalls, with the baby Jesus and without, with angels and without, clothed and unclothed. Some were portraits that reminded me of Leonardo's Mona Lisa (at which I began to wonder . . . .), and some were landscapes both barren and verdant. There were hundreds of these, and I can say with confidence that all the members of my party were clearly as amazed as I was. Perhaps the most amazing thing of all was the outstanding quality of many of these works.

One painting in particular captured the attention of Richard Holmes. I was standing next to him, so I can relate that he was gazing at each of the paintings with great interest, but when his eyes came to this one, I could hear him gasp. His attention was riveted to the piece. He leaned over and examined it and whispered, "My God, Quatermain, it's a da Vinci original. I'm sure of it. An unknown, uncataloged da Vinci painting. It's astonishing. This is not simply a style similar to da Vinci's, I'm sure. It's authentic. It must be! How on earth did it get here?"

The picture in question showed a beatific image of a standing child-like Mary, her head surrounded with a lacy halo. She had on a kind of shawl, black in color, closed at her bosom with a broach in the shape of a rose. In her outstretched right hand there was a scroll tied with a red ribbon. And in her left hand was a chalice, which I supposed was some sort of rendition of the Holy Grail or some such.

"But that's not all, Quatermain! Look where she is standing!" I observed that the artist had chosen to place his Mary in the middle of what was obviously a large and luxuriously appointed library, but one that housed scrolls rather than books. These scrolls were piled in cubbies of which there were three or four dozen or so visible in the background. Holmes's excitement, of course, drew all the others closer and each of them in turn became excited at the genius so evident in the piece—a piece hanging on a wall in an unknown monastery in the middle of an awful desert in a country that Europeans for the most part were barely aware of.

Holmes turned to Tabot. "Please, can you tell me the provenance of these paintings, and in particular this one."

Tabot hesitated. It seemed he was taken off guard by the question. "Please forgive me if I don't have an immediate response. We do, you understand, live with these renderings every day and don't often think about their origins, merely grateful that we have been chosen by God to be their caretakers."

He paused to reflect for a few moments, then continued. "This church began construction in the year 1500 and was finished shortly afterward. As soon as it was completed, all the Christian churches of Ethiopia and, in particular, one of the churches in Axum, St. Mary of Zion far to the north, presented to us, or to this chapel, much of this collection for the glory of Jesus and of his mother, Mariam, daughter of God. The remainder have made their way here over the years, as our existence is not unknown to the other orthodox churches of the land."

Holmes was persistent, however. "This painting showing a collection of scrolls, I was wondering what could have been the model."

Tabot hesitated for the briefest of moments, then shrugged. "No doubt it was inspired by God in the highest."

"I'm sure," muttered Holmes.

Certainly all these paintings triggered a number of thoughts and emotions in the various members of my party, but the upshot of it was that we were still in the dark as much as before.

In any event, we elected to continue our little tour of the church. We came to another opening—this one in the innermost wall of the *k'ane mahlet*—and entered yet another interior chamber. This proved to be still another walkway surrounding yet another interior chamber. This walkway was called the *keddest*, which Tabot explained was a place dedicated to prayer and communion. The central chamber beyond we learned was called the *mak'das*, and it was there that the Holy of Holies was located.

The Holy of Holies was exactly what it sounds like. Only the most senior priests ever could enter the area. This is where something immensely holy called *tabots* were kept. I couldn't help but note the similarity to our host's name, but Tabot avoided answering my questions and it was only after subsequent determined effort that I got him to explain that he was named after the *tabots*, and that they were replicas of the tablets God presented to Moses—that is to say, the stone tablets on which God wrote the Ten Commandments. He also explained that every Ethiopian church was constructed in the same manner, and it had been so since time immemorial—the most holy *tabots* housed within a central Holy of Holies surrounded by concentric circular walkways, so that if seen from above, the whole arrangement would look like a target with the Holy of Holies as the bull's-eye.

We wound back around through the circuits and exited the church and soon were back at our living quarters. As soon as we were left alone, we jumped at the chance to compare notes, to theorize, and the like. I even caught sight of Hans and Bayushtiak off in a corner speaking quietly between themselves (Hans seldom deigned to share his opinions with anyone but me).

In due course, a simple but filling meal made up of honey-sweetened flat bread, onions, and goat's milk cheese was brought in, and eventually we tired of talk and rested for the duration of the night. Cuff, in the meantime, was still being tended to, or nursed, by the priests in an area reserved for such medical requirements.

CHAPTER TWELVE

The Cleft in the Cliff

The next morning, after we had freshened ourselves, a messenger arrived saying that Tabot wanted to see us immediately. In time, we had congregated outside in the rosery since our group was rather large and all the rooms large enough to accommodate us were in use by the monks and priests.

Tabot arrived and greeted us. Then he said the most extraordinary things. "Gentlemen and my lady," he began. "While the Afar had alerted us to your coming, and while we are bound to aid you as necessary, to be frank, your presence here—especially the number of you—is creating a larger problem than expected, as it imposes on our way of life. Last night I prayed upon the problem and in a dream three angels came to me in the form of the Three Kings. Gaspar was the head angel in the dream and he said that my guests were very special and that I should ask them (that is to say, you) for a token, simple as it may be, and that if you had the correct token, then you were to be escorted into the presence of the Holy Mother herself, which is a very rare honor indeed." As you can imagine, at the mention of the name Gaspar, Holmes's and my eyes locked meaningfully.

Someone, I think it was Burton, asked what he meant by a "token" and also, in an uncharacteristically rude fashion, to my mind, what he meant by "escorted into the presence of the Holy Mother," and just who was she?

Unperturbed, Tabot responded, "Why, the token is the key by which you will see the Holy Mother, and the Holy Mother is the mother of God, of course, and you will see her because it is her wish, should you have the token. Are there any more questions?" And then he waited.

Hans whispered about then, "Baas, what is this? It was so simple before—hello and good-bye, have some food, rest a while, but now he is talking about a holy sign, which is different. Even your Predikant father wouldn't talk the way that this priest with a face like granite is doing. And certainly I would rather not see any Holy Mother for fear she might be real."

I for one wasn't concerned whether this mysterious mother was real or not. I was more concerned that it sounded suspiciously as though we were about to be taken somewhere against our own free will. I was about to say as much when the priest held out his hand palm up. This was enough to quiet me.

We all started looking at one another muttering, "A token, what could be a token?" I was thinking that it could be just about anything, from one of Miss Mitchell's hair combs to the cork from Hans's beloved square-face that he liked to sniff and that he kept in lieu of the actual bottle, when that self-same Miss Mitchell inquired, "Perhaps your angels were referring to one of my rocks from the sky?" Tabot merely continued to stand with his hand out. She then inquired in an impatient tone, "Well then, can you please give us an idea of what we are supposed to show you?" Tabot was still silent. Then Peachy Carnehan spoke, "Say, Huxley, I have a notion. More 'an likely what he's lookin' for is something out of the ordinary. Anyone could show a bullet or, say, a compass or handkerchief. What about one of those remarkable bits of bone you found out there in the desert by that cave. Give that a try."

Frowning, Thomas Huxley then unpacked some of the rolls of cotton he had used to store his fossils and unrolled one very carefully. As he was doing this, Will Scott came close, and, forgoing their estrangement for the moment, helped him. In due course, a finger bone became visible and Scott carefully picked it up and showed it to Tabot, who reached for it. But Scott moved it out of harms way. "Look," he said, "but don't touch." At first Tabot was taken aback, but he settled down and bent forward to peer at the bone. Then he grinned and turned smartly around and started walking away from us through the rose bushes, heading toward the entrance of the wall that surrounded the church. When he got there, he motioned for us to follow.

Hans and I looked at one another and shrugged. It appeared that the bone was the key, though at the time I could not fathom why. Later on, I realized that it made sense.

We were soon escorted once more to the open walkway that surrounded the church and where the priests even then were walking in endless circles around the perimeter of the church. From there we were taken into the *k'ane mahlet* where we had seen all the beautiful Madonna paintings housed. It was here that I first became aware of an extremely pungent incense (that later I was to learn was frankincense) and from there into the inner communion circuit, the *keddest*. In the *keddest*, Tabot paused and waited till he had all our attentions.

He pointed to a curtain that clearly entered into another chamber. "This," he said, "is as far as any uninitiated has ever gotten, for beyond this is the *mak'das*, the Holy of Holies where the *tabots* rest, the tablets of Moses." At this moment, several more priests joined us, and Tabot very dramatically and deliberately thrust aside the curtain and bade us enter. I wish I could tell you with some certainty what I saw in that small chamber, but in fact, the incense was so heavy that vision was impaired. Having been told several times that this was the Holy of Holies itself where the *tabots* were kept, I strained to get a glimpse of the sacred objects or their container, but I could see nothing. Whether they were obscured or even removed I never learned. When we were all inside, Tabot motioned to one of the priests who pushed aside another curtain revealing a space no larger than a closet. The priest then pulled aside the rug that was there, thus revealing a wooden door in the floor, which door proved to be heavy if the man's struggles to open it were warranted. This, in turn, exposed stairs leading down. Some of us expressed considerable concern about what this was all about, but we nonetheless let ourselves be led docilely down the stairs, through a short tunnel and then up again, where we emerged into a sort of cave.

That cave opened into what I immediately understood was a cleft in the cliff wall beside which the church had been built. I was already familiar with something of the sort since the horrible Black Kloof, the home of Zikali, "The Opener of Roads," was entered by way of a similar breach in the face of a precipice.

Light poured down from the sun above into what would have appeared to be a crevasse from above, and a well-worn earth path lay before us. With Tabot leading the way, we ten remaining explorers marched forward. We rounded a bend in the path, and the wall suddenly flowered with decorative murals—paintings, carvings, and friezes—depicting various aspects of the Madonna similar to those we had seen in the *k'ane mahlet*.

Holmes was again and quickly beside himself in ecstasy. He reached out to touch one of the figures. But before his hand had moved a foot in the direction of the wall, one of the priests had quickly moved and grabbed his elbow. The normally congenial-appearing priest suddenly wore an ugly scowl, startling Holmes and myself—for I was next to Holmes and was able to observe the priest's expression—so that we both caught our breath. The man's visage was positively horrific!

Thus warned off, we proceeded along the path keeping our hands to ourselves. For perhaps half an hour we moved along the path. Sometimes it was extremely narrow so that we could only progress by removing our kits and sidling along sidewise. Hans, Will Scott, Miss Mitchell, Carnehan and myself had no problem, being either small or thin in stature. Burton, Huxley, Holmes, Dravot, and Bayushtiak found these intervals rather tight going. Other times the path opened up so that the distance between vertical walls might have been as much as ten yards. Above, I was happy to see that the sky still shown clearly through the crevasse.

I couldn't help but wonder what our fates would be if an earthquake happened to hit just then. Would the walls move in and flatten us, or would they come crumbling down—with the same effect but from a different direction?

Finally, we saw light ahead of us and I could see that we were approaching the end of the crack in the plateau. A moment later I saw that it opened up into a kind of wide gorge. A bit more and I stepped into the open and I was so overwhelmed with images that I hardly know where to begin describing them.

CHAPTER THIRTEEN

The Fountain

Totally unexpectedly I saw a crowd of people, perhaps thirty in number, dressed as from another era—my first thought was of Biblical times. Women mainly, with some men and children, most wearing brightly colored striped robes or ankle-length skirts. They were standing, talking or strolling in a kind of village square with a pool and fountain in the center. From the center of the pool rose a statue of a young woman with a great jar in her arms, and from the jar water poured into the pool, splashing noisily. There was something joy-filled and mysterious about the statue and something else, too, but all this was quickly swept from my mind as events unfolded.

Beyond the square, I saw a compact community with connected buildings built of stone. From our vantage point, we could see a main thoroughfare made of rough flagstones held together with mortar leading from the square down, around, and past countless functional stone edifices until it disappeared into the distance.

All this I saw in an instant, and the next instant, the normal harmony of the place was disturbed as you would expect when the priests from the cleft appeared with ten strangers—eight of European origin (one of which was a woman), a Zulu, and Hans.

A woman with authority in her bearing was approaching us. She walked right up to Tabot and they spoke, using what I assumed was the region's Coptic tongue. She was perhaps middle aged, with a cragged but thoroughly noble face. Over her head—which I could see was crowned with the richest of chestnut colored hair—she wore a loosely fitting covering of the deepest blue. The overall effect was quite wonderful. She had been sitting on the edge of the pool in quiet discussion with a group of other younger women when her attention had been drawn to the passage opening where we emerged.

This woman and Tabot had stepped aside some distance and continued to confer. There was much gesticulation with their faces turning in our direction numerous times and all manner of other signs to indicate that our sudden appearance was not altogether welcome.

Eventually they both approached us—or rather me. The priest introduced the woman as Ruth, who was a teacher, and told us that the roles of himself and his fellow priests had been satisfied according to the laws of the matter that had been set down more than four centuries before at the time the church had been established. And without further ado, that whole bunch turned and returned the way we had come, and we wouldn't see them again for some time.

Ruth then faced me and spoke. Her language was quite incomprehensible to any of us, even to the inexhaustible Burton. Then approaching it rather academically, Holmes and Burton conferred between themselves and decided it must be a form of Coyne, the ancient popular form of Greek that long since had faded from the planet—thereby putting to rest my own rather humble speculations as to the nature of the language. In lieu of using her language, between us we tried English, French, Zulu, Dutch (that is to say Afrikaans), and several others to no avail, and all to the clear frustration of all involved.

There came a moment when all the reasonable options seemed to have been used up, and we sunk into a long silence, our collective mood being that of defeat.

Then Burton snapped his fingers! Facing Ruth, he launched into another language that was vaguely familiar to me, probably one of the Romance languages. Suddenly Ruth's face lit up. She took Burton by the hand and took him aside where they whispered together and it was perfectly clear that they were in fact communicating quite well.

When Burton returned to our group, he was grinning ear to ear. "Holmes," he said, "you told us that Salai and Tomasso ventured into these parts in the past. Suddenly I realized that it wouldn't be out of the question if Italian had some currency here."

When Ruth rejoined us, she, too, seemed quite pleased. This time she addressed our group while focusing on Burton. She opened her mouth and out emerged a slow and guttural, yet perfectly recognizable (so Burton affirmed) and passable Italian! Then Holmes himself made inquiries in the modern form of the language, which he had a passing knowledge of, and, eventually, a sort of general conversation was established.

During this interlude, one of the first questions put to her, by me, if I recall correctly, through Burton, was one which had the goal of affirming the assumptions that some of my little group seemed to prize so highly: Why could she speak Italian?

She replied that centuries before, they had been visited by two great men who spoke in this manner and these men had tarried among them for months and spent some of that time sharing their language. Even after they left, by instruction from the Holy Mother—who at the time I took to be some sort of priestess—Ruth's people had handed the language down from novice to novice in preparation for the great day when it would be needed again. In fact, she was extremely disappointed in herself for not immediately recalling the age-old writ that required her people to use the Tongue of the Messengers, as she called it, when confronted by strangers. That we were the first such strangers in some 400 years did not seem to matter.

Nonetheless, she seemed to quickly get over her lapse, then gestured at us in our well-traveled and unfamiliar clothes and giggled. Holmes extracted from her that in her mind's eye she had always envisioned that if she ever needed to use the Tongue of the Messengers in her lifetime, it would be to individuals resembling the great prophets, not to a ragtag group of heathens!

We Europeans smiled at this and I asked Holmes to convey our gratitude and other various courtesies that I had learned over the years after much travel were always well regarded regardless of the culture or level of civilization.

She accepted the compliments and bowed slightly, gesturing with her arm to follow her.

It was at this point that Hans, who had been unnaturally quiet during this whole interchange, chose to speak, this time in Dutch.

"Baas! Mayhap I have been thinking that we are even now within a great hole in the rock, a hole much like the holes made by worms in apples, and just as the worm is in the power of the great beast that presses the apple within its jaws, we are likely to be flattened if the rocks come tumbling down or if the crowds choose to rise up."

"Old fool!" was my response. "Do you think I have not thought of these things? But what can we do? We are here now, and do I need remind you that we are here largely because of your proddings yonder, back in Durban? Nevertheless, though this is all very strange, in its own way it is wondrous and I for one am interested to know what happens next."

Hans appeared to be somewhat chastened by my retort, though, as usual, he needed to have the final word: "Ah, Baas, that may be so, but please don't forget that an apple infested with worms is a rotten apple!"

I suppose I must have looked at him particularly fiercely for he turned on his heels and I lost sight of him, though, of course, I knew in my heart that drunk or sober, angry or not, he would never be far from my side.

Ruth ignored this small drama and motioned for us to follow her. She took us through the throng of people, who parted before us, chattering, much as I suppose the waters parted before Moses. She led us out of the town square and onto the road (which was the only one I ever noted aside from a few paths). This road was bounded on both sides as far as one could see with buildings, that is to say dwellings, and as we passed I saw many women and children poking their heads out of the small windows or watching us from the roofs, on either side. These were one-story structures made of slabs of rock mortared together. Doors were not prominent I noticed but I saw that between every two or three houses there was a narrow alley, which led me to believe that the doors were on the side of the house opposite the street, that is to say in the backs of the houses, which I learned later was a correct assumption.

We walked thus down the main road, which twisted and turned down the middle of what amounted to a great gorge cut through the mountain, for perhaps somewhat more than a mile. Though the gorge was clearly mostly of natural design, there were many indications that certain areas were enlarged or shaped by the hand of man. Perhaps such areas were the quarries from which the towns people acquired their housing materials. I never did ask. Accompanying us the whole length were the homes and structures that made up the village, or perhaps town would be a better word, and of course most of the population, which we learned comprised some two thousand individuals, turned out to get the best view of us.

And, gentlemen, now that I'm recalling all this for the first time in years, I'm remembering that it was while we were marching along this route that a strange thing happened. Will Scott, who had remained perfectly nondescript since entering the gorge, suddenly took off and began running around in a most comical manner, darting off to this side, and then over to the other. The children in the crowds on either side laughed merrily to see him so, but he didn't seem to notice or mind. Whatever he was doing, he was totally absorbed. I kept an eye on him as we walked along, trying to understand his actions, but the more I watched, the more perplexed I became. This lasted perhaps five to seven minutes, then ceased as quickly as it had begun, when he rejoined our group and seemed as placid as ever. Naturally, it was Hans who solved the mystery.

"Yes, Baas, for a time I thought for sure the beardless one had somehow become possessed by a witch and that he was sniffing out the ghosts that must haunt this place. As you know, for we have known many such, these great caverns that have no roofs are full of ghosts, for spirits are easily confused and it is hard for them to find their way out. I watched and listened closely and finally began to hear the voices of these ghosts. Baas! They didn't cry out or moan or shriek as ghosts do. They *buzzed*. Whoever heard of buzzing ghosts? So I stayed close to him, as close as I could, trying to see with his eyes. Then, squinting, I chanced to see one of the ghosts, and then another, and another. But they weren't ghosts, Baas! They were bees. The pup was chasing bees!

I must tell you, the expression on Hans's face as he announced his conclusion was perfectly priceless. My poor Hottentot servant simply could not imagine what would prompt an otherwise sound human being to behave thus. And, frankly, I couldn't either! Nonetheless, once I had put two and two together, it was clear that Hans had gotten to the root of the problem. Indeed, now that it was called to my attention, I saw that the gorge was in fact more than ordinarily full of the little creatures, intent at their busy tasks and minding their own businesses. Still, I had my own pride, so I pretended to mull over Hans's findings as we walked, then made a great show of agreeing with him. Of course, I intended to ask Scott about it later, but thereafter so much happened so fast that the incident entirely slipped my mind . . . until now all these years later! One thing I can say for certain, though, thinking back on the man, is that Scott was, all in all, a most curious fellow!

Be that as it may, at the end of the road, Ruth finally stopped before a temple-like structure that was built on a gentle slope so that it rose in tiered gardens up from the street. I could see through the gate and beyond and saw that encircling the structure was a small courtyard comprising still more gardens with convenient stone benches to rest upon, not unlike the monastery rosery that had so affected poor Cuff. However, Ruth bade us not to enter the interior.

Instead, she asked us to follow her a bit more and she took us a little distance off to the right and up a ramp to a separate building, which proved to be a sort of community building. We were led into an open central court, where we were met by attendants who took charge of us as Ruth went her own way and disappeared. The robed attendants led us to rooms that were distributed among us as follows: young Will Scott and I shared one room, Holmes and Huxley another, and Hans and Bayushtiak another. Miss Mitchell was allocated a room to herself and Burton and the two soldiers shared another. In addition we were shown where we could bathe.

Not that this distribution really mattered at all, for as soon as we were left alone, we all gathered in one of the rooms, that of Burton and the soldiers, as it was somewhat larger than the others, to discuss this totally unexpected turn of events.

Oh! I may have forgotten to mention that as we followed Ruth through the gorge, we learned that this community—hidden away behind the Holy of Holies of the Chapel of the Immaculate Heart and secreted within a great chasm visible only to the birds in the sky—bore the name Sinai.

CHAPTER FOURTEEN

The Girl

You can imagine our riot of talking when finally we were alone. Our experiences were astounding. Burton was certain we had discovered a hidden city of Hebrews who had been cut off from advancing civilization perhaps two thousand years ago. He and Holmes discussed and argued about these people's language, their architecture, their manner of dress, where they could have obtained the bright dyes and materials for their clothes, and any other detail that entered their minds. There were, however, two observations that troubled them deeply. They could not understand the apparent matriarchal tenor of the culture—whereas Hebrews were supposed to be typically and steadfastly patriarchal. Also, they were baffled by the presence of a statue of a young woman in the village square. Old Hebrews, they said, would not have—indeed, could not have—allowed such a "graven image" in their midst.

Finally, in the evening, a messenger came and bade us follow her, and we were are all escorted to a hall in the council building. We had no choice but to stand as there was no place to sit in the spare surroundings. In time, there came the low throbbing of a bell, ringing over and over again. After nearly fifty interminable rings, it ceased and a procession of thirteen women, one of whom was Ruth, marched in—or to be more accurate, twelve women and a girl, and the girl was being held aloft in a kind of litter carried by half of the women. The procession was well practiced and I felt I was watching a performance at the theater or even one of the well-choreographed ceremonies of the Zulu kings.

The women who were not carrying the litter moved to positions around a kind of raised dais. The others set the litter gently before the ramp that led to the dais, then joined their sisters and arranged themselves in the manner of a royal guard. The girl moved quickly up to the bench, sat primly down, turned, and looked out over us all. The entire retinue turned to face the girl with looks of obvious reverence and a great hush fell over the hall. The girl continued to look at us curiously for a time, and I tried to spot some sort of shyness or nervousness as you would expect to see in a young girl in similar circumstances, but in vain for she seemed totally poised. When she had her fill of looking at us, she stood and we were able to get our first really good look at her.

I could hardly believe it: There was before us just a bit of a girl barely four feet tall with a complexion like fresh cream, standing quite calmly. She wore a simple white cloth robe with a belt of golden fabric, and over her shoulders was a blue shawl. I could see ringlets of black lustrous hair falling from under the white scarf-like cloth, or veil, that covered her head. In her hands she held roses, the fragrance of which I perceived even though we were some distance from her. Was she some sort of leader? I thought of India's Dalai Lama* who, I had heard, always began his rule as a child.

Our group stood respectfully before and below her. Then she opened her mouth and spoke. And the voice that emerged from her mouth was the purest most crystalline expression of a human voice that I had ever heard. The voice was a girl's to be sure, but it was also a woman's. It sounded as though it came from above and beyond the firmament and from below our feet from some sort of vast hidden cavern at the same time. It sounded like all these things at once, and what it said was, "My good people, thank you for coming" in English! "I have been expecting you for quite some time."

---

* Editor's note: Quatermain was geographically close. In fact, the Dalai Lama is the spiritual leader of Tibet.—T.K.M.

[At this juncture, it is imperative to note that Bayushtiak, who had been a participant in all this only in the most peripheral manner and who had been watching it all with a jaundiced eye, was clearly taken aback by the ethereal voice emanating from the girl *in what I was to learn later was his own language!*]

The girl smiled at each of us and her smile was truly like sunlight radiating upon us. "I am Mariam," she said. Then she gestured around her saying, "And these are my people. I have brought you here to Sinai from your far off homes [hearing this, several of us looked quizzically at one another with raised eyebrows] to share with you, and through you to the rest of the world, knowledge of the holiest place on earth.

"Long have men sought treasures such as the cup from which they believed Christ drank, which is what I caused you to believe was the object of your quest; or the Ark of the Covenant; or for the true mountain called Sinai; or fragments from my son's tree; and so much more.

"Well, I, of all people, know well what is holy and what is not and what is more holy or less holy, for I am the mother of God, and you have come to this remote spot at my bidding though you knew it not. You, each of you, came *now* rather than before or later because the time is soon coming when the people of this world must learn the truth of their own existence."

Here she paused, probably aware that her each and every utterance was potent, ripe with astonishing concepts, and pregnant with controversy. My impression was that she stopped to allow us to take in and digest the vastness of her brief speech. In a minute, she continued.

"They say that God created man in His own image. There is truth to that, not in the material sense, for the material aspect of God can be better thought of as the entire planet on which we stand, and, by extension, perhaps the Universe without as well. No, man is created in God's image in the sense of 'mind' and spirit. Of all the creatures on earth, man is the only one that can seek God consciously, or who can arrive at God's door through attainment of merit, for God created man to join with and become God—and the destiny of each man, woman, and child is to attain God, whether he knows it or not, wants it or not, needs it or not. And though some men may not consciously strive for this, in time they will arrive there in any case.

"Of all of God's creatures on earth, man is the holiest by virtue that only man becomes God, as a child becomes an adult at childhood's end.

"Have you never gone back to the spot of your birth and wondered at the fact that it was there in that precise midwife's home or there in that very room or there in that exact glade that you came into existence, where you were born into this world? Now I bid you think. At such moments, are you not full of wonder for your very existence, for the miracle of your life . . . ?"

Her pause this time seemed especially prolonged. Then she said, "Well, I have brought you here to make it clear that mankind likewise has a place where it came into existence, where it was born, and it is time that all of mankind learn of that place so that all may feel that self-same wonder.

"The Holy Scriptures tell of the creation of the world and a place that is called Eden . . . . "

Suddenly the girl sagged, and Ruth and some of the other women jumped to her aid in a practiced manner and helped her sit back down on the dais. The girl became quiet as the women fussed over her, and I think we all used the opportunity to reflect further on what we had just heard. I certainly did. And I must say that my conclusions were not very flattering to our hosts. From first to last, this entire trek from Durban to the place called Sinai seemed to have been predicated on lies, deceit, and deception of one sort or another, and the current elaborate charade seemed to fit perfectly in line with all the rest.

When the girl regained some of her strength, she whispered to Ruth, who clearly wanted Mariam to return to the litter, but she held fast and got a set expression on her face. Her attendants moved away and stood at reverent attention as they had before. Mariam faced us again and continued in her mystical voice.

"But first, before I discuss the realm that is the real Eden of the real world, you need to know more of myself. There is skepticism among you, and that is good, for what good would you be as my messengers if you were to believe all that you heard from whomever you heard it. So I will explain somewhat. As all the world knows well, Jesus asked his beloved disciple to care for his mother. That person is myself."

It was, unexpectedly, Carnehan who first reacted to this preposterous announcement. "God A'mighty! Just how are we supposed to believe *that!* I've heard some bloomin' tall tales in my life—" Also, unexpectedly, it was a glare from Bayushtiak that stopped him in mid-sentence.

Mariam continued as though nothing had happened. "Thus, John and I headed north and resided in Ephaesus in Turkey for a time. However, we chose to continue our journey north and settled in what is now the countries you call France and England, but that did not suit our purposes either. We continued our search for a permanent home and then returned south. When we eventually came to this land, which was far more fertile two thousand years ago, the angel Gabriel came to me as he had before and declared that our journeying was finished and that this spot was to be our home. He split asunder the rock cliff, creating this hidden valley, and bade John and me enter. Over the years, mainly by sending dispatches to Galilee, we gathered around ourselves the people who were to become our community.

"I was ninety-seven years old when the great miracle happened. Death came to claim me as it does everyone, and, Lo!, Gabriel was there for me one more time. He told me that our Father wished me to tarry for there was more for me to do on Earth. Thus, at the point of my bodily death my spirit entered the body of a certain twelve-year-old girl and that child became Mariam for a year, that is, my soul, my personality, all that is invisible that was Mariam the mother of Jesus entered that girl and the girl became me. Following that, every year the woman who was Mariam moved from twelve-year-old to twelve-year-old so that the Mother of God is always within the body of a living girl. Through the mind and bodies of these girls, I have lived on."

Here, Ruth interjected: "The blessed Mother of God lives on eternally!" The girl paused again then, and I dared to break the mood by asking a question.

"If what you say is true, why does the Virgin, that is you, trouble twelve year olds?"

Mariam looked at Ruth, who responded for her, "Because that was the age of Mariam when the Angel of the Lord came to her and explained that she would in time to come conceive Jesus through the Holy Spirit, for in those days, and still in our land, that is the age of promise for a girl."[41]

Some of our party looked at one another in dismay at this statement. It was Burton who merely shrugged and reminded us that cultures the world over have different standards.

As Mariam sat quietly gazing over us, Ruth then went into more detail concerning the "possession" of the girls. In brief what she explained is as follows: When a girl ceases to be Mariam, she has no memory of that whole year. It is as though she made the transition from eleven to thirteen with no year between. Sometimes it happened that, when it was time for Mariam to move out of her body, there was no twelve-year old girl to act as her vessel.

It is at those times, as Mariam waits for an eleven-year-old to come of age, that she appears as an apparition in various places around the world for a little time, Guadalupe, Mexico, for one, and more recently in La Salette and Lourdes, both in France, where she shared some of her insights with some chosen children or others in whom innocence abounded. *[Quatermain note: As I was not altogether familiar with the particulars of these incidents, later, when I happened to think of it in Durban, I looked them up. Their respective dates were 1531, 1846, and 1858.]*

Naturally, Ruth went on, there are all sorts of ceremonies built up around the miracle, with parents vying for their daughters to be "the One." The only time when it is guaranteed that a particular girl becomes Mariam is when there is only one twelve-year old girl in the town.

Then Ruth went into the history of the place, noting that when Mariam and John left the Middle East for Europe, they rendezvoused with Joseph of Arimethea who had already obtained custody of the Holy Vessel. When eventually John and Mariam decided to continue looking for a home to the south, they had by then possession of that item. Unfortunately, as they were passing through the land that would eventually include Antioch, they were robbed by brigands, and Mariam lost track of that particular object for about 1,100 years.

In the meantime, in the 4th century, when the Library of Alexandria was threatened, many of its greatest volumes were secretly shipped to this community, since its existence and location were known to the great librarians of the time. Thus, the town of Sinai held close to its bosom the wisdom of millennia.

Then, some eight centuries later, another miracle happened, of which we already knew something. For in the "fullness of time" (an expression Ruth was to use often), following their adventures in the Holy Land, Duke Stephen and his men were able to retrieve their Holy Cup. They took a wide detour and, in the end, came to Ethiopia and, being directed by an angel, sought shelter in this very valley. Of course, once being interviewed, they left the treasure here in the care of Christ's mother before they left.

Then all at once, the girl's posture slumped and her eyes rolled back. At that her entire retinue, including Ruth, went into motion, swooping her into the litter and hurrying her into another room.

Ruth returned quickly to explain that our interview would continue another day, and then she led us some distance to a dining room where we were treated as honored guests, and we enjoyed more of the simple fare of these people. Afterward, we were taken again to our rooms. For some peculiar reason, we did not converse much when left to ourselves. It was as though we were all spiritually fatigued. I do remember that Holmes was irate about something and that Huxley was particularly subdued.

Frankly I cared little about anything just then. I was confused. Nothing I had heard had made any sense, though I could not deny the sincerity of these people. I lay down with my sleeping roll, and the last thing I remembered was that Hans was curled up next to me snoring.

CHAPTER FIFTEEN

Allan's Charge

The following morning our meal consisted of cakes and honey, apples, and raisins, with cool goat's milk to quench our thirst. The woman we had come to know as the messenger came and indicated that I was to follow her. Then she indicated Will Scott and made clear he was also to come. All the others were to stay behind. She took us through a veritable labyrinth of passages when finally she stopped and indicated that we were to enter a particular room and wait.

The room was Spartan as all things were in this land. These people did not seem to have much heart for decorating or for jewelry, bangles, and the like. We did as she bade, making ourselves as comfortable as we could on some cushions that were on the floor. I was wondering why Will Scott and I had been singled out, and he and I whispered about this for about twenty minutes when finally Ruth and some other women entered solemnly, walking slowly. Once again, in the middle of this procession was Mariam, walking this time on her own power. She came to a simple enough chair and sat facing us, her matrons standing in an arc behind her.

"Allan and you who are pleased to call yourself Will Scott—for that is your name, isn't it?" she began mysteriously in that fragile voice, "I have asked to see you two now because, of your party, you two and you two alone are destined to live through the ages, not as I who do here secretly in the desert, but in the minds of men for all time . . . as I survive in the hearts of men who know not my real situation. I wished to see you in order to finish what I began to say yesterday."

Here I had to protest. "But what about Mr. Huxley and Mr.

Burton and Miss Mitchell? Surely they are, all three, far greater than I and—" [and then I realized that Scott was a mere boy and heaven only knew how he would turn out].

"Yes, Allan, in an ideal world, Maria Mitchell and Richard Burton should and would enjoy notoriety through all time, but the people of earth have short memories or are fickle and, sad to say, the time is not far off when these two names will be lost, save for those few historians and practitioners in their fields who may remember."

"But what of Mr. Huxley?" I asked. At that moment, I saw Scott clearly wince.

Mariam continued: "Ah, the authentic Thomas Huxley with certainty will always be mentioned in the same breath with his mentor. Have no fear of that."

"But then you contradict yourself," Scott insisted.

"No. Your 'Mr. Huxley's' destiny without question will be an infamous one. In fact, in various guises, he will be remembered perhaps as long as yourself. But his fate in the balance ledgers of God is quite another one entirely, as perhaps you already suspect."

She paused here. I had the impression that she wanted her last words to sink into Scott's mind. Then she addressed him directly again. "But all that is neither here nor there. Hearken to my next words! When you return, tell your masters what you have heard and what you will hear. The bones you have will bear witness to the truth of your statements. Now listen carefully, for one asset I do not have is strength.

"The Holy Scriptures tell of the creation of the world . . . and they tell of God creating man in the land of Eden and that the act of creation took mere moments. These statements are of course true, but who is to determine what is a moment in the eyes of God, who measures time in billions of years? Indeed, God created man in a moment, a mere few million years, and he did this feat in a place that you can call Eden for want of a better name. I have brought you here to identify that real place to you and thus to all man.

"After John and I left Gaul and journeyed south, there came a time when the Angel of the Lord came to me. It was Gabriel, the same who had revealed himself to me at so many other crossroads in my life. He made me see in my mind a place on the far side of the Red Sea, a spot where I was to reside, and where I was to wait. 'Verily, the spot that I am showing you is holy,' he said, 'more so than Ur was where the Lord spoke to Abraham or the Mountain of Sinai where the Lord spoke to Moses. Though these are surely holy places, the spot I show you is holier still, for it is the holiest spot on earth. And verily, you who are the Mother of God, you are bid to attend this veritable womb of mankind, for are you not the holiest person of the world? Thus is it not right that you should live by and in and protect the holiest place? Are you not also the mother of man? Then it is fitting that you reside by and in and protect the womb of man. Verily, I say to you, the spot I show you is the most holy in the eyes and mind of God.'

"So Allan and Will Scott, the place the angel showed me was a vast valley that ran the whole length of Africa from north to south, a tremendous valley with many lakes. The angel bade John and I to come to this very spot that is under our feet now, which is the northernmost gateway both into and out of the great valley.

"Oh, Allan and Will, let me tell you a wonderful truth. Remember, thee, how the Lord through the burning bush told Moses that he stood on holy ground? Well I say to you that the ground on which you stand is holier still." As she said this last, her eyes grew large and she smiled for the first time, as though savoring her words.

"I am growing weak, for the girl who is my vessel was never strong, but I must share with you the secret that makes this place so holy.

"That spot, which is under your feet, continues south, making up the great valley of eastern Africa, the bowl out of which sprang man, the crucible where the embryonic spirit, or God-in-the-making called mankind, was forged. Will Scott, return to your mentors, to Mr. Darwin and your true Mr. Huxley, and tell them they are quite correct in the long view that humans came into being, not all at once, but in stages over time, for that is the way that God performs his miracles, building from the blocks that are available, the stuff of life."

Just then, some women emerged from a door carrying great censers dangling from golden chains and filled with burning incense. Great clouds of the stuff very quickly filled the room and suddenly, I felt as though I had been absorbed into a dream. But just before I went under, I suddenly understood. Like a bright light, it came to me. The girl, albeit very small and very young, was just another wizard of the Zikali ilk! Just another Old Cheat with more of that horrid magical smoke!

*   *   *

In the dream I was out of doors surrounded by lofty trees of a kind I didn't recognize. The temperature had risen and the air was steamy. Then I began to rise, float upward at an incredible speed until I saw clearly that I had been in a jungle and that the jungle spread over a vast area butting up right onto the sea. Then I saw the forest shrink, not because I was still rising, which I was, but because it was really shrinking and much of it quickly disappeared altogether and turned into savanna.

Then, all at once, I realized what it was I was seeing. I was seeing the east coast of Africa twenty million years ago. Don't ask me how I knew that, I just did. That forest that I had seen was the home of the ape. Apes of every kind, gibbons and monkeys, bush babies and lemurs, even a variety of gorilla.

At that time, the highlands of Kenya and Ethiopia did not exist. But geological forces of astronomical magnitude were beginning to split the continent. Over the next millions of years this splitting from Ethiopia through two-thirds of the eastern length of the continent gouged and tore the earth, shifted rivers and made rivers where they never existed before. Lakes like a string of pearls formed down the rift, lakes that provided in abundance much of what the apes and all the other creatures of that time needed—water and food. In fact, east Africa became a veritable jigsaw puzzle of forest, jungle, desert, grasslands, and meadows. This great variety was a boon to the apes, who multiplied and spread and filled every niche with variations of themselves.

Then I saw that some of the apes were moving unlike apes. These apes were not loping and lunging around using both hands and feet as apes move, but were standing upright, standing tall and walking on their feet hardly different than you or me. This I somehow knew was perhaps four million years ago. There was no doubt that they were animals—just apes of a different sort—and for a million years and more these creatures lived lives not that much different than their cousins, and like their cousins communicating amongst themselves with various noises and hand and arm gestures, a vocabulary of up to five hundred words or more.

I saw that some groups of these walking apes, as all creatures do, met adversity, time and again, droughts, floods, predatory animals, great cold, blistering heat, and millennia of geographical separation from their own kind. And slowly, it became apparent to me that their having the advantage of being able to walk and run solely on their feet had certain side effects. For one thing, having their hands free to manipulate objects allowed a certain facility of invention denied their cousins. Another was that possessing a vertical posture, as opposed to the horizontal posture of four-legged animals, or even the diagonal aspect of typical apes, seemed superior for reasons of safety and stealth. And, in the long-run, these changes proved so advantageous that the creatures were able to overcome many of their adversities.

But adversity is eternal, and for eons these creatures lived as part of the animal kingdom. Because of their small size and slight strength compared to many of the carnivores with whom they were surrounded, these new apes were largely scavengers, competing with hyenas and vultures. Yet, about two and a half million years ago, some of these creatures somehow determined that they could partially conquer hunger through the use of tools—for instance, using specialized bits of stone to crush already scavenged bones to retrieve the marrow and slice the flesh off secondhand carcasses—thus the earliest men came into existence. Crude without a doubt, more naked than not, sometimes cowering and afraid, other times bold to the point of foolishness.

I came to the realization that human beings had thus come into the world (at least as presented in this vision).

It was only then that I began to fall back to the earth; and then I stopped dropping, floating in the air a few hundred feet above the ground. I could see the Red Sea to the east and the jungle to the northwest. Then there emerged from a blowing dust cloud a small group of people, travelers dressed in the Hebrew manner that I had observed in Sinai, men and women, and I knew that two of them were John, the beloved disciple in whose care Jesus had placed his mother, and Mariam, that very mother. I saw the small caravan approach a cliff that opened before them, and they came to a place of safety, a good valley with a stream running through it, and they were comfortable. Thus they stayed, naming their new home Sinai, for it was holy ground.

For 1,100 years, the people of Sinai lived quietly, being bothered by none and bothering no one. It was then that Duke Stephen and his men appeared, being drawn by their own angel and returning to the Mother that which was her Son's. They tarried but a while, then left again. Then one day 400 years later, two men stumbled out of what had become a barren desert and found their valley, having followed those instructions that had been left behind by the crusaders. These two men were Gian Giacomo Caprotti and Tomasso Masini da Peretola, called Zoroastro, who were welcomed, and I saw Salai draw sketches of Mariam, whom they met in much the same manner as we. After the two Italians left, a church was quickly put up hiding the entrance to the valley.

Then, finally, I drifted down and touched the ground, and I was aware of Will Scott beside me. I turned to Will to ask him something, then everything seemed to shift and the next thing I remembered was the sensation of coming out of a deep sleep and regaining awareness of my surroundings—of Will Scott and the slim twelve-year-old girl before me.

*   *   *

By degrees I regained my composure. I noted also that the more awake Scott became, the more elated and proud he became. Finally, he couldn't hold it back any longer. "Everything I just experienced seemed to back up Charles's theories—if only he had been here as well. How will I ever be able to explain it to him?" Then a thought came to him. "But it was only a dream, nothing concrete, nothing at all that I can tell Charles except that I had had a dream." His excitement trailed off and he frowned.

He addressed Mariam. "Dear Lady, that was quite a trick. Certainly I saw just what I would have liked to have seen, painted in vivid color and with the broadest of strokes, Charles Darwin's theory of the descent of man. Yet, how can I trust what I have seen and heard?"

"That is a matter of choice," replied the girl. "You may trust or not trust as you desire. I can only remind you that I brought you here from far-off England to show you that which you have now seen. My purpose was to share the truth of man's origin with those most able to divine it and appreciate its meaning. After all, we"—and here she made an all-encompassing sweep of her arms—"are all the children of God, and God wants his children to grow beyond the quaint stories they tell amongst themselves and to hearken to things as they really are.

"I did this in the only manner I can. What you choose to think of it, that I cannot help. For my part, I am only showing you two chosen ones the earth's most divine truth. All of what you witnessed happened right here and yonder as well." Here she indicated south.

"Listen to me now!"

At this point, her normal ethereal, but nonetheless calm, voice changed, indeed, her whole demeanor suddenly took on a fiery passion.

"If God is as real as, for instance, me, and is by definition divine, and if through the use of the tool called Time, he crafted people in his own image, then it would follow that people are also divine and that the spot where He did his crafting must be holy ground—the holiest of ground.

"I have drawn you here from afar to tell you my wishes. During my incarnations in Guadeloupe, Lourdes, Fatima, and such, I have asked, or otherwise let it be known, only two things of consequence. First, that all mankind turn away from sin, chiefly your disregard for God and, too, the lust for war. Second, that a chapel be built on the spot of my appearance in my honor. Well, now I ask something similar of you. I ask that all the terrain from where you stand to the southern-most reach of the great valley—the vast bowl that is birthplace of the human race—be designated holy ground and be set aside so all people can come and contemplate their existence, to perceive with their own eyes the spot where God's greatest miracle occurred, and this will make them more mindful of one another and of God, as well."

I couldn't help but interject here. "Excuse me, miss, but are you saying that you drew Mr. Scott here from England and myself from Durban and perhaps the others as well, and that you did this with powers unknown to us, for the sole purpose of telling us that you want this barren desert and lands beyond turned into a place of worship.

"Yes, a natural cathedral."

Her words struck me dumb. Finally I was able to gather the resources to say, "My dear lady, what you are asking is preposterous. What you have described is perhaps one-fifth of the African continent, making up the national territories of numerous nations. Even if every leader of every one of those countries could see the same vision we have been graced with, there is no way they could all agree to turn large parts of their countries into contiguous reserves for your so-called holy ground, or whatever you want to call it."

Mariam did not deign to comment, nor change her expression from the beatific smile that she seemed to wear forever. She merely gestured to her hand maidens and prepared to leave. However, just as she was about to disappear behind a curtain, she stopped and turned and said, "Allan, rest assured that in the fullness of time all these things are possible and will be fulfilled! For you are my tool and, therefore, blessed by God!"

Then she focused her attention on Scott and said, "And as for you who today call yourself Will, though it is true that your role in honoring these requests of mine is slight, it is nonetheless also true that your hearing me today has given you much pause. For years to come, you will think on these events and hold them close to your heart. And I say to you now that there will come a time—a score of years hence—when you will be called upon to fulfil a divine obligation for the sake of my son, and thus for me as well. You will remember both my person and my words this day, and you will know how to proceed. For you, too, are my tool and, therefore, blessed by God!"[42]

Then she was gone.

CHAPTER SIXTEEN

The Return

Will Scott and I returned to our quarters in a daze, as one can easily imagine. The entire interview from beginning to end was outrageous, and I felt insulted that the inhabitants of this valley would assume that I would swallow any part of this pretense. They actually thought I would believe we'd been interviewed by the Virgin Mary Mother of God. Then to make matters worse, they drugged us with some toxic substance and wanted us to believe the further nonsense that there had once been a totally unknown and new upright ape that mankind was related to. And finally, the last straw, so to speak, was this astonishing attempt to reveal their desire to turn one-fifth of Africa into some sort of continental preserve.

My attempts to draw Scott out so as to affirm my own feelings ended in failure. I supposed that what he had seen that seemed to vindicate his mentors's theories was not to be criticized, for the moment at least. That the source of this information might be suspect didn't seem to occur to him. I wrote it off as a lingering affect of the incense.

Indeed, I found that even I did not feel compelled to discuss any of this with the others of our expedition, much to their chagrin. The exception was Huxley who pulled Scott aside, and they conferred at great length. Though I couldn't hear them, I could see them well enough, and it seemed to me that Scott's whole demeanor around the older man had changed. While at the start and throughout most of our journey, Scott seemed to revere Huxley, almost embarrassingly so, now he seemed perpetually disturbed by the man and avoided him as much as possible. This seemed to have begun about the time poor Lidenbrock had died. I could not see a connection and, in fact, took for granted that there was none. Whereas their relationship had been clearly one of mentor and student, now they seemed perpetually argumentative as, indeed, they appeared even as I couldn't help but notice during this particular interval. What this change of attitude meant I had no idea, and, as it happened, I never learned the cause of it nor the end of it.

In the meantime, some of the others tried to draw me out, but I would have none of it, and the day ended quietly enough.

The next morning, the messenger came and fetched Richard Holmes, who, it turned out would be gone for days. We were all concerned about this but were continually reassured that he was well, and that, in fact, he was probably never better.

It was during this interval that Cuff passed from us. The priests kindly sent word to us from the chapel. They said there was nothing more they could have done for him except make him comfortable. At this news, some of us remembered his principal passion in life and then put our heads together. We sent back a message asking if Cuff could be laid to rest in a corner of that rosery, or rose garden, he had taken such a shine to. The priests, who had, for some days, patiently weathered the brunt of his delirium and his preoccupation with their garden, said they understood and agreed. They buried him with ceremony, or so we understood, as we were a long way off in Sinai at the time. We all agreed that Cuff would have liked this. I, for one, knew in my heart that he would have liked it very much.[43] I was greatly saddened at his loss, but greatly heartened by the fact that, however briefly, I could say I had known him.

*   *   *

Holmes returned in the afternoon of the fourth day of his disappearance. He merely joined us at meal, walking as in a mesmeric state.

Toward the evening, he became more responsive and slowly we got from him the broad strokes. He too met with Mariam, but as his reasons for being there were of a different character altogether than mine or Scott's, Mariam spoke to him of the Great Library of Alexandria and of the Holy Grail. Apparently, she described in some detail the former and explained the provenance of the latter. Despite all our efforts, though, he remained taciturn about the details of his interview.

After another day, the priest Tabot reappeared and announced that our visit had ended and that we needed to pack and prepare to leave Sinai. The following morning, he and Ruth escorted us through the valley and back to the cleft by the fountain. As before, the townspeople came out in throngs, this time to see us off. All concerned seemed happy that we were at this juncture. Our hosts seemed grateful to be rid of us, and we were grateful to be returning to our homes.

One thing, though. We had to give our solemn oaths that we would never reveal the location of Sinai—the home of Mariam for all those many centuries. [I have kept this oath since I have never brought up this adventure at any time until now, and even so, I have changed a few landmarks here and there so as to muddy the waters; I hope you don't mind.]

Each member of the remainder of my expedition—Miss Mitchell, Burton, Dravot, Carnehan, Huxley, Scott, Holmes, and even Hans and the Zulu Bayushtiak—chose this moment to wish the community well and promised to keep their silence.

But it is the words of Miss Mitchell and Bayushtiak that I recall best. Our learned astronomer asked Ruth to convey a message to Mariam. "Please tell your mistress that now I understand that it was she who instilled in me the strength and determination to fight off the Danakil. Please tell her of my gratitude and say that I will keep her with me always."

Bayushtiak spoke in Zulu, which I translated: "My master, the

Great One, the Opener of Roads, sent me to protect the white man, Macumazahn, from various and sundry threats, and I believe that I have fulfilled my obligation well. Therefore, I leave this spot with a sense of accomplishment, yet there is much more also. I feel that I have been in the presence of the one who is the maker of the very air that I breath and the sunlight that warms my face. Never have I felt so much energy as I have felt here, but an energy, indeed a passion, bent on nurturing rather than the fighting for which I was bred. I know full well that it is your mistress who is the font of all these feelings and blessings, and I will remember her in kind as well as I can, evermore."

Once we all had a chance to say our mind, Ruth closed her eyes and responded, mysteriously, as seemed to be the coin of the realm in that far-off hidden spot, with Mariam's voice: "Thank you for your kind prayers, my children. Now go and forge the changes that I have asked in secret ways of each of you. Go in peace, and believe in your uttermost hearts that all my requests are not only possible, but inescapable."

And then we were ushered out and we retraced our steps through the narrow cleft to Tabot's chapel. After more farewells, and a promise that we would not be troubled again by the Danakil on our return trek, we once again entered that horrible desert.

Thus, this story ends. At that time I didn't know this wouldn't be my only journey to the Red Sea. There was to be another, one that would be forever connected to one of the saddest memories of my life.[44]

Our return to the bay where we would find the *Deborah*, the naval vessel that had carried us to Ethiopia, which was then patrolling the coast of the Red Sea while waiting for us, was indeed uneventful. It took about the same amount of time and effort to get back to the pier as it taken to get to the hidden town called Sinai.

The only aspect of the return journey that proved of interest was that we were finally able to get Holmes to open up somewhat about his experience. According to him, Mariam asked Ruth to take him into another part of the temple where she showed him into a room with eight sides, and in a nook in a wall surrounded by torches that somehow he knew never went out, was the Grail. The look on Holmes's face as he described these events was joyful. He said he actually held it in his hands. However, his description of the object left much to be desired. I simply could not pin the man down as to the description of the cup or chalice or platter, as some say. Yet, despite his peculiar vagueness, he did not doubt for an instant that what he was shown was the real object of so many quests.

From the room of the Grail, he was led down a narrow passageway hewn from solid stone and entered a natural cavern. He was instantly aware of the drop in temperature. It was significantly cooler in the cavern, where he saw numerous tall cases set up and rows and rows of shelves that were crammed with ancient scrolls.

At some point on our shared journey, Holmes had told me that it is said that the library once contained the secret method of extracting awesome amounts of energy from minute sources or how to light vast halls without the aid of fire or gas of any sort. And who's to say if those very scrolls weren't there in front of him.

Ruth confirmed that several thousand of the volumes from the Great Alexandrian Library had in fact made their way to her valley some 1,500 years ago and that there was a certain number of their population whose business it was to copy and recopy the scrolls to preserve their content against the passage of time.

Unfortunately, however, Ruth made it clear that despite his need to study the works, Holmes would have no chance other than the moment at hand. You can imagine his infinite disappointment, as he would have given up everything to stay, or better, to haul away much of what he found there. Ruth made it clear, though, that he and all the rest of our expedition would be leaving in due course. She did ask him if there was anything in particular he would like to see. And he responded immediately by querying about the gospel that seemed to be the source, other than Mark's, of Matthew and Luke. To Holmes's great relief and joy, she showed him the entirety of the memoir written by the magus Gaspar, the very writings that had so excited his hopes and which he had shared with me at the beginning of our journeying.

Whereupon he busied himself copying these pages, furiously scribbling, a task that took him all the days he was gone and utterly consumed him, and some other scrolls as well, which he chose not to share with us. And when we pressed, his only response was, "I cannot say. It is for the good of my country."

[Quatermain note: At this point, my dear Church, I interject myself again. Here we bid farewell to the Danakil Desert with all its terrible volcanoes and infinite sands, and we jump ahead in time.

[After Holmes's return to England and his museum, now and again I would hear a rumor or some other tantalizing word that the translation of Gaspar's thoughts from ancient Ethiopian into English was a continuing project for Holmes and his colleagues. I often wondered during the subsequent decade about the results of that effort and now, prompted and inspired by John's, that is, Dr. Watson's, desire to conclude this memoir with no strings untied, I have only just gotten in touch with Holmes again.

[After reminiscing at length, as you can imagine, I posed the question that was on my mind and he was kind enough to present me with a sort of abstract or "precise" of Gaspar's tract. Once again I take this opportunity to ask Dr. Watson to include here in a logical spot in this narrative that summary of the continuation of Gaspar's statements (Editor's note: To review the introductory section, please refer back to page 71.)

[And Gaspar said:

[Where is the word that tells us how to listen to God, that tells us that God speaks in a special language. When you see clouds in the west, you know that rain will come. You know that wind blowing from the south is always followed by blistering heat. You know the ways of your home and its land and you can read the sky. So why can't you understand the signs that God brings you.

[God's language doesn't use simple words like fig or tree or wall or camel. Instead, he uses symbols. For instance, if he shows you a circle, you know from common sense that a circle has no beginning or middle or end. It is whole unto itself; therefore, if God shows you a circle, you know that he is gracing you with wholeness and completion.

[In the same way, a home or house is where you live your life, where you are aware, and where it is that you know all that you know. So if God shows you a house, you know he is showing you your very awareness, or if he shows you an underground vault or perhaps the depths of the sea, you know these places are lightless and the realm of dark and he has graced you with a warning that you need to beware of that which you cannot see, of that which is below your awareness.

[God communicates to you in two ways. One is obvious and the other is less so. Both are common but only one is spoken of, though even then rarely understood. Through all time, people have spoken about God talking to people in dreams. But what is not said is that, even in dreams, God does not talk in an ordinary way using the dreamer's ordinary language. Dreams are full of symbols that mean something personal from God to the dreamer; it is the dreamer's duty to discover what is being said.

[The other less obvious way that God communicates, the way that people seldom speak of, is his placing symbols in our paths during our waking hours. Most such symbols are ordinary and self-evident. So you ask, how is a person to recognize that this or that ordinary thing is a message from God?

[It is not difficult at all. God causes us to notice such symbols by having them occur in the same space or time as other symbols so that two or more ordinary things coming together is not ordinary at all. When this happens, we feel a jolt of wonder or awe or even love. We all have these experiences, but I tell you, as sure as I am talking to you, that God is thus trying to get your attention, to speak to you. If in your heart you feel such a crossing of paths is wonderful, then I promise God is talking to you.

[Therefore, fortunate are you to see what you see, for these are the visions of the prophets, and many are the kings who wish to see what you see, or hear what you hear. But they never do, for they seek too hard and are not pure of heart.

[In this way, there can be nothing that is covered up or nothing that is secret between you and God. The secrets of your mind are held up to God, and God whispers back, or sometimes shouts, as the occasion deserves.

[But again, it is your duty to understand God's words to you, of what he is saying especially to you! Whether it's easy or hard, God rewards the trying.

[Now think! There are many people in your towns, in your nations, in the whole world. Think of all the people of all the many ages who lived in all those nations. Now ask yourself this: why would God trouble to speak so to you, who is but one person among so many? Why would he send you a sign, or speak to you in your dreams? Why would he trouble himself with you?

[*He does so because you are holy as all his children are holy. But few listen. But few heed. Few trust. Few love God as he loves them. Instead they choose to be blind. They choose to be deaf. They choose to be mute. God speaks all the time, but he is ignored by so many. His signs and dreams are ignored. His messages are ignored.*

[Where is the voice of Jesus that explains how the world works and how it should be observed? Where does it say that God approaches and needs to be approached with a serious heart fully open, that this is how God and man come together and that life ceases to be a mystery?

[Happy are those who show mercy, for, in this life or the next, God will be merciful.

[Happy are those who have open hearts, for, in this life or the next, they will see the face of God.

[Great are the keepers of the peace, for, in this life or the next, they will be called the children of God.

[But where is the voice of Jesus, the voice who held all these wondrous truths? Where are these truths? I do not hear of them from the caravans.—A.Q.]

We reached the *Deborah* without incident, and within a few more days, we all went our separate ways, returning to the lives we were leading before, perhaps richer for the experience, perhaps not. Burton retired to Trieste, as was his plan. Professor Mitchell returned to Vassar College with her precious bits of meteorite. However, I am happy to say that it was not long before our paths crossed again, but that is a whole 'nother tale[45] and this is not the time for its telling. Huxley and Will Scott, bitterly estranged by now for no reason that I ever saw, took away their equally precious bits of bone. The soldiers Danny Dravot and Peachy Carnehan, for all I know, disappeared off the face of the earth.[46] And, of course, Bayushtiak went to report to his master, that horrible dwarf wizard—"the thing that should never have been born"—who, nonetheless, for reasons I can never be sure of, I count among my friends.

[Quatermain note: Finally, Mr. Church, as I look over this manuscript that Dr. Watson has so kindly prepared I see that I have not made clear just why it was that your painting of Constantinople and the fountain in part inspired in me the memory that has become what I fear is a rather self-indulgent tale.

[You see, as I have looked back on all these events over these many years, I have often wondered how much of what Mariam said about the Great Valley was true and how much of my vision then could be relied on. And it has occurred to me over and again, that if there is any kernel of truth in the notion of that long, long valley being the very place where human life came into being, then it follows that the valley can be thought of as the fountain of life, or at least human life, on this earth.

[But one thing that I don't understand is why Mariam asked Will Scott and myself to take on that task of bringing her natural cathedral or her impossible park into being. I can't speak for Scott, but I have been fearfully busy merely surviving since then, and besides, the whole idea was simply too far-fetched to take seriously. I sometimes feel an attack of conscience about this. Still, on balance, I believe that I will be able to meet St. Peter when my time comes with my head held high! —A.Q.]47

J.H.W

Afterword

When I read Quatermain's memoir for the first time and came to the last page, my primary emotion was that of thankfulness that, with regard to Allan himself, none of Hans's evil omens came to anything.[48] Of course, poor Cuff and Lidenbrock might have thought otherwise. In addition, it seems a good thing that Bayushtiak came along, for he proved quite effective at least twice as described in this narrative.

Beyond these visceral first reactions, other thoughts come to mind. Despite Quatermain's and Watson's desire to tie up all the loose ends, clearly there were many more such ends than they ever knew, and which we can see now through the gift of hindsight.

For one thing, we never learn why Sherlock Holmes was using an assumed name in Ethiopia. While technically "Will Scott" comprises two of his actual names, they are two that few are familiar with.

We can, nonetheless, use the little that we know to delve into the matter a bit more. For example, we know enough now, through the celebrated efforts of both Watson and Baring–Gould, to make the fair assumption that the "British Government" referred to so often in the memoir may be simply the person of Sherlock Holmes's older brother Mycroft, who we have met in "The Greek Interpreter" and subsequently learn in "The Bruce–Partington Plans," that, in Holmes's words, he "occasionally *is* the British government."

Which brings us to the conundrum that we meet in the manuscript as "Thomas Huxley." Despite the fact that Quatermain diligently reports numerous inferences, instances, and clues that should have raised "red flags" for him and given him much pause, he never really addresses the mystery of the man. Personally, I give Quatermain the benefit of the doubt and believe that he was in such spiritual and sensory overload during this adventure that many nuances just went over his head. Or perhaps, in relating the story to Watson and Church, he was merely being circumspect.

Again with that marvelous gift of hindsight, we know now that the man identified as "Thomas Huxley" was nothing of the sort.

Beginning with Quatermain's casual observation that Huxley and Will Scott bore an odd resemblance to one another, and later with his observations of the familiar ease with which they could squabble in public, we can assume that Huxley is Holmes's older brother. Yet we know from "The Greek Interpreter" that no force on earth would move Mycroft out of his comfortable surroundings.

Thus, using Sherlock Holmes's own methods, if we eliminate all possibilities, that which remains must be the solution, however improbable it may seem. Hence, we are left with the conclusion that "Huxley" must in actuality be Holmes's *other* older brother, Sherrinford, and that he, as Sherlock himself often did, was participating in this game in disguise and under cover.

From all this, we can conclude that for reasons unknown to us, Mycroft Holmes, with the full authority of the British government, dispatched his two brothers off to Ethiopia for some secret purpose, the nature of which we never properly learn. Despite all their stated goals, even that of locating the Holy Grail, we sense that there was something more.

Still, this does not get down to the bottom of the man we have identified as Sherrinford Holmes.

There is much more to it.

When discussing astronomical phenomena with Professor Mitchell, we note that "Huxley" suddenly waxed passionately about asteroids and their dynamics. From this alone, we can easily deduce that "Huxley" must be none other than the criminal genius Professor James Moriarty, whom Holmes identified in "The Final Problem" as "the Napoleon of crime" and who three years after this Ethiopian adventure would publish *The Dynamics of an Asteroid*, a work we are told in *The Valley of Fear* ascended to "such rarified heights that no man in the scientific press was capable of criticizing it."

Therefore, it is impossible to escape the conclusion that Sherrinford Holmes and Professor Moriarty are the same man.

That Sherrinford/Moriarty and Sherlock were not yet, at least at the start of our story, the bitter enemies they would become, is quite clear. The relationship between the two is described in the most cordial terms, even that of a student revering his mentor. Indeed, this makes perfect sense since Baring-Gould tells us that Moriarty was once Holmes's tutor. This fits in the context of the story, for despite what else they claimed to be, they would have still been student and mentor. Yet, couldn't that relationship also be interpreted as that of a younger brother worshipping his older brother? I believe so.

Nonetheless, we are now beginning to see that Sherrinford Holmes was a "bad seed" and that he took the path opposite of his two siblings.

Case in point: All the information we have surrounding the death of Axel Lidenbrock leads us to the conclusion that he was murdered, as opposed to being the victim of the Danakil sortie.

With only this to go on, I will make a leap of deduction. I conclude that Sherrinford killed Axel. For what reason, you ask? Simply because Lidenbrock's unexpected arrival was not part of the equation and, beyond that, he was completely expendable. I conclude that Sherrinford murdered the man for the pure fun of it.

Furthermore, I think Sherlock quickly came to the same conclusion and confronted his brother, who could muster no remorse. This then was the beginning of the rift that would become legendary[49] and which would end at their famous encounter at the falls of Reichenbach.

T.K.M

Notes

1. Michael Crichton's 1980 novel *Congo* is a clear pastiche of Haggard's *King Solomon's Mines*, even to the extent that the last sentence in *Congo* reads thus: "The projected intersection point now marked a field of black quatermain lava with an average depth of eight hundred meters—nearly half a mile—over the Lost City of Zinj." The name "Quatermain" is sufficiently close to the geological term "Quaternary" that some readers, to be sure, would have missed the *homage*.

2. Judy-Lynn Del Rey, with her husband Lester, took over the editorship of Ballantine Books' science-fiction and fantasy lines in the mid-1970s—shortly after Ian and Betty Ballantine sold to Random House the publishing house that bore their name and which they started in 1952.

3. Indeed, Haggard went so far as to write in his autobiography *The Days of My Life*: " . . . I always find it easy to write of Allan Quatermain, who, after all, is only myself set in a variety of imagined situations, thinking my thoughts and looking at life through my eyes."

4. During the three decades before the popularization of television, and serving much the same purpose that TV does today, a profusion of magazines full of colorful stories with vivid, even lurid, covers flourished. These were what we call today the pulp magazines because of the poor-quality paper they were printed on. Whatever your taste, there was a pulp magazine for you, including *Detective Story Magazine, Western Roundup, War Stories, Pirate Stories, Railroad Stories, Amazing Stories, Love Story, New York Stories, Racketeer Stories, Fight Stories, Baseball Stories,* and countless others. One of the most enduring was *Weird Tales*, a magazine of horror

and supernatural stories that began publication in 1926. (Indeed, an incarnation of it is still being published today.) Whereas most of the stories and authors published in all those other magazines have long faded from both popular and critical consciousness, some of the *Weird Tales* writers still have fervent followings, foremost among these being H.P. Lovecraft, who died in 1937 at the age of 47. Lovecraft is remembered today principally because of the efforts of two of his young protégés, August Derleth and Donald Wandrei. These young men started a publishing company in Sauk City, Wisconsin, called Arkham House (named after a recurring town in many Lovecraft stories) for the sole purpose of reprinting Lovecraft's work within the dignity of hardcovers. Though sales were slow to start, the paperback reprints took off during W.W.II and now H.P. Lovecraft is considered by many to be one of America's foremost writers of horror—equal in stature to Edgar Allan Poe. In time, Arkham House began publishing collections of other *Weird Tales* authors and is still a viable publishing house to this day. Following Derleth's death in 1971, James Turner became publisher and editor.

5. From 1825 to 1875, there arose a style of uniquely American landscape painting known as the Hudson River Valley School. These works were astonishingly photographic in detail while at the same time rendering nature in such romanticized and noble hues, with such immaculate emphasis on light and atmosphere, that the paintings were like windows into paradise. As the sobriquet would indicate, many of the original paintings depicted the Hudson River Valley in upper New York State. Among the foremost practitioners of this school—such as Thomas Cole, Albert Bierstadt, Asher Durand, John Kensett, and Thomas Moran—was Frederick Church, whose vast canvases portraying Niagara Falls, towering South American mountain ranges, and erupting volcanoes inspired awe in those who

viewed them. Toward the end of his career, Church built his home high on a hill overlooking the Hudson River. Designed to resemble a Persian palace, he called it Olana.

6. Derleth and Wandrei felt compelled to leave out chunks of Lovecraft's correspondence for a variety of reasons (irrelevance, length, etc.), replacing the deleted prose with glorified ellipses.

7. Saratoga Springs was where Lovecraft's wife Sonia H. Greene (S.H.G.) convalesced from nerve problems and other symptoms following a stressful employment episode.

8. Lovecraft had a fierce interest in astronomy. Over the years, he provided many articles on the subject to the *Pawtuxet Valley Gleaner*; the Providence, Rhode Island, *Evening News*; and the Providence *Tribune*.

9. Many people, Lovecraft included, believe that "The Colour Out of Space" is his finest work. The story details the horrific events that follow the arrival of a meteorite in the area "west of Arkham."

10. In the course of his 60 biographical sketches of Holmes, clear references are wanting regarding the location of Watson's war wounds, the number of his wives, and the chronological sequence of the narratives, among other proofs that the good doctor had his own share of foibles.

11. At the end of the nineteenth century, the expression "romance writer" had a completely different meaning than what we are used to today. During that era, the term "romance" conveyed the meaning of "imaginative adventure fiction."

12. Notwithstanding note 10, Watson explains in *A Study in Scarlet*, " . . . I served at the fatal battle of Maiwand. There I was struck on the shoulder by a Jezail bullet, which shattered the bone and grazed the subclavian artery."

13. Church's marvelous landscape *Cotopaxi*, which features a distant violent Mexican volcano, was exhibited June–August 1865 at McClean's Gallery, London. There is some indication (though this is more difficult to corroborate) that the painting made an encore appearance at McClean's during February-March 1870, which would fit nicely into the chronology of Quatermain's life, being the first time he had visited England since he was three years old [see *Allan and the Holy Flower*].

14. That Church chose to share the privacy of his family's personal sitting room with Quatermain and Watson is telling of his admiration for them. Yet this admiration must have been based solely on their immediately observed characters since neither had attained at that time the prominence that the future held for them. Quatermain's name would have meant nothing to Church, since Quatermain's memoir *King Solomon's Mines* had not yet been published, and wouldn't be for four more years. And Watson's first biographical memoir of Sherlock Holmes would not see print for another six.

15. During his prime, Church traveled far and wide through Mexico, South America, the Arctic, Europe, and the Middle East, so with regard to worldliness, Church would hardly be called an amateur.

16. El Khasne, the ancient treasury house, made cameo appearances in at least two delightful fantasy films—Ray

Harryhausen's *Sinbad and the Eye of the Tiger* (1977) and Steven Spielberg's *Indiana Jones and the Last Crusade* (1989).

17. *El Ayn (The Fountain)* (also known as *Constantinople*) is currently part of the collection of the Mead Art Museum, Amherst College, Amherst, Massachusetts.

18. Of the Khoisan people indigenous to South Africa.

19. It is important to mention that Quatermain lived in a world of empire, a world and a time whose values were far different than those of our so-called "color-blind," "politically correct," and enlightened culture. It would not have crossed his mind that his choice of expression, the words he used, might be demeaning or hurtful. But, putting this bias of the period aside, Quatermain was as fair-minded as a human being could be.

That said, it is likely that Quatermain did not dwell on the subject of his servant as he related the story in Church's sitting room. Furthermore, it is improbable that Watson knew much of Hans so early in his friendship with Quatermain. Perhaps Watson did not, in ignorance, trouble to consult with Quatermain, who otherwise "indulged him by responding to his every question" during the voyage home, or, perhaps Watson did inquire only to be rebuffed by Quatermain for private reasons. Or perhaps it is as simple as the fact that the document was being prepared as a rather informal record of a private conversation with Frederick Church and intended for him as the principal audience as opposed to a formal book. In either case, as Hans is not introduced with any detail in this narrative, though in pages to come he will have an important role, I have chosen to place here passages from two of Quatermain's 19 previously known memoirs that were recorded during his retirement in England, *She and Allan* (which describes an adventure following the one in hand chronologically by about one year) and *The Ivory Child* (which follows this one by seven years), describing Hans in some detail not only in a physical manner but also in terms of his relationship to Quatermain.

S&A: "Hans, I should say, was that same Hottentot who had been the companion of most of my journeyings since my father's day. He was with me when as a young fellow I accompanied Retief to Dingaan's kraal, and like myself, escaped the massacre . . .

"One good quality he had, however; no man was ever more faithful, and perhaps it would be true to say that neither man nor woman ever loved me, unworthy, quite so well.

"In appearance he rather resembled an antique and dilapidated baboon; his face was wrinkled like a dried nut and his quick little eyes were bloodshot. I never knew what his age was, any more than he did himself, but the years had left him tough as whipcord and absolutely untiring. Lastly he was perhaps the best hand at following a spoor that ever I knew and up to a hundred and fifty yards or so, a very deadly shot with a rifle . . . "

TIC: "The truth is that after the death of Hans . . . there was no more spirit in me. For quite a long while I did not seem to care at all what happened to me or to anybody else. We buried him with honor and when the earth was thrown over his little yellow face I felt as though half my past had departed with him into that hole. Poor drunken old Hans, where in the world shall I find such another man as you were? Where in the world shall I find so much love as filled the cup of that strange heart of yours?

"I dare say it is a form of selfishness, but what every man desires is something that cares for him *alone*, which is just why we are so fond of dogs. Now Hans was a dog with a human brain and he cared for me alone . . . Now Hans never cared for any living creature, or for any human hope or object, as he cared for me. There was no man or woman whom he would not have cheated, or even murdered for my sake. There was no earthly advantage, down to that of life itself, that he would not . . . forgo for my sake . . . That is love *in excelsis*, and the man who has succeeded in inspiring it in any creature, even in a low, bibulous, old Hottentot, may feel proud indeed. At least I am proud and as the years go by the pride increases, as the hope grows that somewhere . . . I may find the light of Hans's love burning like a beacon in the darkness, as he promised I should do, and that it may guide and warm my shivering, new-born soul before I dare the adventure of the Infinite."

20. There is irony here insofar that January 6 is Sherlock Holmes' birthday, according to Holmsian scholar William S. Baring–Gould.

21. By the Portuguese explorer Vasco da Gama in 1498 on his epic voyage to India.

22. In recent decades, there have been serious attempts to show that Sherlock Holmes manifested symptoms of Marfan's Syndrome, a hereditary condition affecting ligaments, muscles, and the skeletal structure to the degree that its sufferers possessed excessively tall, lean body types and long thin fingers.

23. Luna Holmes played a preeminent role in Quatermain's life. Indeed, she is an essential element in four of his memoirs, *Allan and the Holy Flower*, *The Ivory Child*, *The Ancient Allan*, and *Allan and the Ice Gods*. Insofar as it has never been shown that she was *not* a relative of Sherlock Holmes, I think it can be safely assumed that he and she were cousins not too distantly removed, which would account for his presence at Castle Ragnall.

24. The bones in question, the genus *Australopithecus*, are still housed at the British Museum, and recent potassium-argon dating has shown them to be 3.4 million years old.

25. In the decades following the time period of this memoir, scholars began calling this hypothetical document the "Q" document, Q being short for *quelle*, which means "source" in German.

26. Scholars, as a rule, assume that Gaspar, indeed, all the Magi, or Wise Men, did not exist at all, and was created out of whole cloth by Matthew and later elaborated on.

27. Recall that Quatermain's name first came to public attention with the publication of *King Solomon's Mines*, which was a memoir of a journey that followed a map, the origin of which his second wife, Stella, at least, considered dubious at best.

28. Two or three years after Quatermain's visit to Olana, he recounted the entire adventure of Heu-Heu to Sir Henry Curtis, Captain John Good, R.N., and H. Rider Haggard while they all rested after a long day's sport at his estate. Immediately afterwards, Haggard wrote down the tale from memory. Forty years later, a delay that need not be detailed here, that transcription came to be printed under Haggard's byline as *Heu-Heu or The Monster*. As an aside, it is worth noting that this book contains some scenes similar enough to scenes in the classic films *King Kong* and its sequel *Son of Kong*, that there has been speculation that the printing of *Heu-Heu* may have actually inspired the creation of those two now-classic films, at least to some extent.

29. Quatermain's first wife was Marie Marais, the daughter of Henri, and Maraisfontein was where they met as children. Such was the pain associated with her demise and this whole chapter of his life that he seldom ever referred to it. Even the brief mention here was unusually candid, but it nonetheless sheds

some light as to why he would hang an unused swing from his porch. See his memoir *Marie* for further details.

30. Sir Richard Burton was one of the great European explorers of the nineteenth century. He was the first to discover most of the great lakes of central Africa. But it is his 1853 adventure into Mecca and Medina disguised as a wandering dervish, or slightly mad holy man, for which he is most known. Within these venerated cities, he visited the most sacrosanct shrines of Islam, adventures which he documented in his *Personal Narrative of a Pilgrimage to Al-Madinah & Meccah*.

31. Burton was fluent in 29 languages and a dozen additional dialects.

32. This list of supplies for a desert trek is very similar to a list compiled for chapter 5 of Quatermain's *King Solomon's Mines*, from which we can deduce that he had a tried-and-true method for desert travel and stuck to it.

33. As described by Quatermain, two-fifths of this adventure took place in what is now the nation of Eritrea, which officially split from Ethiopia in 1993.

34. Now former editor, both because he left Arkham House to begin his own publishing concern, Golden Gryphon Press, and also as he passed away in 1999.

35. Tomasso Masini da Peretola's nickname was "Zoroastro," a name given to him by Cardinal Ridolfi because he was a dabbler in everything arcane.

36. It was this entire episode of the meteorites that seemed to capture H.P. Lovecraft's imagination to the highest degree (see

the "Preface: The Prodigious Phone Call."). As editor, I deliberated at length whether to retain his revisions in this volume, but in the end decided that to include HPL's unedited, sometimes florid passages would be a radical change of style that could only be obtrusive within Quatermain's pragmatic narrative. Perhaps in a future edition, I will include an appendix that will focus on these passages and relate them to "The Colour Out of Space."

37. Wolfram von Eschenbach wrote the epic *Parzival* around 1200, wherein he says, "A valiant host lives there, and I will tell you how they are sustained. They live from a stone of purest kind. If you do not know it, it shall here be named for you. It is called lapsit exillis. By the power of that stone, the phoenix burns to ashes, but the ashes give him life again."

38. Indeed, there is much discussion among biologists and exobiologists today that the amino acids that helped generate life on Earth may have been delivered by meteorites that were derived from comets and, most especially, from cosmic dust.

39. Today these nomadic people are called the Afar, which is what they call themselves. They are a pastoral people but can be ferocious when angered. Their way of life has changed little since Quatermain's experience with them.

40. Matthew 7:13. Indeed, Luke 13:24 says much the same thing. It is ironic, therefore, that the verse that popped into Quatermain's mind is, in fact, one of those that are conjectured to be Q material.

41. In verifying this, I found references to Jewish marriage customs of two millennium ago. Typical of these is the essay

entitled "The World of Jesus" by Roland de Vaux (Director from 1945-65 of the École Biblique et Archéologique Française) that appears in *Everyday Life in Bible Times* published by the National Geographic Society: "Boys marry at 18; girls when they reach puberty, officially at twelve and a half." In addition, one can find in the extant copies of the *Infancy Gospel of James* (Christian Apocrypha—originally written no earlier than 150 A.D.) references to Mary's age when she was visited by the Holy Spirit that vary from 12 to 17, depending the manuscript.

Furthermore, in 1858, Bernadette Sobirous consistently described her Marian apparitions at the French town of Lourdes as being a girl about twelve, a description that the press, clergy, and other commentators refused to accept because it was wholly unorthodox and too dissimilar to popular Marian iconography. As a result, the media of the time steadily increased the apparent age of the "Immaculate Conception" (as the apparition called herself) until that age settled at "about twenty," at which point everybody became content.

42. Though nobody can know just what was on Mariam's mind with regard to these words to "Will Scott," her reference to "two score years" does coincide with the events recorded in Leo Vincey's *The Great Detective on the Roof of the World; Or, The Adventure of the Wayfaring God* wherein Holmes' path happens to cross that of a mysterious Issa, who, it is suggested in that book, may be Jesus Christ.

43. In *The Moonstone*, Cuff tells an acquaintance, " . . . the roses get it. I began my life among them in my father's garden, and I shall end my life among them if I can."

44. Detailed in *The Ivory Child*.

45. Quartermain's further adventures in the company of Professor Maria Mitchell will be documented in the forthcoming book *The Great Detective at the Dawn of Time; Or, The Adventure of the Star of Wonder.*

46. Word has it that these two became inspired to visit far off Kafiristan in central Asia, at least this was reported by Rudyard Kipling in his East Indian newspaper *The Backwoodsman* in a piece titled "The Man Who Would Be King."

47. It is worth noting here, as an aside, that four years after his delightful evening with Church and Watson, Quatermain encountered another "rose of fire," one of an entirely different sort to be sure. As recorded in his final memoir, *Allan Quatermain*, having tired of retirement, he returned to Africa in search for adventure. His journeying took him into an underground river where he experienced:

"[A] huge pillar-like jet of almost white flame . . . sprang fifty feet into the air, when it struck the roof and spread out some forty feet in diameter, falling back in curved sheets of fire shaped like the petals of a full-blown rose. Indeed this awful gas jet resembled nothing so much as a great flaming flower . . . Below was the straight stalk, a foot or more thick, and above the dreadful bloom . . . , which gleamed fiercer than any furnace ever lit by man . . . For yards and yards round the great rose of fire the rock-roof was red-hot . . . My eyes seemed to be bursting from my head, and through my closed lids I could see the fierce light . . . [I]t roared like all the fires of hell . . . "

48. It must be noted here for the record that when my editor read this remark, his marvelous reaction was: "You mean to say that after reading of the discovery of the Grail and the living Virgin Mary and a lost valley containing the Library of Alexandria and

the missing link and a lost gospel, your primary emotion was *only* that Hans's evil omens didn't come true?"

49. But I will take this logic one step further. Quatermain's description of the probable weapon used to kill Lidenbrock, that of a sharp instrument such as a scalpel, and also the description of the wound, along with Sherrinford/Moriarty's apparent total lack of concern, all ring familiar. I believe that it is quite likely that another chapter of Sherrinford's life would play out sixteen years later on the streets of Whitechapel—a chapter that would attain its own very special and infamous notoriety.

Acknowledgments

Thank you to Jayne and Douglas, my wife and son, without whom none of this would have any meaning. Also to my mom, who was a most "prodigious" lady.

A special thanks to Nicholas Meyer and the editors of E.P. Dutton & Co. for opening up the flood gates in 1974.

A formal and most appreciative bow to Ian and Betty Ballantine and Lin Carter who introduced me to Rider Haggard in 1973 with the Ballantine Adult Fantasy publication of *The People of the Mist*.

Thanks also to Walter Sullivan, who brought the Afar Triangle and the Danakil Desert to my attention, also in 1974.

And a special appreciation to Umberto Eco, who, in 1980, showed me just how far afield you can take "the world's first consulting detective"!

Aside from the works of those knights of the realm, H. Rider Haggard and Arthur Conan Doyle—which works I admire more than it is possible to convey—various and sundry compositions by many writers and editors provided invaluable research material for this novel in the form of color, historical and biographical perspective, inspiration, speculation, and insight. These include Isaac Asimov, Carl Barks, William S. Baring-Gould, Marcus Borg, Jorge Luis Borges, Raymond E. Brown, Slater Brown, Richard Burton, Raymond Chandler, Nicholas Clapp, Arthur C. Clarke, John Clute, Wilkie Collins, Thomas B. Costain, S.L. Cranston, Michael Crichton, Clive Cussler, Charles Darwin, John J. Delaney, Nelson DeMille, Chrétien de Troyes, Lloyd C. Douglas, Robert B. Downs, Cy Enfield, Bart Ehrman, Eldon K. Everett, Harry Geduld, Stephen Jay Gould, Beatrice Gormley, Ronald Gottesman, Robert A. Haag, Peter Haining, Richard Halliburton, Graham Hancock, Ruth Harris, Michael Harrison, Donald Johanson, C.J. Jung, Joseph Head, Herman Hesse, Franklin Kelly, Rudyard

Kipling, Richard E. Leakey, Roger Sherman Loomis, H.P. Lovecraft, Mary S. Lovell, Burton L. Mack, Arthur Machen, Geddes MacGregor, Harold G. Marcus, A. Merritt, Geoffrey of Monmouth, Alan Moorhead, Talbot Mundy, Peter Nicholls, J.I. Packer, Robert Payne, John E. Pfeiffer, Mark Powelson, David Pringle, R. Reginald, Ray Riegert, Brian Roberts, James Anthony Ryan, Carl Sagan, Irving Stone, M.C. Tenney, Wilfred Thesiger, Jack Tracy, Jim Turner, Peter Tzou, Anne Vail, Jules Verne, Wolfram von Eschenbach, Irving Wallace, Lew Wallace, Franz Werfel, Bahru Zewde, and Sandral Zimdars-Swartz.

Without doubt there are many others as well, but in the more than a quarter of a century that this book has been brewing and the fifteen years since it was first announced, I've experienced, viewed, and read much, to be sure, and the mind is at times a sponge and at others a sieve . . . I apologize to anyone I may have inadvertently left out.

I would be remiss if I didn't call attention here to the boundless enthusiasm heaped on my embryonic efforts by Norman Siringer and Michael J. Thornton, my principal writing teachers at Hillsdale High School, San Mateo, California, from which I graduated Class of '63.

Thanks to Sheila Marie Comerford for her cover artwork for this book, and also to Linda Villareal, who designed the cover and etched the cover illustration for *Sherlock Holmes on the Roof of the World* in 1987.

Thanks also to Tammy Johnson, who rescued my poor map.

Chapter VI of this book, "The Relection," was first published in slightly different form as "The Fountain" in *Inferno*, No. 1, a publication of the JPL Writers Club, copyright 1992. This same material and various elements in the present novel associated with it had earlier helped me earn my bachelors degree in English (with an emphasis in Creative Writing) in 1982 from San Francisco State University.

Thanks to all those who read and enjoyed the first work, especially Susan Foster, Michael Karman, Jim Rich, and Melissa Mullen, whose kind comments encouraged me to continue with this second effort. Thanks to Jesse Theodore, Mima Horne and Daniel Horne for their moral support.

Thanks again to all those who read and commented on the work in progress: My two brothers, Jerry and Rodger; my two closest friends, Gary von Tersch and Gail Morgan Hickman; my copyeditor, Peter Manley; and Shelly Sommer and Rick Schneblin (who, though he does not agree with some of the points I wished to make in this book, graciously allowed me to include his name nonetheless).

And most especially, for their wonderful and limitless enthusiasm, thanks to Mike Phoenix, Matt Artz, and Carol Oveross.

I am grateful to Henry Nkosi and Patrick McKivergan of GIMS (Pty) Ltd., Johannesburg, South Africa, who helped me with Zulu translations. GIMS was established with the sole aim of implementing and supporting geographic information management systems (GIS).

In addition, I wish to gratefully acknowledge my friend Tabot Debretion Araia, who helped me better understand his home nation of Eritrea.

And finally, I must acknowledge John Betancourt, my publisher, who shocked this author in August 2002 by literally *instantly* growing attached to this work, and to Sean Wallace, whose labors turning the manuscript into a book have been Herculean.

About the Author

Thomas Kent Miller has, for more than three decades, nurtured his interests in Sherlock Holmes and H. Rider Haggard by conceiving pastiches featuring elements from the canon of the former and the works of the latter. His first short novel, *Sherlock Holmes on the Roof of the World*, was distributed by Borgo Press in the 1980s and became one of that publisher's best sellers (which Wildside Press plans in due course to reissue as *The Great Detective on the Roof of the World*). Tom is now working on a third volume in the sequence titled *The Great Detective at the Dawn of Time.* He resides in western California with his wife and their son and a menagerie of cats and dogs. Formerly a documentation specialist with NASA, he has now for more than a decade been editor-in-chief of the longest running continuously published periodical devoted to geographic information systems. Beyond the passions listed above, he became a dyed-in-the-wool science fiction movie aficionado beginning in 1953 and has been a multichannel music and home theater enthusiast since 1991. He welcomes your correspondence at millerslighthouse@earthlink.net.

Printed in Great Britain by
Amazon.co.uk, Ltd.,
Marston Gate.